Silvermo

HAVE A COLLECTION
OF 50 GREAT NOVELS

OF

EROTIC DOMINATION

If you like one you will probably like the rest

A NEW TITLE EVERY MONTH
NOW INCLUDING EXTRA BONUS PAGES

Silver Moon Books Ltd
PO Box CR25 Leeds LS7 3TN

Silver Moon Books Inc
PO Box 1614 New York NY 10156

Distributed to the trade throughout North America by
LPC Group, 1436 West Randolph Street, Chicago, IL 60607
(800) 826-4330

THE PENITENT first published May 1998

CONTENTS

THE PENITENT by Charles Arnold

CHAPTER ONE - INVITATION

Kathy was still half asleep when she heard the sound of chains clanking. She rolled over on her side and put both hands between her legs, pressed hard against her pubic bone. Her hands were together as if in prayer except that her fingers pointed down. The edges of her hands rubbed slowly between her legs.

She was a little girl in her dream, sliding up and down against a hickory post in her uncle's dark basement.

It seemed to her she had always lived in the rectory with her uncle, who was the village priest. Like in the other dreams, she was aware of his shadowy figure behind the cellar stairs, watching her. He was always there, watching. She began to whimper in her sleep. Her hands moved more quickly, and her pelvis ground against them in a circular motion.

Before she had a chance to climax, there was an explosive roaring in the street. She woke up, trembling, and went to the window.

Outside, a man stood next to his rumbling grader and pissed on the steel treads. His stream ran down a crack between two treads and dribbled onto his shoe. He pulled twice at his long flaccid cock before stuffing it back in his jeans.

She couldn't actually see the man's cock, but she knew what he was doing. Her nightgown was bunched up around her waist as her small fingers stroked her clit. As she came, she stood on tiptoes and pushed her open cunt against the window. But the man's back was towards her. She sat down on the bed, shaking. She remembered her uncle's cold blue eyes and her fumbling attempts to pull up her panties, and his voice, always the same, admonishing, 'Shame, Katherine, shame. God will punish, God will punish.'

It had been something like a game between them, a contest that had never been resolved. She knew he would watch her. She was obvious about going to the basement. She waited until she felt his presence there on the top step. Knowing he was there made it exciting in a way she could not understand. Knowing he would say 'shame' and 'God will punish' caused a fluttery feeling in her stomach and made her wet between her legs. She would take down her panties and rub herself against the post. After awhile, he would step out of the shadow saying, 'Shame! shame! God will punish!' Then she would run to her bedroom, fall upon her knees reciting the catechism while waiting for punishment neither her uncle nor God ever administered.

Outside, the grader started up again with a roar that shook the house. All morning the huge yellow machine lumbered back and forth, cutting a wide flat clearing in the brush and scrub oak of the vacant land across the street. This was the way such things begin: with a tall, solitary man and his machine pushing over trees and disturbing the morning with smoke and noise.

It was quiet when she crossed the street. She held a cold bottle of Iron City with both hands. Her cutoffs were tight. She could feel them pressing the dampness of her cotton panties into the crease of her ass and the crease of her pussy. Her nipples pushed against the loose tee shirt she wore.

John Wallowitz sat in the shade beside his grader. His shirt was soaked with perspiration. He could feel the sweat in his crotch, and the seat of his pants stuck to the bony flatness of his ass. His lunch box was open beside him. Too fucking hot to eat, he thought, and threw the sandwich back into the box. When he looked up she was standing before him holding out a bottle of beer. "Goddamn!" he said, "you surprised me."

But he didn't look surprised. He squinted his eyes and looked up at her, seeing long dark hair, the brown eyes, small delicate face, full mouth, the quick rise and fall of her breasts, the tiny waist, the way her shorts molded her firm ass and crept into the crack, her beautifully shaped legs and small hands and feet. She looked like a little girl with a woman's tits and ass. He could feel his cock slide in sweat against his leg. He still hadn't reached out for the bottle.

"I - I thought you might be hot," she said, and immediately reddened. He raised one eyebrow and smiled. She noticed that his teeth were yellow stained and the front one was broken. A dark purple scar extended in a half-circle from his right eye to the edge of his mouth. She continued to blush and stammer, "I mean..."

"You mean you felt sorry for old Wally out here in the sun and decided to bring him something nice."

"Yes, well, I thought..." He reached up and took the bottle from her, quickly twisted off the cap, and drank. She watched his Adam's apple bob up and down. Some of the beer spilled over his chin.

"Ahhh!" he sighed, holding up the half empty bottle, "that's where the gusto is supposed to be, right?" She smiled and nodded her head. He leaned forward and clamped his big hand over her foot. She was wearing thongs, the callused skin of his hand suddenly tight against her bare foot shocked her. She tried to draw back, but he held her firmly. She could feel her toes curling, and the grit on his hand was like sandpaper against her flesh. "Do you really think that's where it's at?" he asked. "I mean the gusto of life?" He studied the bottle. "No," he continued, "it ain't in a bottle." He looked hard into her eyes, then let his gaze drop slowly and settle on her crotch.

Suddenly it seemed as if there were a movie playing in her head. She saw her fingers lightly tracing the horrible scar. Then she was bending over him, holding his face between her hands. She kissed his eyelids and the pink tip of her tongue followed the livid curve of the scar, lovingly, tasting his sweat. Then she slipped her tongue into the corner of his mouth feeling it explore the yellow teeth, rubbing it against the edge of the broken one. The movie stopped. He released her foot and she almost fell. She was trembling and breathing hard. Her mouth felt dry.

"Thanks for the beer," he said. "You know, after work I usually stop down in Hawthorne and have a couple more. I owe you one."

"Oh, no!" she said. Her voice sounded strange, as if she were hearing someone else do a bad imitation of her. "I'm married you see -"

"Wally," he interrupted. "My first name's John but everyone calls me Wally." She nodded. "It's the only bar in Hawthorne," he said. She started to go. "Hey!" he yelled, "what's your name?"

She turned back to face him. "Kathy," she said.

"You have nice legs, Kathy." The colour rose to her cheeks. He smiled, "Harry's Bar." She walked quickly, then half ran toward her house. "In Hawthorne!" he shouted.

Later in the afternoon it began to drizzle, one of those August rains that go on for days, muggy and hot. She wore a nylon blouse and a slim tan skirt. She was about to put on her raincoat, but she returned to her room and, from deep in the corner of a dresser drawer, pulled out a silver chain. Attached to the chain was a Saint Christopher medal. She placed it around her neck and fastened the clasp. Before backing the car out of the garage, she removed her bra and panties and stuffed them into her purse. On her feet were white high heels.

Hawthorne was ten miles down route eighty-six in a depressed area of the county. Long ago the coal mines had been worked out and the freight depot closed. Harry's Hotel

Bar was seldom frequented except for alcoholic pensioners and itinerant construction crews.

She pulled into a parking space and got out of the car quickly, not allowing herself time to think. In her stomach was a hollow, sinking feeling. Five men were grouped together at the bar, and one old drunk slept at a table in the far corner. The light was dim. An overhead fan turned lazily. Her heels clicked on the bare wooden floor. All of the men at the bar turned toward her.

"Hey, well Jesus H. Christ!" shouted Wally. "I told you guys she'd show!"

She stood before them now. Except for one man, the rest had swivelled around to stare at her, but no one had moved to offer her a seat. "Harry, you better ask for proof," someone said.

"Yeah, Harry," Wally laughed, "looks like you got a minor here." His eyes were bright. She could see that he was excited. "Hey, what's your name again?"

"Kathy," she said, feeling her face grow hot and red.

"Right, Kathy." He turned to the huge black man on his left. "Look at them legs, Cliff. She's got the best damn legs I ever seen!" He waved his arm toward two empty tables. "Kathy, walk around the place. Let the boys have a look."

"No, please!" she began.

"Go on, do it!" Wally said. "Stuff like you never pays us a visit here in Harry's."

No one smiled. The men continued to stare at her. The only sound was the soft whirring of the paddle fan. Kathy looked down at the floor. After a moment she walked over to the sleeping drunk and returned. She knew that they were undressing her; that they were pushing their cocks between her bare legs. "You're all right!" Wally shouted. He was confident now, arrogant and drunk. He stood up. She hadn't realized how tall he was, or how thin. Through her mind flashed a picture of her on her knees in front of him. She would need a stool to kneel on or pillows, like a little girl at communion. The thought startled her. She had never touched a man there with her mouth, not even her husband.

"Kathy here ain't no shanty Irish," Wally was saying. "She lives up in Cedar Grove, big house, couple hundred thousand, right, baby?" He put his arm around her waist and reached up to cup her breast in his big hand.

"Yes," she said, "it cost about that." She wanted out of here. These men were ugly and mean. They had been drinking. Wally was the worst of them. But his hand was hot on her breast. She felt her nipples swell.

"And little Kathy here brung old Wally a cold beer in the middle of the morning and damned if she wasn't wearing the tightest shorts you ever seen." Wally shook his head and grinned.

Cliff, the big black man, sipped his beer, but did not take his eyes from her. His head was shaved. There was a gold ring in his left ear. Wide leather straps were buckled tightly around his thick wrists. There were metal studs and heavy loops embedded in the straps. The wide bracelets could easily circle her ankles. A cord could be put through the loops to pull her legs apart, to open her.

Wally tapped the arm of the man at her right, the one who had not yet swivelled around to look at her. "This here's Ezra Stein," Wally said. "He's a fat, dirty old bastard, but smart. Ezra reads a lot." The fat man nodded as he turned lazily to stare at her. His little eyes were set deep in his face. His belly hung over his belt. Several buttons were missing from the lower part of his shirt. She could see the pale flesh of his belly and a trickle of sweat. His hands were soft and puffy, the spatulate fingers swollen at the joints. His pig-eyes glanced first at the Saint Christopher's medal, then rose to meet hers. She felt, all of a sudden, very cold and frightened. She tried to look somewhere else but couldn't. He smiled slightly. The pudgy hands twitched. He turned his back to her.

Wally pointed to the empty stool between Cliff and Stein. "Sit here," he said, and took his place standing behind and to one side of her. The cracked plastic seat felt damp and sticky against her bare legs. She ordered a beer and paid for it herself. As she lifted her glass to drink, Wally's hand slipped under her raincoat. She drew in her breath and quickly put down the glass. She glanced toward the door, but did not move to get up. She wondered if he would unbutton her blouse and rub his rough hand across her breast. The men, except for Stein, watched Wally's hand as it moved beneath her coat. "Jesus," Wally said, squeezing her breast, "they ain't big but they sure are perky." He laughed, looking around at the others and winking. "No bra, neither," he said. The colour rushed to her cheeks.

Cliff reached for her hand. She pulled back, upsetting her purse on the bar. Wally spotted the panties and dug them out. He waved them back and forth. She clenched her hands in her lap and stared down at them, her face red. Wally held her panties over his head. "And, Goddamn, nothin' under her skirt!" he laughed. "Who wants a sniff? Only one buck for a sniff!" He put them to his nose. "Ahhh, a real lady!" The men began laughing and shouting.

"I'll take them," Cliff said, and held out a ten-dollar bill.

"They're yours for free!" Wally shouted. Cliff stuffed the panties in his pocket. "I pay," he muttered quietly and placed the ten in Wally's hand.

"No!" Kathy cried. "Please Wally!" Suddenly, under her coat, his fingers gripped her nipple. He dug his fingernails into it. The unexpected pain was sharp and searing. She gasped. He swung her around, still cutting with his nail into her nipple. She was about to scream, but a look in his eyes stopped her.

"It's Mr. Wallowitz," he said squeezing tighter. "Mr. Wallowitz," he repeated. Tears came to her eyes. Stein still had his back to her, but the others watched silently. In spite of the pain, she felt a hot rush between her legs. "I ain't givin' you leave to call me Wally. Who the hell do you think you are? Just another rich bitch in heat, right? Ain't that right?"

"Yes!"she gasped.

"Yes, what?"

"Yes, Mr. Wallowitz."

"Tell the boys why you're here. What you want from Mr. Wallowitz." He eased the pressure on her nipple. She caught her breath and forced back the tears.

She couldn't think.

"Speak up, Goddamn it!" He twisted her throbbing nipple. "Tell them."

She looked up at him. The ugly scar had deepened. The pockmarks were angry red. "I - I want you to -" she paused. "I want you to come to my house and -"

"Say it right!" he shouted. The men waited.

"Do it to me," she whispered, looking down at the bar, her voice on the edge of breaking.

He tore open her coat and ripped her blouse down the front. Her hands flew up quickly to cover her bare breasts. Wally took both of her wrists in one hand and held them against the bar. "Show," he said, nodding to the men at the bar. He let go of her wrists. Still not looking up, she slowly lifted her hands to cup each breast. She held them out first to the men at her left, then turned to the fat man. Stein placed his hand lightly on the breast closest to him. His white flesh was cold and wet, yet his touch left a burning sensation that caused her to tremble. He slid his hand under her breast and lowered his head toward it. She thought he was going to take the swollen nipple between his thick lips. Instead, he spit on it. His spit was cold. She watched it slide, like a pale yellow snake, over her nipple and down the side of her breast.

"Ohhh," she said, softly, "ohhh!"

Wally spun her around to face him. He placed her tiny hands on each side of his face. She pulled him down to her, pressing her bare breasts against him. Before their lips met, her mouth was open to accept his tongue.

Wally's face between her hands was rough, his skin bumpy. Her fingers found the scar. She followed it with her fingertips. Wally shuddered and pulled away, shaken. With her right hand, she reached up and jerked violently at the Christopher medal breaking the chain. The room was silent as she closed her coat and fastened its belt.

"When?" Wally asked.

"Friday night," she said, trying to keep her voice under control. The men knew she was hot. They could smell her heat. It hung in the humid air. It was as penetrating as the soft rain which whispered against the plate glass window. "Friday," she repeated, "around nine. My husband won't be back until Saturday."

"I'll be there," he said.

Turning toward Stein, she placed the medal next to his glass. He stared straight ahead, ignoring her. She picked up her purse and walked quickly to the door, knowing that behind her were at least four hard cocks. As for Ezra Stein, she wasn't at all sure.

CHAPTER TWO - WALLY

That night, in bed, she told her husband what had happened. She left several things out, but it was clear that she had taken Wally a beer, accepted his invitation, and been subjected to some abuse at the Hawthorne bar. It was also clear that she had asked Wally to come to their home on Friday, when Jeff would be in Philadelphia. When she finished, she waited for what seemed several minutes. Finally, Jeff stirred beside her.

"Here?" he asked. His voice was little more than a whisper.

"Yes. If I can't have him here, I'll meet him somewhere."

"You want him that much?"

"Yes. I don't know why. It's not just for sex. It's something else, something that goes back a long way. At least, that's part of it, I think. I'll know afterwards, and I'm sure this will be the first and last time. It's - it's something I have to do, Jeff, something I have to find out about myself, or more like something I have to resolve."

"And what about me?"

"I don't know." There was a long silence. She didn't expect him to rage and strike her, but it was possible. How she wished he would. Even gentle Jeff must have a breaking point. They had been college sweethearts at a time when it was cool to sleep around, to experiment. But she and Jeff weren't cool. They were the exceptions. Their relationship was old-fashioned and proper. On her wedding night she had been a virgin and so, she knew, had he. Since their marriage, she had never even kissed anyone until this afternoon. Sex between them had been satisfactory for a while, but as her sexual needs grew stronger, his diminished. She propped herself up on one elbow, "This past year -" she began.

"Yes, I understand," he said. He closed his eyes. "If you can promise me you'll be safe, then I guess it's OK, if that's what you need, if it's what you really need."

Odd how sometimes the simplest things can become impossible and how the most complicated things can suddenly become simple.

"No recriminations? No sending me on guilt trips?"

"No, I promise."

She trusted him. He had never gone back on his word. She also loved him. Except for the sexual disappointment, her marriage had been all that she'd ever hoped for. Jeff was intelligent, handsome, caring, and gentle. They shared the same interests: books, the theatre, tennis, golf, the country club. They were open with each other and happy. They laughed together, often and easily. Why, then, had she taken the beer to Wally? Why had the hour she'd spent in Harry's Bar been one of the most exciting she'd ever experienced?

It did not stop raining until late Friday afternoon. Wally's grader sat where he had left it, a silent but imposing reminder. Just as well, she thought, I'd have gone crazy watching him.

At six o'clock she began to prepare herself. A long hot bath, then a shower, her hair, the painting of her nails, her fingernails filed to sharp brilliantly red points, her body perfumed and rubbed with oil. She took meticulous care with her make-up: the lining and shadowing of her eyes, the careful outlining of her lips, accenting their fullness. Over the rich red lipstick she smoothed a transparent oil that made her mouth glisten. Her face and body were nicely bronzed. Yesterday, before he left for Philadelphia, she had asked Jeff to shave her pussy. She'd remembered Wally liked young girls. She wore no panties or jewellery.

She put on a white sheath skirt that buttoned up the front. The skirt restricted her movements but sharply outlined her legs and pulled tight against her buttocks. Her blouse was shear white nylon. Her breasts and pink nipples were clearly visible through it. Unlike the blouse she had worn to Harry's Bar, this one had no buttons. Thin spaghetti straps were tied in bows at her shoulders. A slight tug at each bow, and the blouse would fall away. Her spike heels were new. They enhanced her tiny ankles and the swelling curve of her calves, and the hard round firmness of her ass.

She had never prepared for any occasion with this much consideration. Every choice was calculated, every decision reviewed, every final touch refined. She wanted to make herself as beautiful and as desirable as it was possible for her to be. She wondered how she might dress to entertain fat Ezra

Stein. The thought of those pig-eyes, the cold puffy hands, the sweating pig's body made her tremble. Why - why had the old and ugly fat man disturbed her so? Stein, she concluded, would no doubt instruct her what to wear should he condescend to visit her.

But it was Wally she was expecting...

At eight-thirty she was ready. She had chilled the wine and seen to the candles. She had also placed several bottles of beer in the ice bucket and arranged two pilsner glasses and napkins on a try. Finally, she had heated and perfumed a plastic bottle of baby oil. She placed it on the night stand beside the bed.

At nine-fifteen, she began to pace. At nine-thirty she was looking for the phone number of Harry's Bar when she heard a car in the driveway. "Oh, thank God," she said aloud. Before Wally was halfway up the walk she had opened the door. He didn't look any different than he had on Wednesday: blue sweat-stained shirt, jeans that hung loosely from his hips, the same dirty work shoes she had seen him piss on.

She stepped back from the door. He closed it behind him and stood looking at her. She could see he was impressed. She knew he'd never had a woman as beautiful. This tall, skinny, homely man had never had anyone remotely like her even in his dreams. "How's your tit?" he asked. She crossed to him and took his hands in hers. Looking up into his eyes, she raised his hands to her breasts. The nipple was still sore, but when he touched her the hot rush spread downward. He reached up to pull the bows on her blouse.

"Not yet," she said. She unbuttoned his shirt. His thin chest was white and pimpled. With her tongue she circled his nipples until they stiffened. His hands were on her ass, pulling her into him. She could feel the length of his cock pressing against her belly.

"Do you like that?" he asked, thrusting his prick against her.

"Yes," she said, "yes, I like it."

"And whatcha gonna do with it?"

She looked up at him, her red mouth glistening.

"Suck it, say you're gonna suck it."

"I'm going to - going to - to suck it, Wally."

His bony chest was rising a falling rapidly. His hands moved to unbutton her skirt. She spun away from him and walked quickly to the ice bucket offering him a beer. He took it. His hand was shaking.

"Slowly, Wally, please. Let's make it last." She held the glasses out to him. He filled them and sat down in the big leather chair to drink. She turned off the lamps so the room was bathed in soft candle light. The CD player clicked and a jazz album fell into place; just flute, bass, and drums in a slow primitive rhythm. In front of the leather chair stood a sturdy glass topped coffee table. Kathy stepped up on the table and faced him. As she began to move to the beat of the music, she unbuttoned several of the bottom buttons of her skirt, enabling her to move more freely.

"Take it out," she said. He fumbled at his fly. His monstrous penis emerged like a red and purple snake. She had felt it earlier and knew it would be large, but its length surprised her. She unbuttoned her skirt to a point just below her shaved crotch. He began to stroke himself, his cock continuing to swell and harden.

"No," she said, "no hands, Wally."

She sat on the edge of the table, opening her legs as she place one foot on each of his knees. With both hands she spread the lips of her cunt. He drew in his breath sharply. She pointed her toes and thrust the gleaming butterfly toward him. "My shoes, Wally," she said. He didn't seem to hear or understand. "My shoes," she repeated, "take them off." Gently, he removed her shoes. "I think it's time now," she said. She stood before him and unfastened the four remaining buttons on her skirt. It fell to the floor. Then, with a hand on each shoulder, she pulled at the bows that held up her blouse. It dropped around her feet and she stepped over it.

Wally put a hand on his cock. "Suck it," he said.

She had never sucked a man's cock, not even her husband's. But she had thought about it. She thought about it on that first morning when she took him a beer. He was waiting. She got to her knees before him. She took his cock in her small hands and leaned down to circle its rim with the tip of her tongue. Her lips were wet and red, and her mouth was hot with saliva. She closed her mouth over the head of his cock, leaving a red mark around the glans. He eased himself back into the chair moaning with pleasure. She withdrew his cock from her mouth and stood up.

"Carry me," she said.

He lifted her easily. She put her arms around his neck. He carried her down the hall and into the candle lit bedroom. He stood, for a moment, beside the bed holding her in his arms as if she were a child. She kissed him, sliding her tongue deep into his mouth. Then she kissed his scar and ran the tip of her tongue down its ragged length. He placed her on the bed and looked down at her. "Take your clothes off, Wally," she said. He removed his pants. His cock swung back and forth awkwardly, like a long red stick. She watched it, then slowly spread her legs.

"You want it?" he said.

"Yes, yes, I want it." Wally tried to pin her down, but she slid out from under him. She handed him the heated oil. "Rub me," she said. He poured the hot oil on her breasts. She winced slightly and shuddered. His hands spread the oil over her body, down her belly, and along the slit of her shaven pussy. "Not inside," she said. Gently, he rubbed her legs and feet. She turned over and squirmed as he smoothed the oil on her ass. In the soft light, her splendid body glowed. Still on her stomach, she reached back and spread her ass cheeks.

He rubbed oil into the pink and brown pucker of her anus. Then, tentatively, he began to push the tip of his long bony index finger into her. “No!” she said quickly turning away from him. “Not there.”

Slowly she rolled over to face him as he knelt above her. “Jesus, Kathy, you’re beautiful,” he said.

It was all wrong. Everything was wrong.

She waited a moment then, staring directly into his eyes, challenged him. “Mrs. Ryan,” she said. “It’s Mrs. Ryan, Wally.”

“What?”

“Mrs. Ryan. Say it, Wally. Say ‘Mrs. Ryan, you’re beautiful’.”

He understood but hesitated. She pulled his face close to hers. “Say it,” she repeated.

“You’re beautiful, Mrs. Ryan,” he said, as he tried to push his cock into her.

“No,” she turned away, “later.” She pushed him onto his back and turned around, positioning her head at his crotch. She spread her legs so that Wally could see the glistening cum ooze along her crack. He reached for her pussy. “No,” she said, “just look.” His balls were small but hard. She cupped them in her hands, then bent her head to lick them. With the tip of her tongue, she drew circles on his balls and with her pointed fingernails she gently raked the underside of his cock. Then she sucked his balls, taking them one at time into her mouth, careful not to hurt him. She had not yet placed her lips on his cock.

She spread her own legs wider, jamming one of her small feet under his arm. He began to gasp, turning his head back and forth on the pillow. She dug the fingernails of one hand into the base of his cock and scratched her toenails hard into his armpit. With her other hand, she squeezed his balls and pushed the sharp point of her nails into them. Wally cried out in pain but did not resist.

At several places her fingernails broke through the skin and drew little flecks of blood. His cock grew harder and deepened in colour until it was almost purple, the thick veins bulging and pulsating. She drew the skin back tighter at the base of his cock, increasing the pressure of her grip. Then she began to run her tongue up the underside of his throbbing prick, lingering on the spot just beneath the swollen head, pausing, digging in her nails, hearing him whimper, feeling him pull back, squeezing his balls, and once more the exquisite laving of his cock, if only he were forcing her, now moving her lips as well as her tongue along its slimy length, feeling her lips swell and her mouth fill with hot spittle, feeling in his balls and along his cock the beginning surge of an orgasm. Stopping then. Digging in her nails. The stabbing pain followed by the tender ministrations of her mouth.

"Let me cum," he cried hoarsely.

"Say 'please'," she said. She flicked the tip of his cock with her tongue.

"Goddamn it!" he yelled, and began to reach for her head. She clawed his balls and jerked the base of his cock his cock back fiercely.

"Beg, Wally," she whispered. She did not look up at him. She concentrated instead on his cock, her lips lightly touching it as she spoke. "Beg," she repeated.

"Please!" he cried, "please!"

"More, Wally," she said.

"Suck me, please, Mrs. Ryan, suck me!"

She opened her mouth wide and closed it over the ugly head of his cock. Putting both hands on its shaft she worked it up and down in rhythm with her head. He came immediately, not in short hot spurts but in a long flow of warm mucus. She held his cock away from her, milking him with one tiny hand. He tossed his head from side to side. She turned again and smiled down at him, "For shame, Wally, for shame," she said. In less than a minute Wally's cock went limp in her hand.

Wally lay on the bed and did not move. A wimp could never satisfy her fully, she knew. This was not what she had expected. But in a way it had been marvellous, touching his loathsome cock with her lips and tongue, then taking it into her mouth. Jeff had a beautiful cock and she had never done this for him. She tentatively touched her pussy. It was very wet. She spread her legs and looked down at her shaven cunt. Her vaginal lips and clitoris were red and swollen. She drew her finger over her clit and shuddered. She hadn't felt like this since those dark afternoons in her uncle's basement.

She disappeared into the bathroom, and when she came out, wearing a white nylon robe, Wally was in the living room completely dressed. She handed him a beer. "For the road," she said, leading him to the door.

"But what about next time?" he said. "I want to see you again!"

She smiled and opened the door. "Yes, Wally, but there's a condition. I've been thinking about Harry's Bar. One of your friends was interesting." For a moment she felt a wave of fear, the sure knowledge that she was starting down a dark path toward something that she could not control.

"Stein," she said, "bring Ezra Stein to me Wally."

CHAPTER THREE - MISTER STEIN

Kathy thought continually about Stein. Would he come on Saturday? Each evening she went to bed early and slept late. She was sure she had disturbing dreams, but except for feeling they included her uncle, she could not remember them. Her cunt was constantly wet, but she did not touch herself.

The weather turned bright and hot. During the day she

could hear Wally's grader across the street, but she didn't look out of the windows. In fact, she pulled the drapes shut. Once, he came to the door, but she did not answer.

When Jeff returned from his trip to Philadelphia, he wanted to know all about her Friday night. Although he had accepted the arrangement, he now seemed very jealous and hurt. She told him her evening with Wally was OK but nothing special. He wanted to make love, but she invented an excuse. She half wished he would slap her and then throw her down and pound his cock into her. But, of course, he wouldn't do that, not Jeff.

"I'll make it up to you this weekend," he said. "My next trip is in two weeks."

"No, no." She almost panicked. "No, be away! I'd rather be alone for a little while. Can't you rearrange it? Please!"

He was reluctant but he agreed, understanding as always.

She bathed twice each day and spent hours brushing her hair. She found herself wishing her summer tan would disappear completely. She wanted her skin to be perfectly white. She had an intuitive feeling that Stein would want to see the thin, blue tracery of her veins. The thought caused her to shudder, but at the same time she became hot and excited.

On Tuesday she decided to remove the polish from her nails. She cleaned and filed them, meticulously rounding the points that had dug into Wally's scrotum. She experimented with a very light shade of lipstick and a colourless gloss. She washed and pressed her white silk robe and cleaned her white heels. But, then, she put the heels away, thinking that he might find shoes somehow offensive. She would wear the white robe and nothing else.

She never thought of the night with Wally except for his parting promise to talk to Stein. She spent her waking hours recalling the fat man's smooth puffy skin, his quick, bright eyes full of cunning and hate, the pendulous lips, the coagulating glob of cold saliva that had seemed to sear her breasts as it slid between them. She found herself touching, almost reverently, the place where he had spit on her. Sometimes she repeated aloud her uncle's admonition, 'Shame, Katherine, shame.'

Late Wednesday afternoon she called Harry's Bar. Her hand trembled so much she got the wrong number and had to try a second time. She asked for Ezra Stein. Instead, it was Wally who came to the phone. "Stein wants you to write him a letter," he said.

"Won't he talk to me? Is he there?"

"He's here but he won't come to the phone. He says to write him a letter. Mail it at the local post office tonight. Send it here, to Harry's Bar. He will get it by Friday and decide after he reads it. Send it to Mister Ezra Stein, care of Harry's Bar. Stein also says for you to get your husband to go away just in case he decides to come to your place."

"Thank you, Wally, tell him I've done that already." She replaced the receiver and sat back in the chair, trembling.

She wrote several drafts of the letter until she produced one that satisfied her. She told him about her Catholic childhood, the deaths of her mother and father, the hickory post, the priest-uncle watching but reprimanding her only after he had seen her cum. The peeping priest who punished her with no more than 'Shame! shame!' She told him about her marriage. She wrote that, hard as it was to believe in these times, she and Jeff were virgin bride and groom. She wrote of her love for her husband and of his gentle nature and his kindness, her disgust at Wally's submissive pleading. She ended: I am Yours, Katherine.'

When she thought about the possibility that Stein might be here in this house, her heart began to race and the warm flow oozed from her cunt. She could feel the blood rush to it, swelling its lips, gorging her clit. She felt that she could make herself cum simply by brushing her finger over her clitoris. Her mouth would suddenly go dry, then just as quickly fill with saliva, making her swallow rapidly.

On Saturday morning Jeff left for the airport without waking her, but she heard the garage door shut and then the sound of his car backing down the driveway. She did not bathe until late Saturday afternoon. She shaved her pussy again and rubbed it and her body with scented oil. She made up her eyes, startled at how large and softly luminous they seemed. She applied the pale lipstick and a shiny gloss. Stroking the familiar place between her breasts, she watched her nipples harden beneath the light touch of her trembling fingers. Finally, she put on the white silk robe and at seven o'clock sat down in the living room to wait. She refused to let herself consider the possibility that Stein might not come.

At ten-fifteen she heard a car in the driveway. As she opened the door, the car was backing out and Ezra Stein, in spite of his weight and age, was moving quickly and, she thought, gracefully up the walk.

She stepped back from the door. When his short bulky frame filled the entrance, she turned to face the wall. She waited. She heard him close and bolt the door, place something on the coffee table, and cross to stand behind her. She turned to face him. His eyes were as she had remembered: hard and bright and cruel. There was a slight hint of a smile on his thick lips. He looked at her and nodded. "Always follow your instincts, Mrs. Ryan. It seems they do not misdirect you."

"You approved of the letter?" she asked, bowing her head slightly and lowering her eyes.

"Yes, the letter and also how you've prepared yourself. I approve of both."

"Thank you, Mr. Stein." She felt herself blushing. She lifted her head but was afraid to look directly at him. "Won't you sit down," she said. The burning in her crotch became intense.

He chose Jeff's large leather chair and put his feet up on

the ottoman.

"May I get you something?" Her voice trembled and was so low she wasn't sure if he understood.

"No, not at the moment."

She sat on the edge of the couch, her bare feet peeping out form under the hem of her robe. She saw him looking at them, and the colour rose to her cheeks again as she quickly pulled her feet back.

"I also find shoes uncomfortable," he said. He shoved the ottoman out of the way and placed his feet on the carpet. He sat looking at her, waiting. She didn't move. He glanced down at the floor and tapped impatiently.

"Oh!" she said, jumping up, "forgive me." She knelt at his feet, unlaced the black, worn shoes and slipped them off. His socks were thin black nylon. Carefully, she removed one, then the other. His small feet, like his hands, were soft and white. She rubbed them gently. The smooth skin was cool and damp and smelled faintly of sweat and talcum. This was the first time she had touched him. It seemed right, somehow, that it should be this way, kneeling before him performing this humble act of tenderness and contrition.

After a few moments, he stood up. "Does you husband have a dressing gown?" She nodded. "Bring it, please." She returned immediately with Jeff's velvet robe. He took it from her and held it up. "It is long, but I like the colour, burgundy. Is the bathroom down this hall?"

"Yes, and to your left."

After several minutes, he was back. The robe dragged on the floor, and the sleeves were turned up in two wide folds. He had pulled the belt tight across his huge stomach. "And now, my little penitent, there is nothing but a thin piece of cloth between my flesh and your adoration of it." He chuckled. "And nothing but a thinner piece of cloth between your flesh and my use of it. Or would 'abuse' be a more precise word?" He stared at her. "Abuse, I think." He lowered his bulk into the leather chair once more.

She took her place on the couch, the coffee table between them. She thought of his naked body under the robe, his white distended belly, his cock and balls, his words about adoration and abuse, his absolute authority over her, and his undisguised contempt for her. This fat, ugly, pig of a man had come here to humiliate and, no doubt, hurt her. Yet she was prepared - how might her uncle have phrased it? She was prepared to celebrate his body and, if need be, consecrate her own. 'Celebrate' and 'consecrate' - how often had she heard those words! The desire between her legs was almost painful. She had the urge to rip open her gown and rub her throbbing cunt, the wish to masturbate for him. Instead, not daring to look up, she asked, "How did you discover what I need?"

"It was obvious right from the start. The way you subjected yourself to that fool Wally. And, of course, your letter: the guilt you felt about your parents' deaths, the strict Catholic home, the voyeuristic uncle who refused to give you what you really wanted. What exactly was it you longed for after those steamy sessions in the basement?" He did not wait for her reply. "You wanted to be beaten. You wanted him to remove his belt and whip you with it. You wanted him to punish you for your sins. And then there is your weak husband jumping through whatever hoop you hold up. Did he have to be absent this weekend or did you send him away?"
"I sent him away."

"Ah, yes. And finally there was Wally begging for your kisses. Three men in your empty life and all of them emasculated."

She lifted her head and for the first time looked directly at him. "I knew that afternoon in Harry's Bar, that you were different. I knew you would not be like other men."

He leaned forward, his eyes narrow slits. "Of course you did. You understood that to me you are nothing. You are of no earthly use other than to be used. Your face is beautiful, but I'm not interested. Your small, young body is exquisite, but it doesn't excite me. Your innocence is as rare these days as honesty, but it is of little consequence to me, except..."

He left the sentence hanging, incomplete. The colour had risen to her cheeks. She looked away from him. He smiled. "Tell me," he said, "You've had no children?"

"No," she said, "I - I can't."

His eyes bore into hers. She could not look away. "Then, it seems, the delight in nourishing another life at your breast is to be denied you forever." He smiled slightly. "If I recall," he leaned forward, "you have such healthy breasts, small but full and firm."

She was suddenly conscious of the blood pulsing in her nipples. Abruptly, he got up and crossed to stand before her. He untied his robe and it fell open. After a moment, she slid off the couch to her knees. Her face was not six inches from his crotch, which was as hairless as her own. His cock hung limp and fat like a pale sausage. His testicles were enormous smooth white globes. The skin drawn tightly over them seemed almost transparent. She could see the network of their blue veins crisscrossing and intersecting like a detailed road map.

She inched forward to lick him. He slapped her, not hard, across the face. More surprised than hurt she fell backward. She huddled between the couch and the coffee table like a frightened child.

"I am not your uncle or your husband or Wally," he said. Unable to speak, she nodded. He lifted his dead, white cock and let it go. "You want to suck this?"

"Yes," she whispered.

"And these?" He cupped his huge testes.

"Yes," she said, getting to her knees.

"How much?"

The burning between her legs was unbearable. She shut

her eyes and clasped her hands together to keep them from shaking. "Very much," she said.

He closed his robe and retied the cord. Then he returned to the leather chair. "There is a jar in that paper bag on the table. A gift for you."

It was a squat wide-mouthed glass jar with a screw-on lid. It contained approximately two quarts of murky water and three flat worm-like creatures. Two were brown-grey and at least six inches in length. The third was longer and brightly coloured with bands of orange and yellow and blue. The sudden light caused all of them to expand and contract. They propelled themselves listlessly, sliding against the curved surface of the glass container.

She drew back, pulling her robe together, her hands instinctively covering her breasts. She stared at the leeches, the bloodsuckers, hypnotized by their slow contractions. Even through the dirty water the light glinted on the slime that covered their bodies. Stein watched her intently for a few moments then sat back and folded his hands over his stomach again, apparently satisfied.

"My pets," he said, "phylum, Annelida; class, Hirudinea; common name, leech. But they are most uncommon, don't you think?" She continued to gaze at the jar, hardly hearing him. "They have a tiresome diet, subsisting on just one food. Can you guess what it is, Mrs. Ryan?" She did not answer. "Mrs. Ryan," he spoke forcefully, "I've asked you a question!"

"Yes," she said, her face gone pale, "yes, I know what it is."

"They are hungry, Mrs. Ryan, not weak yet but hungry nonetheless. It's been about five months since they've eaten." She shuddered visibly. "Do you really want me that much?" he said, pointing at the jar. "Does the disgusting thought of holding this limp, white, shrivelled cock between your lovely lips excite you that much? Are you so anxious to lick these," he lifted his testicles, "that you would..." He did not finish the sentence.

She stood up, facing him, the coffee table and the jar between them. Her trembling hands loosened the belt of her gown. Her high firm breasts rose and fell rapidly. Without taking her eyes from him, she unscrewed the lid of the jar.

"Yes, Mr. Stein," she said, "I would like to feed your pets."

If her response surprised him, he did not show it. "Come here, Mrs. Ryan." She stepped around the coffee table and stood between his open legs. He reached up and squeezed her nipples between his thumbs and index fingers. At his touch she gasped and her breath came faster. "Yes," he smiled up at her, "they will enjoy these." He pointed to her crotch. "Let me see it."

She spread the lips of her shaven cunt for him. The pink membranes were dark with blood, and he could see the cum beginning to ooze from her vagina. Her clit stood up, red and hard. He pressed it with his forefinger. She thrust her hips forward. He quickly withdrew his hand and looked up at her angrily.

"I'm sorry," she said, "I couldn't help it."

"Perhaps we can take care of that." She glanced at the jar and drew in her breath sharply. She shut her eyes. Stein watched her closely. "Yes, Mrs. Ryan, I'll leave it up to you. I will always leave the choices up to you. Tell me, how many of my little companions do you want?"

Why didn't he tie her down or something and drop them on her? Why must she help? Why must she agree? Her eyes were still closed and her head bowed. "Two," she said softly.

"What?"

"Two. I want to feed two."

"Well, Mrs. Ryan, you are very kind indeed. Feed them, that's what you said, wasn't it, feed them? Feed them from your sweet virgin breasts?"

"Yes."

"But they don't subsist on milk, to they?" She didn't answer. "However, I'm sure they will find some nourishment, Mrs. Ryan. Won't they?"

"Yes," she whispered.

"Shall we go to the bedroom?" he asked.

"Yes," she said.

"Will you take them?" He motioned toward the jar. She picked it up carefully but did not look into it. From the paper bag, he removed a pair of rubber gloves and followed her down the hall. "Oh," he said, entering the bedroom behind her, "candles. How thoughtful. Will you light all of them, please?"

She placed the jar on the end table and, in a few moments, the room was flickering in candle light. He switched off the floor lamps. "Good," he said, "bright enough to see and yet softly romantic." He touched her arm. "Perhaps, in these matters, you have the habit of making last minute preparations?"

She sat at her nightstand and took up her lip gloss. Her hand trembled, but she willed herself to steady it. She brushed her hair and turned to him holding up a vial of perfumed oil.

"Yes," he said.

She began to rub the oil over her body. Her skin glowed, reflecting the warm light. "Is this what you do before receiving a lover?" he asked.

"I, yes, I want to look attractive."

"For them?" he pointed at the jar and chuckled.

"Yes." She cupped her breasts as she had done that afternoon at Harry's. She crossed to the jar and, kneeling, pressed one of her nipples to it. Perhaps sensing the change in light or heat, all of the leeches stopped circling and hung suspended in the water just opposite her breast. They undulated slowly. She stared at them. They were flat, narrow at one end and wide at the other.

Stein watched her. "The broad posterior contains the primary sucker," he explained. "It is large and serves to attach the body firmly to its host." She could see the suckers sticking to the glass. "The head and mouth are at the narrow end," he continued, as if he were giving a lecture. "There is a smaller but very powerful sucker at the head as well as three small teeth. The punctures they make heal very quickly." She stood up, almost knocking over the jar.

"Are you afraid?" he asked.

"Yes, very,"

"Well, then, why do it? You have a choice, you know. We can simply put the lid on the jar and I will go."

"No!"

"Good," he smiled. "I must admit, Mrs. Ryan, you surprise me. Yet, there is something of the Old Testament in this, don't you think? I mean, the beautiful and innocent Eve seduced by the serpent." He pulled on the rubber gloves. "Will it be necessary to restrain you?"

"No."

"Then perhaps you'd better lie down. They have been waiting for a long time." He patted the side of the glass and turned to her. "Are you ready?" All week she had been thinking of him, of Stein, knowing that he would do something, would be different, would understand what she needed. But no one could possibly have imagined this - this giving herself to those slimy bloodsucking creatures, offering them her breasts, making herself beautiful for them, the lip gloss, the perfume - Good God, it was insane!

She pushed the robe from her shoulders, and it fell to the floor. "Yes," she said, "I'm ready." She lay on the bed, her arms at her sides, her legs slightly parted. She heard him reach into the water with his gloved hand. As he leaned over her, she felt drops of the warm water on her stomach. Her nipples seemed twice their normal size. Under her breast she felt a cold stinging sensation as the sucker adhered tightly to her skin. Then, she felt the long glutenous body stretching over the curve of her breast.

Stein pressed the leech's head against her nipple. "Here, my pet, is what you've been waiting for. What both your and your gracious hostess have been waiting for." She felt a slight pinch as its teeth punctured her skin. He attached the second leech in the same manner to her other breast.

Lying back, she closed her eyes and gave herself over to the subtle but oddly powerful sensations that the feeding leeches produced. Gradually, at her breasts, there was a quiet subsiding of tension and, in a way she could not understand, her initial feelings of revulsion changed to tenderness. With the index finger of each hand, she began to stroke their bodies. They squirmed slightly under her touch but continued to feed greedily. The pressure of their suckers increased. She spread her legs and reached down to touch her clit.

Stein quickly pushed her hand away from it. "I was hoping," he said, "that the other one might be invited to feed there."

Stein's voice seemed far away. She shook her head. "No, no, not there," she whispered.

"Very well, then, perhaps some other time." She did not respond. She closed her eyes and concentrated on the leeches at her breasts. She could feel the flow of juices between her legs. She lay like that for several minutes before opening her eyes. At the foot of the bed stood Stein, his pig-eyes bright, his robe open, and his flaccid cock beginning to stiffen. It seemed to her that she was starting to cum, but it wasn't like any orgasm she'd ever experienced. It was slow, almost imperceptible but nonetheless a tickling and burning coupled with a delicious draining at her nipples and between her legs.

She began moving her hips and making small whimpering sounds. At one point she bent over her breasts and brushed her lips against each of the feeding leeches. "There, there," she whispered softly. As they sucked, she became aware of the increased weight of them. They had embedded their heads deep into her nipples. She could feel acutely the pressure at the points where they were anchored to her body. And all the while there was this euphoric flow inside her cunt, seeming to be drawn out in a long thin strand, a liquid thread, opalescent and shimmering in the candle light.

She closed her eyes again. When she opened them, Stein was standing over her removing one then the other bloated creature from her breasts. "You've been generous," he said, dropping the thick leeches back into the jar. "They will not require feeding for a very long time."

"And what about me?" she asked rolling on her side and reaching out to touch his cock. It had become limp again. The skin covering his huge testicles was tight. She drew her fingernails lightly across it. His skin felt smooth and dry like rice paper. He looked down at her. "Do you think you can make me hard?"

"I can try. But first I want..."

"What?" he asked. "What is it you want?"

"The other one. The big one with the bright colours." The two she had fed lay quietly on the bottom of their container. The third still clung to the glass, its extended body almost circling the jar.

"It's quite large," Stein said. "A Pisciolidae. They are different. Teeth bigger and sharp. The suckers are very strong and their appetite, well, it's voracious."

She lay back on the bed again and spread her legs. "Here," she said, and she raised her pelvis. Stein put on his gloves. He had some trouble detaching the leech from the glass and was forced to hold it with both hands. She could see it wriggling and the light glinting off its brilliant colours. She moved to the edge of the bed so that Stein might have easier access to her cunt. He was preparing to position it so that its head would be on her clitoris.

"No," she said. Stein paused, thinking she had changed her mind. "No," she said again. "I mean turn it around." He looked puzzled. "Place the large sucker on my clitoris. Direct the head up there - up inside me."

Stein stared at her.

"Yes," she said. "I want it inside me, deep inside."

The posterior sucker covered her clit and immediately fastened itself with such force that she could feel her clitoris swell with blood. Stein didn't have to direct the head. Sensing the warm, dark, liquid place, it slid quickly into her open vagina. She watched as the snake like creature oozed into her. She could feel it move in the dark passage, pulling itself along by attaching and releasing the smaller sucker. Finally, it was stretched tight against the furrow of her cunt. Three-fourths of its length had disappeared inside her. She felt the head sucker anchor itself firmly. She waited. As it bit into her vaginal wall, she winced and cried out.

When she looked up at Stein again, his cock was thick and hard as a club. Very carefully she got to her knees, keeping her legs well spread. Her mouth filled with hot saliva. She licked his dry balls until they dripped with it. Bending her head lower, she licked the underside of his cock, first with the tip of her tongue, probing and flicking the base of his glans, then long teasing runs down its thick length, circling his balls, gradually lapping at the underside of his cock, stroking and licking it with her tongue. Finally, she opened her pretty mouth wide and took the head of his pale cock into it.

Between her legs she felt the drawing sensation of the large sucker and an exquisite draining. She felt the engorged body of the leech swelling deep inside her cunt just as Stein's engorged cock filled her mouth. She placed her hands on his smooth white belly which hung above her. As he moved, it brushed against her hair. She took more of him into her mouth. His pudgy fingers gently directed her, pushing her head slowly into his hairless crotch and pulling it back just as slowly, her tongue sliding along the base of his cock, her lips and teeth stretching the skin tightly over its head at the end of each pull and firmly skimming it back as she moved her head down his shaft. The ugly man and the beautiful young woman moved rhythmically together in slow motion. All the while she could feel the thing between her legs growing thicker.

Stein came in her mouth with several short hot spurts. She dug her nails into his stomach. He stumbled back and sat down on the bench behind him, his cock going limp, the scratch marks flaring like welts across his white skin. She had hardly been aware of his coming. Her clawing at his stomach at the moment of his orgasm was accidental, a reaction to the intensification of desire between her legs. Her feelings were centered on her own vagina, the wet slit of her cunt and her clitoris.

Now, she fell writhing to the floor, her legs spread wide, her hands grasping and pulling at her nipples. The leech was the thickness of a cock. She squeezed her vaginal muscles. Perhaps somewhere in the dark recesses of the creature's mind there existed a dim memory of another life that caused it to respond to her rhythm. Or perhaps the primordial patterning of its genes insisted that it move as she did. Perhaps it simply squirmed in fear. She felt it extending and contracting, swelling and moving there inside her. The suckers alternately drew and released. The large sucker covered her clitoris completely. It was like a small but powerful mouth, sucking hard at her clit, drawing it in and out. As she squeezed, the body squirmed inside her. The pleasure she felt was unbearable. The creature's head buried itself deeper into her, and the swelling, undulating body filled her and slid up and down against her slit.

There was no man pressing her to the floor, no electrical device jammed into her opening, no dead hickory post rubbing between her legs. But, instead, this living thing moving with her contractions, the fierce mouth glued to her clit, opening and closing over it, sucking it.

Her orgasm exploded in a fury of spasms. She thrashed and screamed. The thing between her legs, sensing danger yet not satiated, increased its pressure to adhere, drawing her clit deep into its sucking mouth. Pain coupled with pleasure. She arched her back, shouting unintelligibly, tossing her head from side to side, squeezing her breasts. Orgasm after orgasm welled up inside her and flowed over and around the tumescent leech that finally released her and slid from her cunt blind and flopping about on the rug as if she had just given birth to it.

After a moment, Stein rose unsteadily and put it back into the jar. He then helped her to the bed where, immediately, she fell into a deep and quiet sleep.

CHAPTER FOUR - REUNITED

Jeff did not come home - he died suddenly of food poisoning far from home. An airline meal - it caused quite a problem to the airline, but that meant little to the distraught Kathy. She could not bring herself the visit the funeral home. After each drugged sleep she woke to the terrible knowledge that it was she who had persuaded Jeff to do this trip. It was her insane desire to see Stein. And Stein, too, was guilty. Even before he decided to see her on Saturday, he had told her to send Jeff away. The thought of him sitting in Jeff's chair and wearing Jeff's robe was driving her crazy. And in the bedroom she and Jeff shared - this old, fat, pervert had been there with his horrible leeches. He was as guilty as she. It seemed to her that together they had made a pact with the Devil to kill her husband.

It rained on the morning of the funeral. By the time the entourage reached the cemetery, however, the rain had stopped. But a solid, gray cloud cover continued to mask the sun and sky. Since the news of Jeff's death, she'd eaten almost nothing, but on the morning of the funeral she awakened ravenously hungry. After eggs and ham and several cups of coffee, she showered and then carefully selected her clothes: a black skirt and suit jacket, a white tailored blouse, black stockings and pumps.

She had not been in the sun for several weeks. Her face was pale, but in spite of the past few days, she looked serene. Her skin was tight and smooth, almost translucent. The redness had gone from her eyes. As she applied her mascara, she noticed that her hands were quite steady. She'd been given a small black hat and veil which, after some hesitation, she decided to wear. She pinned it on, arranged the veil, and carried her raincoat.

Jeff's parents picked her up and took her directly to the cemetery. They arrived shortly after the hearse and the cars carrying relatives and friends. The people standing around the grave site parted to make way for them. Among the mourners were Brian, who had been their best man, and his wife Cordelia. Brian approached her but she quickly bowed her head, not wishing to talk to him or look at the casket.

The priest began speaking. Several times she heard him say Jeff's name, but the words were meaningless sounds. She and Jeff had known each other since high school. Until this past month of insanities, he had been her world. The fact that he was gone was just beginning to register. Tomorrow he would not be running up the front steps, happy and laughing, and calling out her name. He would not come home tomorrow, or ever, not ever again. She felt faint. The priest had paused in his eulogy.

She raised her eyes and there, across the gleaming mahogany lid of the casket, was Ezra Stein's head. For a moment she thought she had gone mad. The head seemed dismembered. From her angle of view it appeared to be resting on the casket like a pumpkin. She gasped and quickly looked away. Her father-in-law felt her trembling and took her arm.

After a little while, she turned and looked up again. Stein had stepped back, but he was no more than six feet away from her. Only Jeff's body and the grave separated them. The fat man wore a shabby black raincoat that was pulled tight across his huge stomach. His pig eyes stared at her across the little distance. She looked away once more fearing, for a moment, she might be sick. Her cheeks reddened with anger. There was a shovel beside the mound of dirt. She wanted to swing it in one terrible blow that would cleave his evil face like an apple.

When she looked up again, he was still staring directly at her. She looked back at him, a scream of rage swelling in her chest. Then his heavy lips began to form silent words. She wasn't sure at first what they were. He repeated them.

"Will you leave with me?"

She looked again at the ground, hoping it would open up at her feet and swallow her just as it was soon to close over Jeff. Dimly aware that the priest had come to the end of his speech, she heard him ask for a moment of silent prayer for the repose of her husband's soul. She knew Stein was watching her, waiting for her answer. She nodded her head in assent.

Before she could collect her thoughts, a blur of people began to crowd around her offering sympathy and expressions of their sorrow. Jeff's father directed her down the path toward their car. Behind them she could hear the casket being lowered. She was aware of Stein up ahead, waiting. She took a firm grip on her father-in-law's arm, determined to ignore Stein. But when they were next to him, she heard herself introduce him as an old and dear friend of Jeff's. He offered to drive her home, saying he lived in the neighbourhood. She accepted, quickly explaining to Jeff's parents that the trip back to her house would take them out of their way. They protested for a moment but, anxious to begin the long drive back to Boston, they left her there standing in the road with the rather shabby fat man.

As soon as they started to drive away, Stein pushed her back against the side of his car. He leaned his fat bulk into her.

"I hate you!" she hissed, raising her hands to strike him. Just before their car turned the bend, Jeff's father looked into the rear-view mirror and, although Kathy was not visible, the fat man's arm was lifted as if he were waving. His blow caught Kathy on the side of the head, slamming her against the car. Her cheek carried the imprint of his hand. She bit her lip, holding back the tears.

"You will never do that to me!" he said, fighting to control the anger in his voice. She leaned against the car sobbing. "Never," he repeated. She nodded her head. He opened the car door and, pointing to the passenger side, slid behind the wheel. She got in and sat next to him. As they drove away, she glanced back. Two men were shovelling dirt into her husband's grave.

Stein drove slowly and cautiously like someone who had just been granted a license. The car was an old Chrysler. The seats were greasy and wads of cotton fiber hung from the torn fabric. On the floor behind her, beer bottles rolled back and forth clinking together. Even though the afternoon had turned muggy, Stein did not open the windows. Under the smell of spilled beer was the faint odour of vomit. Stein did not speak until they reached an open stretch of highway. "Tell me, Mrs. Ryan," he said, "what did you think about when you heard your husband was dead?"

"Killing myself," she answered.

"And killing me?"

She waited a moment wondering if it would be better to avoid the truth. "Yes, and you too," she said, realizing it was impossible to lie to him.

"Guilt again," he chuckled, "major, world-class guilt. Only this time you like to think we are both guilty, we both killed your husband. And now you want to avenge his death?"

"Yes," she said.

"Well why don't you do it? Why don't you kill me?"

She did not respond. He pulled slowly to the side of the road and stopped. "Here, I'll make it easy for you." He reached under his seat, fumbled around, and withdrew a tire iron. "Take it." He placed it in her lap. "One hard blow right here," he tapped his temple. "I'll look the other way. You can say I tried to rape you. Plead self-defence. The lovely widow defending her honour on the day of her husband's funeral. My guess is that they won't even make you stand trial."

She didn't move for several minutes. Then, with both hands she picked up the tire iron holding it firmly at one end. Stein turned away from her and looked out at the passing traffic. She raised the heavy bar and, with a sob, put it down on the seat between them.

Stein turned back to face her. She stared ahead, her body rigid. "I'm surprised, Mrs. Ryan," he said smiling. "Here it is not more than half an hour after burying the man you so dearly loved. I've given you the opportunity and the means to avenge his death and you refuse." He placed the tire iron beneath the seat. "A short time ago we were treated to the sad sight of the pretty widow dressed in black weeping at the grave of her beloved husband. And now she is sitting in a car with the man she believes is responsible for his death. And she's hot. Isn't that right Mrs. Ryan?" He placed his puffy white hand over hers. She drew in her breath sharply at his touch but did not move. "Do you think I'm responsible?" he waited for her reply.

"Yes," she said, not looking at him.

"After you came to the bar that afternoon did I try to contact you?"

"No," she said quietly.

"Well then, Mrs. Ryan, how did we manage to get together?"

"I phoned you."

"And pleaded with me to visit you, isn't that right?"

"Yes."

"Then you wrote a letter to me asking me to come to your home?"

"Yes."

"And because of the rather unusual nature of our relationship, who suggested that your dear Jeff go off to Washington? Did I?"

"I'm not sure," she said. "You told me to send him away, but I had already done it."

"Have I ever forced anything on you?" His voice was almost a whisper. "Isn't it true, Mrs. Ryan, that you've always had the option to say 'no'?"

"Yes!" she cried, turning abruptly away from him, leaning against the side window, the tears welling up in her eyes. "Yes!" she cried again. "I can't help it. I can't, I really can't."

"Help it or not, the choices have been your own. It is a hard fact of life, Mrs. Ryan, that we must live by the choices we make. I suggest you learn to live by yours."

"Or die," she said softly, looking straight ahead.

"That, too," he answered.

They sat in silence for a few moments. She stopped crying and wiped her face with a handkerchief she'd taken from her purse. Stein leaned back in his seat and sighed. "That's settled," he said. "Now, I would like you to do several things for me but only if you wish."

"What things?" she asked. He waited. "I'm sorry," she said, "what would you like me to do, Mr. Stein?"

"That's better." He tapped the steering wheel with both hands. "I do not like driving. I am not good at it and this is a borrowed car. I'd like you to take me home." She reached for the door handle. "Not yet," he said. "Are you wearing anything under your blouse?"

"Yes, of course," she said, "a brassiere."

"I would like you to remove it and the blouse as well. And your stockings."

"Pantyhose," she said.

"Yes. I would like you to be naked except for your hat, jacket, skirt, and shoes."

She hesitated. To do as he asked, now in this place at this time would be unthinkable, worse, even, than accepting the leeches. This obscenely gross degenerate was partly responsible for her husband's death. She had watched them lower Jeff's casket into the grave less than thirty minutes ago. She should have killed Stein. She should have crushed his skull with the tire iron.

"Yes, Mrs. Ryan, or no?" he asked.

Without a word, she removed her jacket, her blouse, and her bra. Then she put her jacket back on and buttoned its single button. The swell of her breasts was clearly visible between the deep V of the jacket. She slipped out of her shoes and stripped off her pantyhose. Her white legs contrasted sharply with the black skirt. After she had wiggled her bare feet into her shoes, she waited. During all this time, Stein had not looked at her. "Did you want to do that for me?" he asked.

"Yes, Mr. Stein," she said softly.

"Now, one more thing. Draw the index finger of your right hand along the outer lips of your cunt and across your clitoris, then hold it up for me to see." She reached between her legs and did as he asked. He glanced at the finger she held up. It glistened with her cum. "Ahh," he said, his small eyes staring into hers. "When was the last time you were like that? The truth, Mrs. Ryan."

She folded her hands in her lap and looked down at them. "On that night."

"Mrs. Ryan, I do wish you would learn to be more specific."

"On the night you came to my house."

"And when did this begin?" he said, pointing at her hands.

"The cemetery."

"Precisely when at the cemetery?"

"When I saw you there."

"So, across your dear husband's coffin you see Ezra Stein, this fat, ugly, evil old man and your dry cunt suddenly becomes hot and wet. What does that tell us, Mrs. Ryan?" She was silent. "Never mind, I think we know." He motioned toward the door. She got out and walked unsteadily around to the driver's side. He'd gathered her blouse, bra, and pantyhose together. As she slid behind the wheel, he opened the door again and dropped them to the gravel. "Show me your breasts," he said. She spread her jacket and he leaned closer to peer at her nipples. Each had a tiny triangular scar where the leeches had fed. He smiled and sat back in his seat, his pudgy hands clasped over his stomach. "Too bad all the pets have been fed," he said. He gestured toward the ignition and nodded. She started the engine. "Do you recall what you said when I last phoned you?"

She was afraid to answer. "I don't remember." But she did remember. The day after the leeches he had called her and she had rejected him.

"You told me you were absolved. You said, 'It's over, Mr. Stein'. You said it twice, then you hung up on me." She could hear the anger in his voice. She moved to shift the car into gear, but he grabbed her wrist tightly. "That was a mistake, Mrs. Ryan, a bad mistake. No one ever speaks to me like that." His grip tightened on her wrist. "It is just one more mistake to atone for, Mrs. Ryan." A cold fear made her tremble. "Yes, Mrs. Ryan," he let go of her, "your disrespect for Ezra Stein and your husband's untimely death, two tragic mistakes. I should think you have much, very much, to atone for. You are far from being absolved. Isn't that right, Mrs.

Ryan? A heavy penance to be paid?"

"Yes," she said, "I'm sorry Mr. Stein. Truly sorry."

"But being sorry isn't enough is it, Mrs. Ryan? For you it is never enough."

"That's right, Mr. Stein. It is never enough," she answered.

He smiled. "I'm glad to see that you agree. Now, let us drive slowly and carefully to my place. It is an old warehouse next to the abandoned mines out on route 519, a few miles south of Hawthorne."

CHAPTER FIVE - THE WAREHOUSE

Kathy put the car in gear and eased out onto the road. Stein sat back and closed his eyes. They drove in silence for several minutes, and a soft rain began to fall. She remembered the day when she met Stein at Harry's Bar in Hawthorne. It was an afternoon much like this one.

"You must be tired after such an eventful morning," Stein said. "If you wish, you may stay the night at my place."

She did not answer for a long while. Finally, without taking her eyes from the road she said, "Thank you, Mr. Stein."

He dozed beside her, waking soon after they'd passed through Claremont. "Look for Sconzo's Wrecking," he said. "It will be on your left. Then take the next left after that. It's an old dirt road that dead-ends at the mine. I'm the only one who uses it now."

Sconzo's was a ramshackle wooden garage which, in better days, had been a gas station. Behind it were scattered the rusting bodies of wrecked cars. "Vinnie Sconzo is my only neighbour," Stein said. "In fact, this is his car. He let me borrow it today." The garage looked empty but the front window was so dirty she couldn't be sure. Stein glanced over at her and smiled. "Mr. Sconzo knew how anxious I was to pay my last respects to an old and dear friend. Isn't that how you introduced me to your late husband's parents?"

She felt the tears coming to her eyes but held them back. "Yes," she said.

"Go easy here," Stein cautioned. "The road is hard to see." He leaned forward peering through the rain. "Poor Vinnie is burdened with a retarded son. I let the boy work for me and he stays at my place so Vinnie owes me lots of favours." He pointed ahead and gestured, "There."

She had slowed down but almost missed the turn anyway. The narrow road twisted, and the old Chrysler lurched through the pot holes. "I understand there's a good deal of evidence to suggest that the airline was at fault," Stein said. "The chicken he ate, was it?"

"So I was told," she answered, easing the car out of a rut.

"You mean you're not going to sue?"

"I hadn't thought of it." She was afraid the irritation was noticeable in her voice.

"Well, Mrs. Ryan, you should think of it. You could be in for as much as five million."

"I'm not interested in the money," she said. Up ahead she could make out the warehouse, a large rectangle of corrugated steel, dark gray against the barren hillside.

"I think you ought to be interested." Stein had turned in his seat to look directly at her. "For both our sakes," he said. "Pull up next to the door at this end of the building. All the other doors are welded shut."

She followed him out of the car. Beside the heavy metal door, he took out a ring of keys and opened a small steel box set into the wall. He pressed some buttons and she heard a faint clicking noise coming from the second floor, then a louder click on the other side of the box.

"You said your late husband was from Boston?" he asked, pushing open the door.

"Yes."

"Many, many years ago I went to school there, M.I.T., electrical engineering. I designed the complicated locking system for my humble abode here. It also works from the inside." He stepped back pointing to the narrow iron stairwell that led to the second floor. She started up, noticing that the first floor held nothing but rusted mining equipment.

Stein was behind her. "Tell me, Mrs. Ryan, under your jacket and skirt are you naked?"

She could feel her face redden. "Yes," she said.

"Say it," he demanded, "say that you are naked and why."

"Under my skirt and jacket I am naked, Mr. Stein, because - because you asked me to remove my bra and pantyhose."

"Did you want to do that for me?"

"Yes, I wanted to do it for you."

At the top of the stairs was another steel door. Neither it nor the one on the first level had handles or windows. "I unlocked it from below," Stein said, "just push." Inside was a dimly lit passageway at least a hundred feet long. On her left was a windowless outside wall. Ahead was what seemed to be a large open space. "Down there," he said, pointing to the end of the passageway. Her heels clicked on the bare concrete floor. To her right was a series of four doors spaced at equal intervals.

"Storage," he said, as they passed the first door. "The second is for my hobbies and next is the pet room." He took her by the arm. "Would you like to see your little playmates?" He inserted a key in the lock.

"No." she said, pulling back. "Please, Mr. Stein, no more pets."

"Of course, you're tired. So am I." They passed the fourth door. "And this is Richie's room, Vinnie's son. He will be along later. I think you might take to Richie," Stein chuckled. "He's probably just a few years younger than you, I would guess. He certainly will be impressed by your intelligence and charm." The hallway opened into a room about fifty feet square. There were no windows. Kathy wondered how he ever knew what kind of day it was. The air smelled greasy, like fried onions. But in spite of the humid weather, the high ceilinged room felt cool.

To her right was a kitchen sink and some cupboards along with a thick round table and several mismatched chairs. To the right of the stove stood a metal partition. The open door revealed a sink and toilet. In the far corner of the main room were a huge unmade bed and several old chests. Before them was an area which contained a soiled maroon couch and a large vinyl chair with a hassock. There was also a television set and, beside the chair, a large wooden desk. A few dirty rugs were scattered about, but most of the floor was bare concrete. Two large steel columns supported the ceiling beam. She noticed eye bolts about ten feet up on either side of the column. She was surprised to see several small TV cameras suspended from the ceiling. Also, in front of Stein's chair, a TV monitor hung down from the ceiling.

On the floor, near the centre of the room, was a large foam rubber pad and on it stood what looked like a big nail keg, heavily padded on the top and sides. The keg rested in a metal cradle which stood on four angle-iron legs, the pair at the front shorter than those at the back. These supports were anchored to the floor and welded to the base of each leg was an eye bolt similar to those in the column.

Stein had lowered himself into his chair and propped his feet up on the hassock. "I'd like a beer, Mrs. Ryan. The refrigerator is over there." He pointed. "And bring a glass." She went to the kitchen area, found a bottle of Iron City, opened it and set it, along with a glass, on the desk beside his chair. Stein looked up at her. "I think you should go to the bathroom and freshen up," he said. "Do you have your lipstick?"

"Yes, here in my purse."

"Use it. You have a nice mouth." She crossed to the bathroom. "Leave the door open," he called. "No matter what you do in the bathroom, leave the door open. In my house, you have no privacy, none at all." She did not close the door.

"I'm not accustomed to waiting around in cemeteries all morning. My feet are hot and tired," he called to her. She had to urinate. He did not look in her direction. She splashed her face with cold water and applied fresh lipstick. "Do you remember," he asked, "how you made me comfortable on the night of our meeting in your house?"

"Yes, I remember," she answered, crossing the room to stand before him. She experienced, just as she had on that night, the sinking sensation in her stomach. He smiled up at her. His beady eyes stared into hers, and then he slowly raised his pudgy hand and with a blunt forefinger he pointed to the floor.

She got down on her knees. Against her bare skin, the cement floor was cold and gritty. She began to untie his laces. He wore the same black shoes as before, dirty and cracked. "Ahh, yes," he sighed, leaning back. She rolled down his socks and carefully slipped them over his heels and slid them off. His small white feet were warm and damp. As before, mixed with the fetid odour was the smell of baby powder. He smiled slightly, his eyes closed. "Mrs. Ryan," he said, "what were you doing at eleven o'clock this morning?"

She stared at his small fat toes, not looking up at him. "I was attending the funeral of my husband."

"I see. And did you love your husband very much?"

"Yes, I did. I loved him very much." She swallowed, holding back the tears.

"And am I at least partially responsible for his death?"

It was several moments before she could answer. "Yes, Mr. Stein, you are."

He opened his eyes and peered at his watch. "It is one

o'clock, just two hours after your husband's funeral. What are you doing now, Mrs. Ryan?"

"This," she said. She quickly wet her lips with the tip of her tongue. Then, she bent over his toes and tenderly pressed her soft mouth to them.

He closed his eyes again and smiled, "Yes, Mrs. Ryan, on your knees to kiss the feet of your husband's murderer. Penance, Mrs. Ryan. You need that don't you?"

For an answer, she lifted his other foot to her lips.

"A few more questions, after you unbutton your jacket." She fumbled with the button. Her jacket fell open. With his eyes still closed, he motioned for her to lean forward. He pressed his right foot against her breasts. His toes were almost even with her chin. "Mrs. Ryan," he said quietly, "do you know what it means to French?"

"Yes," she looked up at him, her arms at her sides.

"Would you explain?"

"You put your tongue -"

"Ahh, the tongue," he interrupted, "a remarkably sensitive instrument. I seem to recall that you use yours extremely well." She looked down at his foot resting lightly against her breasts. "Your tongue, Mrs. Ryan," he said softly.

She could feel the sticky wetness between her legs. The pressure against her breasts increased slightly. She held his foot in both hands and bent her head down to it. She sucked his toes as if they were tiny cocks. Her pink tongue slid over and around each of them. "Between, Mrs. Ryan, lick between." And she did.

"Good, Mrs. Ryan," he said. "You have a loving mouth."

She licked and sucked the toes of one foot, then the other. When she finished, she removed her jacket and dried his feet with it.

"Exquisite, Mrs. Ryan." He placed his feet on the floor and looked down at her. "We will have to indulge ourselves in that delightful way more often."

A ringing bell startled her. Quickly she put on her jacket and buttoned it. "That will be Richie." He switched on the TV monitor above his head. "Yes," he said, "it's Richie." He pushed some buttons on the side of his desk. She heard the metallic clicking of both doors, then someone climbing the stairs and shuffling, it seemed, down the hall. Both she and Stein waited.

CHAPTER SIX - RICHIE

She wasn't sure what she'd expected, but certainly nothing as grotesque as the figure who appeared in the doorway. She felt herself staring at him with a mixture of pity and horror. He was her height, perhaps a little taller, and very skinny. There was something wrong with his left side. It seemed to be only partially under his control. He moved like a puppet whose strings on the left were slightly longer than those on the right. His head was cocked to the left. Both his left eye and his mouth turned down on that side. His left foot twisted inward, causing him to drag it so that he walked with a lurching movement.

He wore a dirty sweat stained tee-shirt and loose fitting olive green trousers that had obviously once belonged to a much larger man. The cuffs were rolled up revealing dirt caked ankles and torn sneakers. Thin strands of straight black hair reached almost to his shoulders. His pinched face was dominated by a large thin nose. His fingers, too, were long and thin, with dirt and grease ground into the chafed skin. From the corner of his mouth she noticed a small formation of saliva that suddenly spilled over and dribbled down his chin. He paid no attention to it. His eyes were intent on her. She had to look away.

"Richie," Stein said, "it's not polite to stare. This is Mrs.

Ryan. She's come to pay us a visit." Richie grunted something unintelligible. "You see, Mrs. Ryan," Stein continued, "Richie is somewhat mentally deficient. Several years ago he got into trouble with two young girls and the authorities had to put him away for a little while. Isn't that right, Richie?"

Kathy turned to face him. He stared at the exposed upper swell of her breasts. "They - they ast for it," Richie stammered. His hand on the outside of his baggy pants was pulling mechanically at his cock. Kathy turned away again.

"Are there any mice?" Stein asked. Richie grunted. "I think you should feed the pets now," Stein said. Kathy began to protest, but then realized he was not speaking to her but to Richie. She heard him shuffle down the hall. "We keep a small supply of mice, but when we run out Richie is kind enough to provide their nourishment himself." Stein paused, smiling up at her. "You and the young man already have something in common." The implication in the 'already' caused her to shudder. "Richie seems to disturb you, Mrs. Ryan. Do you find him attractive?"

"No!" She shook her head."He frightens me."

"Yes, well, Richie can be a problem. The girls I mentioned were quite young and the crime was sodomy. Do you know what that is, Mrs. Ryan?"

"I'm not sure," she said.

"It can mean several things, but in Richie's case it meant anal penetration. Aside from masturbation, that seems to be his preference. Have you ever experienced it? I mean anal penetration?

"No," Kathy said, feeling a clutch of fear in her stomach. "I'd like to go home now."

"Certainly. We will get you a cab. But first come here. I want to show you something." Stein lifted his bulk out of the chair and led her to the barrel set in its cradle. "I just had this made yesterday. Richie's father is a master welder. The cradle seems like a mistake with the two front legs shorter than the rear ones, but that's the way I designed it. Notice how nicely it's padded. Richie's mother did the leather work and the stitching. She's a remarkable woman. Some day you will meet her." He patted the top of the leather covered barrel. "Do you see the eye bolts at the base of each leg? It's a toy, a gift for Richie. But so far he hasn't been able to play with it."

"I don't understand."

"Well, Mrs. Ryan, suppose someone were to lie on it face down, their head at this end." He pointed to the shorter legs. "And suppose their wrists were fastened to the eye bolts in the floor and their ankles to the base of the longer legs that support the back of the cradle? Do you get the picture?"

"Yes," Kathy said, turning away.

Stein returned to his chair. "I see you don't appreciate Richie's little toy." He eased himself into the chair. He opened a drawer in the end table. "Look at this," he said, "I've had a gift made for you, too." From the drawer he took four leather bracelets. Each was about two inches wide and four inches in length. Each had a heavy metal buckle at one end and several evenly spaced holes strung out along the opposite side. Welded to the buckles were iron rings. "I wasn't sure of your size, but I remembered you have tiny ankles and wrists. I'm sure these will fit. Would you like to try them on?"

"Oh, please, I'm exhausted. I couldn't, I just couldn't. It's impossible." The vision of Richie taking her like that, her legs spread, her wrists and ankles secured, and that filthy retarded pervert touching her, coming up behind her... She began to tremble, her breath coming in sobs.

"There, there," Stein said, "no need to be upset." He placed the leather straps on the table beside his chair. "I can see that you are tired and that you find Richie repulsive. I must confess he appears that way to me also. I can't get him to bathe much less teach him manners. However, he is helpful and doesn't ask for much." He gestured toward the bathroom. "Would you like to freshen up again before I call a cab?"

"Yes, thank you." She breathed easier and even managed a smile. She picked up her purse and went to the bathroom remembering to leave the door open.

"It does seem a shame, though." Stein raised his voice so she could hear. "I hate to keep bringing it up, but you did bury your fine young husband this morning." Kathy's hand began to shake as she tried to apply her lipstick. "I really can't see that you've done much today to atone."

Kathy tried to answer but could not. There was a tightness in her throat and, once more, the tears began to form.

Stein watched her carefully. "You might consider how you caused our Richie to become excited," he continued. "Richie tends to forget the lessons of the past when he's that way. And, as we know, there are always little girls running around the shopping malls."

Kathy wiped away the tears and applied fresh lipstick and light mascara. She crossed the room and stood before him. "I can't," she said. "I can't do it." Her voice was firm and, for once, she was able to look directly at him as she spoke.

"Very well," he sighed, "perhaps some other time. But when you are safe at home I hope you will remember Richie's condition."

He went to the phone, sat down heavily, and flipped through an index of phone numbers. Then, he began to dial.

"Wait," she said.

When he looked up she was holding one of the leather straps out to him. "You will have to help me," she said.

CHAPTER SEVEN - CONTRASTS

Stein smiled., "Ahhh, Mrs. Ryan, you keep surprising me. Just when I'm sure you've reached your threshold of self-debasement, you cross it - if you will just place your foot here on the edge of my chair." Carefully, he attached one of the ankle cuffs. The leather was several layers thick and the iron buckle heavy. He pulled it tight, but not so tight as to be uncomfortable. "From now on, you must always wear heels, very high heels," he said as he felt along the firm muscle of her bare calf.

"Ahh, yes, such slim ankles and such finely proportioned legs. I expect you are athletic?" She didn't answer. He looked up at her but she averted her eyes. "I see you've lost your tan completely." He continued to stroke her calf. "Your skin is so smooth and white." His pudgy hand moved up along the back of her thigh until his fingers touched her sex.

She drew in her breath but stood still, the toe of one foot touching the chair edge, her cunt open to him. "So damp, Mrs. Ryan!" Slowly he slid his blunt finger along her furrow. "Do you know, in the matter of the leeches I was sure you chose them because you wished to be cleansed of old imagined sins. But now I'm not certain. Do you ever wonder how much you are motivated by guilt and how much by a curious kind of pleasure?"

The thought had occurred to her, but she'd refused to consider it. It was true that Stein and his perverse choices made her excited, made her excited in a way that was coupled with fear and disgust, but excited nonetheless. It was as if she had given her body and mind to some force over which she had no control. Or had her will somehow been taken from her? Did this disgusting man have some kind of messianic power over her? In this respect, she was not much different than Richie. Stein was waiting for an answer to his question. "No," she said, "I never wondered. There is no pleasure. Only the penance of humiliation and pain."

"It is of no consequence." He secured the second wrist cuff. "Yet to desire Richie, to encourage him to, ah, to take you in that way." He shook his head and smiled. "It will be painful. I suggest you lubricate the opening. We are out of perfumed oil, but Richie is hardly accustomed to such subtle refinement." He waved his hand in the direction of the kitchen. "Bacon fat will do. There's some in a can beside the stove."

She crossed to the kitchen area. "I think you had better remove your skirt first, but leave your jacket on. The black contrasts nicely with your skin." She unbuttoned her skirt and stepped out of it. After applying the lard, she wiped off her hands and walked back to stand beside the padded barrel. From his desk Stein took four short chains. On both ends of each chain was a steel spring lock.

She lay face down on the barrel and extended her arms along the front legs of the cradle. Stein grunted as he stooped to lock the chains to each cuff and attach the other end to each of the eye bolts. He secured her ankles in the same way. The shape of the barrel and the angle of the supports served to pull the cheeks of her ass apart, exposing the tight pink and brown pucker of her glistening anus.

Under her, pressing against her crotch, was a raised welt in the padded leather covering. She squirmed against it and felt it moisten with her juice. Although her movement was severely restricted, neither the cuffs nor the chains were excessively tight. "To think," Stein began, "only this morning you buried your husband, and who are you with now, Mrs. Ryan, on the afternoon of your dear husband's burial?"

"With you," she said softly.

"And is it your desire to be with me?"

"Yes."

"For a long time?"

She waited then said, "Yes, Mr. Stein, for a long time."

"And together we will sue the company whose negligence caused your husband's death?"

"Yes."

"Good. Before I summon your new lover, Mrs. Ryan, I'd like you to describe to me exactly where you are and what you are doing."

Without turning her head to look at him she said in a flat monotone, "I am in your house."

"And?"

"Leather cuffs are fastened around my wrists and ankles. They are attached with chains to bolts in the floor. I am lying face down on a leather covered keg. Except for my jacket and shoes, I am naked. I have lubricated my anus."

"Why have you done that?"

"So it will not be as painful."

"Be specific, Mrs. Ryan. So that what will not be as painful?"

"When Richie puts it there..."

...she heard a door open and murmuring voices, then Richie's shuffling gait. "There," Stein said, taking Richie by the arm and gesturing toward the keg, "is the surprise I promised you."

"Fuh me?" Richie stared in disbelief at the high round cheeks of Kathy's bared ass, her splendid legs spread and chained, the black jacket pulled tight at her narrow waist, her wrists and ankles secured to the eye bolts in the floor.

"She's yours, Richie," Stein said. "She's a virgin. You see how smooth and clean she is. She has even shaved her cunt hair off for you." Richie attempted to say something, but only succeeded in making guttural sounds. Behind her, Kathy heard him take off his shoes and pants. She gasped as cold wet hands grasped her waist and instinctively tightened her sphincter muscle.

"Wait, Richie," Stein ordered. "Mrs. Ryan needs to relax. Why don't you show her what you are going to fuck her beautiful ass with?" Richie lurched around the keg to face her. Her face, supported by the keg, was level with his knees. She squeezed her eyes shut. "Look at him," Stein said. She lifted her head and opened her eyes.

Richie's cock was almost as dirty as the hand that held it, but neither long nor thick. It looked like a fat cigar. "Yuh want this up your ass?" Richie stuttered. She closed her eyes again and, after a moment, nodded her head.

"Mrs. Ryan," Stein said, "I've been trying to teach Richie the most elementary rudiments of courtesy. Won't you be good enough to set an example for the poor boy?"

"Yes, please Richie. It's what I deserve."

Stein sat down in his chair and swung it around to face them. He nodded to Richie. In a moment Richie's fingers were again digging into her waist. She felt something wet drip onto the small of her back and run down her side. At first she thought he'd gone off before he had a chance to push his cock into her, then she realized that the warm glutenous liquid was saliva seeping from the crooked corner of his mouth.

She felt his cock probe her anus once. Then, with a single powerful thrust, he buried it in her as far as it would go.

She was conscious of a high piercing noise which momentarily blocked out the searing pain. Then she realized that the noise was her own scream. As his cock slid in and out of her opening, she experienced waves of pain and nausea. But in addition to the pain, she was aware of her wet cunt sliding along the welt of leather. In order to rub her clit against it, she began to raise her ass and push back, matching the rhythm of Richie's thrusts.

His spittle sprayed her ass and her back. She pushed back harder against him. He grunted, each forward thrust becoming faster and deeper. She could feel her explosive climax building when suddenly Richie's fingernails cut into her skin as he came.

She continued to move her open cunt against the keg, crying more in frustration and anger than pain. Stein quickly went to her. He unlocked the chains and rolled her off the keg. "No!" he shouted. "Save it, save it." He yanked her wrist chains up and dragged her across the floor to one of the steel columns where he'd placed blanket and pillow. With Richie's help, he pulled her arms back over her head and chained her wrists together behind the pole. She lay on her back unable to touch her cunt or rub it against anything, and it became dark...

CHAPTER EIGHT - VINNIE

In her dream she sat on a velvet covered throne. Kneeling at her feet was her uncle, dressed in sacramental robes. He begged to be allowed to lick her cunt. She lifted her satin gown and closed her eyes waiting expectantly for his tongue. But as he was about to touch her, she awoke not knowing at first where she was.

Before her, silhouetted against the dim light from the kitchen area, were three figures. Stein and Richie stood on either side of a huge man. He towered over both of them, his massive stomach bulging out over his belt. Because of the light, she could not see him clearly, but as he turned to say something to Stein, his face was no longer in shadow. He appeared to be almost bald, with heavy jowls and a thick neck. His large eyes bugged out of his head. He was unshaven and spoke in a low whiskey voice.

"Looks Goddamn small," he was saying to Stein. "You sure she ain't no fucking kid?" They were not aware she was awake. She closed her eyes. Her arms ached, and she longed to move them but she didn't dare.

"Here, let me show you," Stein said. He bent over and took the bottom edge of the blanket, then pulled it down slowly to reveal her.

"Jesus," the stranger said, "that's some woman. Look at them legs and that ass."

"I fu-fucked her in the ass," Richie said proudly.

Stein kicked the bottom of her shoe. "Wake up, you have company." When she opened her eyes, the large man was unbuckling his belt and pulling down the zipper of his trousers. "This is Vinnie Sconzo, Richie's father. He was kind enough to lend us a car for your husband's funeral. I think we owe him a favour."

Vinnie had stepped out of his trousers and was holding his hardening cock. It looked like a club, thick and long. "Richie," the big man ordered, "open her coat." Richie leaned over her and unbuttoned the jacket, pushing it aside exposing her breasts. She had not taken her eyes off Vinnie. He took a step forward and began to stroke his cock slowly.

"You look like some rich bitch girl, but I bet you love to fuck, right?"

Her wrist chains scraped against the iron column as she drew her knees up, keeping them pressed tightly together. She squeezed her eyes shut and shook her head. "No, no," she whispered, "go away, let me alone."

She looked up at Stein who was staring down at her. "Open," Stein said, "show Vinnie what you have for him." Still looking at Stein, she slowly spread her knees, revealing her glistening pussy.

Quickly Vinnie knelt between her legs and then fell forward on her, shoving his huge cock into her. The force of his heavy body drove her back toward the post. His chest was pressed against her face. He smelled of sweat and whisky. His stomach rode up almost to her breasts. But his great cock sliding in and out against the wet lips of her cunt, his hard shaft pressing on her swollen clit, that was all she really cared about. She began to groan immediately, frantically trying to wrap her legs around his body, her heels digging into his sides.

"Richie!" he shouted, "Unlock them damn chains." Richie unsnapped the locks. She tried to pull Vinnie to her but her arms would not go around him. She dug her fingers into his flabby back and thrust up at him, wanting him deeper inside, feeling once more her orgasm begin to mount. Suddenly he withdrew his cock and leaned back, holding it in his hand. In the dim light it was dark purple and glistened with her juices. His quick movement had surprised her. She continued to writhe on the floor. Her hands went to her cunt. Before she could touch it, he had grabbed both of her wrists in one hand. "You hot for it, baby?" he laughed, moving his cock back and forth a few inches from her cunt.

"Yes," she gasped, "Oh, God, please, please."

"Well, moan for it you little bitch. Cause that's all you are, a rich bitch in heat."

"Please... please," she begged.

"I didn't say for you to ask for it. I said moan. Moan like a fuckin' animal. I want to hear you like you was an animal."

She began to whimper. He tightened his grip on her wrists. "Moan, Goddamn it, or I'm gonna chain you back up and leave you here." She groaned deep and low. The voice did not sound like her own. "Louder!" he yelled. He needn't have said anything. Already the pitch and volume had increased. Soon the room was filled with the unearthly sound of her moaning. Her eyes were wide open and she rolled her head back and forth on the hard floor. She continued to thrust her cunt up at him.

Richie had taken his cock out of his pants and was now cuming in long spurts. Even Stein had begun to stroke himself inside his trousers. She moaned louder now. A thin stream of spittle ran from the corner of her mouth. Suddenly Vinnie plunged into her, and in a wild frenzy of powerful thrusts they both came. But she kept cuming long after he finished. She gasped and pleaded with him to keep it inside of her where she continued milking him until she came again. Stein had orchestrated the entire day toward this end. It had been, he concluded, a splendid success.

They let her rest for a few minutes. Vinnie went to the bathroom. Stein got her a glass of water. "Well, Mrs. Ryan, you've had a rather full day. I think you'd better get dressed while I call you a cab."

She rose unsteadily and started toward the bathroom. Vinnie came out of it ignoring her. She picked up her skirt. "Remember, leave the door open," Stein said. Richie slouched in the doorway watching her pee. Vinnie clapped Stein on the shoulder. "That's some wild cunt you got there!"

"I thought you'd approve," Stein said.

"You ain't gonna let her get away?"

"She's free to go. She has a nice house of her own and will soon be a very wealthy young lady."

"But, Christ, Stein -"

"Don't worry," Stein's voice rose so that it would carry into the bathroom, "I'm sure Mrs. Ryan will be anxious to pay us another little visit." The three men laughed. She wanted to scream, to get a knife, to get a gun. She wanted to kill them all. She had pulled up her skirt and buttoned her jacket. She came out of the bathroom and crossed to the phone. Richie followed behind her.

"I was telling Vinnie that you're always welcome here, Mrs. Ryan," Stein said. "I expect now that your husband is gone time will weigh heavy on your hands. Would you enjoy the pleasure of our company some evening in the near future?"

Not answering him, she reached for the phone. He quickly put his fat hand over hers. "I'll do it," he said. She stepped back and turned to face them. Her legs were trembling and her mouth had gone dry.

Stein stared at her, his hand still on the phone, "In case you've forgotten, the question was, would you like to pay us a return visit and perhaps stay a bit longer?"

She looked down at the floor and nodded her head.

"I don't think we heard you," Stein said.

"Yes," she whispered, "yes I would."

"Jesus," Vinnie said, "some bitches can't never get enough." He took Richie by the arm and led him toward the hall. "She's sure some wild cunt," Vinnie said again, shaking his massive head.

"She even ast m-m-e to fu-fu-fuck it," Richie was saying as they disappeared down the hall.

Stein called for a cab, then pulled another chair up to his desk. "One more thing while we're waiting." He motioned her toward the chair. "I happen to know an excellent lawyer. Really, one of the best. Very expensive. But he owes me a big favour, several big favours." He opened a drawer and took out a folder which contained neat packets of legal looking papers. "He's agreed to handle the suit for us." She looked puzzled. "The three million dollar suit we're bringing against the airline."

"Oh, yes," she said, "I'd forgotten."

"I know you don't want to get involved in matters of litigation but, Mrs. Ryan, you must admit three million is a tidy sum."

She looked down at her hands. "Couldn't we discuss this some other time? I'm so confused, so terribly ashamed - and tired Mr. Stein, very tired."

"Of course, but we must act on this quickly."

"I don't know." She shook her head, trying hard not to cry. "What I did today. I don't understand. That person you saw here wasn't me. I must be crazy. And my husband, my husband, Mr. Stein -" She turned away from him holding her head in her hands and sobbing. "Oh, God, I wish I could die!"

"Tell me, Mrs. Ryan, when you were a little girl and your parents were killed in that car accident. Where were they coming from?"

"It was just before Christmas. I was six. I wanted a new bicycle. They had been to the mall to buy it for me and were on their way home."

"How did they know you wanted a bike?"

"I guess I was spoiled. I kept after them about it even though I had a good bike."

"And after they were killed, you went to stay with your uncle, the priest?"

"Yes."

"And that's where you read the books about guilt and saw the pictures of the penitents?"

"Yes, my uncle was always reminding me that my parents were dead because I insisted they buy me a new bicycle. And later he kept telling me how bad I was and that I should be ashamed."

"And who sent your wonderful husband off to Washington?"

"You know that I did."

"It seems, Mrs. Ryan, when you send those you love off to do something for you -"

"They die," she said.

"You're not crazy, Mrs. Ryan. "Somewhat oversexed, perhaps, and addicted to guilt." He shuffled the papers on his desk. "Now, this other matter will take only a minute. Just sign these documents. They give me power of attorney for you. I'll make the decisions and, if necessary, appear in court on your behalf. My friend has agreed to take the case for a small percentage. He's sure the airline will agree to settle out of court. We're asking for five million and expect to get at least three." He chuckled. "I understand they are no longer serving chicken sandwiches!"

CHAPTER NINE - ESCAPE

When Kathy arrived home she showered and then slept until late the next afternoon. She awoke feeling well rested and, although the pain of grief and guilt was constant, she took comfort in the knowledge that it would pass. She was also sure that had it not been for the events of yesterday she would now feel worse. She had serious doubts regarding Stein's suggestion that she enjoyed the humiliations he subjected her to, but there was no question about the cleansing and healing effect of penance. However, that did not really surprise her. After all, the Church had operated for centuries on the principle of atonement for guilt through humiliation and pain.

During the week she answered calls from solicitous friends but declined invitations and invited no one to visit her. By Saturday she found herself wishing Stein would call. The memory of the day of Jeff's funeral kept returning, every time more vividly. Each morning she dressed as Stein had suggested: a tight skirt, shear blouse, and heels. She wore no panties, so that when the images of that night caused her to become hot, she had ready access to her cunt. She reached orgasms quickly, and they provided some relief but were far from satisfying. It was several days before the soreness in her anal opening subsided.

On the Monday of the third week, she decided to visit Jeff's parents in Boston. Surprisingly, Stein's hold on her had weakened. She remembered clearly the events of that terrible day and night, but they no longer stimulated her in the way they had. At times she felt as if the experience had never occurred except, perhaps, in a dream. On the morning of her decision to go to Boston she flushed Stein's phone number down the toilet. "There," she said aloud, "that's just where you belong."

The prospect of her trip excited her. Jeff's younger sister, Mary Margaret, would be back, for awhile, from Europe. They could do things together. Boston was interesting and fun. She might even look around for an apartment there and inquire into job possibilities. The idea of a clean start in a different place seemed to infuse her with new life. How easy it had been to dismiss Stein and the past. It was like recovering from a serious illness. Three weeks after it's over, the pain, the medications, and the smell of the sick room are all forgotten.

She was just about to dial Jeff's parents when the phone rang. She picked up the receiver immediately. It was Stein.

"I was going to call Jeff's parents in Boston." She spoke matter-of-factly, surprised and pleased at her self-control. The old feelings were indeed gone. Stein could have been someone trying to sell her a magazine subscription.

"Would you mind repeating that?" There was a hardness in his voice. She didn't care. He couldn't frighten her.

"Yes," she said, "I'm planning to visit Jeff's parents and his sister. I may decide to move to Boston."

"I see." There was a long pause. "And just when do you expect to leave?"

"Tomorrow," she said, even though she hadn't planned to drive up until Friday.

"Then I suppose I'd better come over to see you this evening," Stein said. "The insurance claim. The airline settled out of court for three million. You are rich woman."

"Oh!" she said, the old fear welling up inside her again. "You'll come alone and it's just the signing of papers?"

"Yes, just that - and perhaps a little proposal which, of course, you are free to reject. Nine o'clock. It won't take long. I'll have the cab wait for me."

She decided not to call Jeff's parents. She'd drive to Boston, check into a motel and phone them from there. Although she was sure Stein's control over her had been temporary, she knew it would be best to get away from him as quickly as possible.

She recalled the meticulous preparations she had made for his first visit: the white gown, the scented oil, the candles. And she remembered his recent instructions as to how she should dress. What a fool she'd been. At eight o'clock she showered and afterward put on, for the first time since the day of Jeff's funeral, a bra and panties. She found a pair of loose-fitting slacks and a large gray sweater. 'No more bare legs and spike heels,' she thought, 'thick wool socks and penny-loafers.' She picked up her lipstick, but, recalling Stein's instructions that she keep her lips moist and red, she put it down again. No make-up either. She would sign Stein's papers, send him on his way, get a good night's rest, and leave for Boston in the morning: a new woman, independent and strong, starting a new life.

A little before nine Stein was at the door. She waited until he had rung twice before she opened it. She was relieved to see the taxi parked in front of the house. She knew his visit would be short. This time instead of a brown paper bag, Stein carried a new leather briefcase.

"Well, well, Mrs. Ryan," he said stepping inside, "even in your college girl outfit you are a beautiful woman." It was the first genuine compliment he'd ever paid her. She found herself blushing.

She opened her mouth then closed it abruptly, suddenly aware that she was about to invent an excuse for not wearing the clothes he'd told her to wear.

He lowered himself into Jeff's big chair. "It's quite all right," he said, as if she had made an apology and he was graciously accepting it. He placed the briefcase on his lap and snapped it open. "Here are the papers. Everything is is order." He held them out to her. "If you will sign where I've indicated."

She took the documents and signed her name quickly, not bothering to read them. "There were legal expenses," he said, "and I subtracted my fee which was rather modest considering the amount of the settlement. A check for slightly more than a million and a half will be deposited in your bank account by Friday."

She put down the pen and handed the papers to him. "Thank you. I'm sure it will give me options I wouldn't otherwise have. Perhaps I can do some good with it."

Stein sat up. "I hope you're not planing on subsidizing a home for stray cats or anything of that sort." She shook her head and began to get up.

"Just a few more minutes, Mrs. Ryan," he said softly. "Please sit down." She hesitated, then did as he requested, trying to hide the fear that had been growing inside her. She knew her pussy had quickly become warm and wet. "That's better," Stein said. "I used some of the money to renovate my living quarters. Really quite a number of interesting improvements. You will have to pay me a visit."

"Thank you, but -"

"Ahh, yes, I keep forgetting. You are going off to Boston. Jeff's parents and his sister. How old did you say she was?"

"I didn't say. I think she's seventeen or eighteen."

"And her name?"

"Mary Margaret."

"A good Christian name. She wasn't at the funeral?"

"No, she'd been on a bicycling tour of Europe. She's going to school in London. Her parents couldn't get in touch with her until after -"

"Until after we buried your poor husband."

"Yes," she looked down at her hands folded in her lap.

Stein placed the papers in his briefcase and locked it. "Your generosity has enabled me to increase the size of my own family," he said. She looked up, puzzled. "Do you remember Richie?" he asked. A wave of nausea passed over her. The thought of Richie made her sick. She nodded her head. "I've adopted him," Stein said. "He's now my son. He will, however, retain his own name. But he's mine nevertheless, all proper and legal."

"Oh?"

"Of course I had to pay his father to part with the dear boy," Stein continued. "I've also had him re-examined and the poor young man has been judged legally incompetent."

Kathy wished he would go. She hated being reminded of Richie and his horrible father. She started to get up. Stein gestured for her to stay seated. "Dear, dear, Mrs. Ryan, you are anxious to see me on my way. Are you expecting someone? Have you given up on Richie and taken another lover? Is he due to arrive at any moment?"

"Of course not!"

"Too bad," Stein said, "a lovely widow and now a very wealthy one, and no man in her life. Too bad, Mrs. Ryan. You certainly should think about finding a lusty substitute for your wonderful but recently deceased husband - this morning when we spoke I mentioned a proposal."

"And I said I'd sign the papers, then you were supposed to leave."

"First the proposal," Stein said sharply. He stared at her for a moment. She nodded, trembling. Stein leaned back again and closed his eyes. "It is in your own best interest, Mrs. Ryan, that you have a man, a husband. I'm afraid in your present state of emotional stress you might be taken advantage of by some unscrupulous swindler whose chief concern is your back account. You must be careful. Then there's the matter of your somewhat strange sexual needs which seem to be tied up with guilt. It will require a rather special husband to meet your unique requirements. Don't you agree?"

Stein leaned forward, his pig eyes burning into her. "Mrs. Ryan, I have not only made you almost two million dollars,

I have found what I believe to be the perfect replacement for your late husband." She squeezed her eyes shut and put her hands over her ears trying to block out what she knew he was about to say. "It's my son, Richie." She wanted to scream but couldn't. She was unable to speak. She sat there shaking her head from side to side, her hands still covering her ears, her eyes shut. "You don't have to decide this minute. Give it some thought and phone me later," Stein said. She continued to sit there shaking her head long after he had gone.

She was vaguely aware of packing her suitcases and loading them into the car. It wasn't until she'd been on the Pennsylvania Turnpike for several minutes that she realized with a great surge of joy that she had escaped. Stein's last proposal had been exactly what she needed. It cleanly severed the cord. She was free!

She couldn't remember when she'd felt so happy. She needn't return, ever. Wally, Stein and his horrible pets, Richie, Vinnie, all of them were part of a nightmare that was over. Her loose sweater felt comfortable. She glanced down at her sensible shoes and warm socks and laughed. For the first time since Jeff's death she was able to look at her wedding band without feeling the wrenching pain of loss and guilt.

The humming engine of the car soothed her. There was a comforting familiarity in the dark landscape that rushed by: signs promising food and rest at the next exit, the lighted windows of farm houses, the gently rolling hills bathed in the soft light of a full moon. This was the world as it should be: safe, predictable, natural. She smiled to herself, thinking that each minute increased the distance between her and the insanities of Stein's warehouse.

She laughed aloud. She was totally free of him. The morning would find her in Boston, a fresh beginning in a new place. Jeff's parents, old fashioned and steady and protective, his sister, beautiful, and sweet, and fun. Yes, a complete sea-change. She would get a job, establish a daily routine, make new friends. She felt wonderfully independent for the first time in her life. She had a sense of purpose. Her life would be secure and normal and best of all, she would be in control of it.

Her headlights picked up a green and white sign, "Harrisburg 140". She felt as if she could drive straight through to Boston. The night was clear and the bright October moon silvered the roofs of the barns and farm houses that snuggled against the gently rolling hills.

Could Stein really have expected her to marry that slobbering imbecile? Of course, he must have. He'd gone to the trouble of adopting Richie and then having him declared incompetent. If she were Richie's wife, then he would have control of the settlement money, or at least half of it. Whatever was hers would be Richie's: her house, her money, her body...

She shuddered at the thought. But at the same time she felt her clit begin to swell and, in her stomach, the tingling sensation edged with fear. With her right hand she rubbed her left wrist where the leather strap had been. She could feel them again on her ankles and hear the locks snap into place. She could sense Richie behind her, his spittle sliding down her back. She could hear Vinnie shouting at her, his thick cock inches from her writhing cunt, and she could hear her own voice moaning like an animal. She glanced at the speedometer and quickly slowed down. She'd been doing ninety.

At one o'clock she was pulling off the turnpike at the Harrisburg exit. She felt worn out. She'd check into a motel and get a fresh start in the morning. She stopped at Howard Johnson's for coffee. The counter girl was a large pale woman not much older than herself. Kathy ordered coffee.

"Hate this shift," the waitress said. "But it gets me away from the kids and the old man. You married?"

"No, no I'm not," Kathy said, covering her wedding band

but not before the waitress had seen it.

"Lucky," the woman said. "Sometimes it might work out OK, but most times it's so Goddamn boring." She wiped the counter next to Kathy. "You know, it's the same damn thing day after day." She lifted a tray of dirty dishes from beneath the counter. "Boring," she repeated, "married is boring and from what I seen, single ain't much better." She rested the tray on the back counter and leaned toward Kathy. "You know what I wish? I wish I had lived in the time of the Indians and I wish one of them would have come and taken me off to be his woman. Life might not have been so Goddamn boring that way, you know, not such a waste." She turned and grunted as she lifted the heavy tray and disappeared into the kitchen.

Kathy finished her coffee, left a tip, and crossed over to the cash register. An older woman with blue-grey hair took her check and money. "Getting off the turnpike here?" the woman asked.

"No," Kathy said, "I'm anxious to get home." She concentrated on tucking the bills carefully into her wallet. After a moment, she looked up. It was another person speaking, surely, not her. "I'm going home to be married," said the voice.

CHAPTER TEN - HOMECOMING

Kathy arrived home exhausted. Her hand shook as she put the key in the garage door lock. It was four A.M. The drive back was a complete blank. She poured herself a small glass of brandy and sat down next to the telephone. She felt much as she had when she first saw the pets circling slowly in the murky water. The brandy burned her throat but did little to quiet her nerves. Her fingers pressed the phone numbers Stein had given her. They were burned into her brain, but, like her voice, they seemed to belong to someone else, for she surely had no wish to speak with him. He picked up on the first ring.

"Mr. Stein?" she could hardly say his name.

"Yes, Mrs. Ryan. I've been expecting you to call, but the hour is rather late."

"Yes," she said, her voice dry. "I started to drive to Boston. I got as far as Harrisburg and," she felt tears starting, "and, well, I decided to come back." The tears ran down her cheeks. She didn't bother to wipe them away. "You want me to - to, I mean you want Richie, Richie and me to..."

She couldn't finish.

"Mrs. Ryan," Stein began, "you are quite mistaken. I don't want you to do anything. You are absolutely free to go to Boston or San Francisco or any place that suits your fancy. I have no desire whatsoever to interfere with your life. All I did was remind you that you are now without a husband and that the young man I introduced you to is an eligible bachelor."

"I don't want the money!" she cried. "It's yours. You can have it."

"That's not the point, Mrs. Ryan. The issue here is your misunderstanding of my suggestion. Even though I might benefit considerably if you and my adopted son were husband and wife, whatever you and Richie decide is a matter of complete indifference to me. To be perfectly honest, in spite of your readiness to give yourself to him, I can't see why you would consider marrying the hopeless creature. I mean your late husband was handsome and brilliant and charming while Richie, well, we're both aware of Richie's shortcomings."

He did want her to marry Richie. She was sure of it. And no matter what he said, he wanted control of the money. "The choice is mine?" she asked.

"Why certainly. In matters of the heart how could it be

otherwise." He paused. "Surely you didn't call me at this hour to tell me about your aborted trip to Boston? I take it you've made a decision regarding Richie?"

He waited.

"Mrs. Ryan? Are you wearing the same clothes you had on earlier this evening?"

"Yes."

"Perhaps you would like to remove everything except your sweater?" Without answering she put down the receiver and did as he requested. When she picked up the receiver again he asked, "Were you wearing panties?"

"Yes."

"And?"

"They were wet. The crotch, it was wet."

"And do you remember just when, on your journey, this wetness began?"

"At Harrisburg."

"When you decided to return?"

"Yes."

"Please put your fingers on your cunt and, as you explain why you've called me, rub them over it, slowly, very slowly."

"Yes," she said, and gasped as her fingers made contact with her swollen clit.

"Now then, I assume you wanted to talk about Richie, is that right?"

"Yes, about Richie," she said. Her fingers began to move in a circular motion.

"He has none of your husband's sterling qualities. Isn't that correct?"

"None," she said.

"But he must have something that attracts you. Perhaps the way he makes love? I seem to have forgotten; just how did he demonstrate his affection, Mrs. Ryan?"

"He took me from -" Her fingers slid over her clit and into her vagina. "He took me from behind," she said quickly.

"He did it to me like that."

"And did you enjoy the way he did it to you?"

"No!" she almost shouted. "No, I hated it!"

"Then why did you change your mind about Boston? Why did you do that, Mrs. Ryan? Why did you call me? What is it you want?" The hot juice oozed from her cunt. She pressed harder against her clit and began to moan softly, yet she could not bring herself to answer him. Once the words were said there would be no turning back. The door would close and the heavy bolts slide into place.

"Where is your husband, Mrs. Ryan?" Stein's voice was soft, conciliatory.

"He's dead. Salmonella poisoning from something he ate on a plane."

"Perhaps you want a new husband?" came Stein's voice.

She didn't answer for a long while. Finally, "Yes," she whispered, "yes, I want a new husband."

"And this new husband you have in mind, will he please you as much as the first one, the one you buried so recently?"

"No, oh God no!" she said quickly. Stein waited. "It's different," she continued. "I mean, he will not please me, he couldn't, not ever. It's - it's different."

"Certainly, but not all together different. As his bride I'm sure you will want to do all those affectionate things new brides anticipate with such excitement and joy? Kiss him, Mrs. Ryan, part your warm soft lips for him."

"Yes,I will kiss him."

"Lovingly?"

"No! I mean, yes, yes, lovingly."

"I expect you will want to undress before him?"

"Yes."

"And offer your tender breasts to him?"

"Yes."

"Perhaps you will even learn after a time to enjoy, as you say, being taken from behind... but most importantly, Mrs.

Ryan, as this is to be an old-fashioned union, will you obey your husband? Will you be a submissive and obedient wife to my son Richie?"

Once more she was slow to answer. She knew she should slam down the receiver, disconnect the phone, seek help. 'Obey' Stein had said, be an obedient and submissive wife to that cruel, mindless, perverted monster. Her fingers slid over her clit. "Yes, I will obey him," she said.

"And you are willing to change your name?"

She hadn't thought of that. The idea of giving up Jeff's name caused the tears to flow again. "Yes," she whispered.

"But Ryan is such a nice name. Are you really anxious to change it?"

"Yes."

"And what will your new name be? I'd like to hear you say it, Mrs. Ryan."

"Mrs. Richie Sconzo."

"Again, Mrs. Ryan."

"Mrs. Sconzo. Mrs. Richie Sconzo."

"I think we should plan a formal wedding," Stein said, but her orgasm was so powerful she dropped the phone and didn't hear him.

CHAPTER ELEVEN - CONFRONTATION

She awoke late in the afternoon. The weather had turned warm again. Across the street construction crews were beginning to erect the new condominiums. Just two months ago Wally had been pushing over the first trees with his grader. Exactly sixty-five days had passed since the afternoon when she impulsively interrupted his lunch.

She remembered the waitress at Howard Johnson's - what was it she'd said, 'Boredom is the worst of all, day after day, after day, the same damn things.' Kathy had realized immediately that the woman was right. It was this understanding, not Richie, that had sent her rushing home.

Her afternoon thoughts were interrupted by the ringing of the phone. She'd told her friends that she was going to Boston and staying for several weeks so it had to be Stein.

"I trust you slept well, Mrs. Ryan."

"Yes, I did, thank you."

"You have not, I take it, changed your mind."

She thought before answering, "I really haven't had time to think. I'm not ready to make a final decision." She had decided but was afraid to tell Stein. She'd just procrastinate for awhile and hope that he would get the message.

"I must remind you, Mrs. Ryan, that your decision last night sounded quite final."

"Yes, but I was tired."

"And you drove all the way back from Harrisburg to masturbate over the telephone," He paused. She could not say anything. "I'm not anxious to make another trip over there but arrangements must be made. I've been busy all morning and now there are things we need to discuss. The date has been set, October 10th, that's next Saturday."

"I can't, Mr. Stein. Really, it's impossible. I must have more time."

Stein cut her off, "It's after five o'clock now. I still have things to do here. I'll be at your house at ten." He hung up before she could reply. Kathy sat beside the phone for a long time. She thought back over the events of the past two months. She felt her resolve melting away. She touched her pussy. It was wet. Not Richie, absolutely not Richie. But there was another possibility.

Kathy dressed quickly and drove to the village mall which housed a cluster of expensive shops. She bought several pairs of shoes, a black negligee, a red one, and a number of other revealing gowns. She also purchased a variety of lipsticks, eye shadows, glosses, soaps, oils, and perfumes. There was just enough time to have her nails done and her hair styled. It framed her face and curled under at the nape of her neck.

At home again, she showered and shaved the slight stubble of pubic hair that had begun to grow back. She rubbed her body with the familiar mixture of Shalimar and oil. The black negligee was transparent and held together at her waist by three small hooks. She selected a pair of the new shoes, black with a very high heel, thin as a nail. They had narrow ankle straps which she pulled tight remembering Stein's wide leather cuffs with their steel rings. She took care with her eyes and lips, the dark mascara and bright red lip gloss in striking contrast to her pale skin.

At ten o'clock a cab pulled up before her house, discharged its passenger, and waited. She opened the door before Stein was half way up the walk. He pushed the door closed behind him and stood looking at her. "Yes," he said, "much better. Tasteful, provocative, expensive." She smiled, pleased at his words of approval.

He sat down in the chair which she no longer thought of as Jeff's. It seemed to belong to Stein. It was as if she and Jeff had purchased it long ago expecting that one day Stein would appear to claim what had been his all along. She adjusted the footstool so that he could easily place his feet upon it. He sank back in the chair, sighing contentedly.

He watched her for a moment. "Yes, Mrs. Ryan," he said, a gentleness in his voice that she had not heard before, "if you must look like a whore, and I think you should, then it's best you look like a high priced one."

"But I'm not!"

"No, of course you're not. I didn't mean that the way it sounded. You do not accept payment. You give of yourself how and when it pleases you." He stared up at her. "Indeed, you are an exquisite example of proportion and grace." Until now he had never spoken to her in this way. She felt flattered and, to her surprise, touched.

"Rather like a piece of Oriental sculpture," he continued, "a rare Ming vase." She smiled at him. "Do not be deceived. I can appreciate your form and admire your beauty, but you are only an object, a uniquely beautiful one, but an object all the same. To me you will never be more than that." She felt the colour rise to her cheeks. "Do you know what a vase is, what it really is no matter how precious or rare?" She shook her head. "It's a receptacle, Mrs. Ryan, just a receptacle, that's all."

"But -"

"Enough!" he said, sharply. "There are matters we must attend to."

She crossed behind the coffee table to sit opposite him. She took a deep breath and spoke, quickly, a speech she'd been rehearsing all evening. "Mr. Stein," she said, "I can't marry Richie. I've thought about it and it's out of the question. If you want the money, I'll give it to you. You can have it. Or, if you're agreeable, I'll -" she paused and looked away.

"You will what, Mrs. Ryan?"

"I'll marry you!"

His burst of laughter was so loud it startled her. He rocked back and forth shaking his head. "Mrs. Ryan," he said when he'd caught his breath, "I never gave you credit for having much intelligence, but occasionally you struck me as being slightly perceptive. It appears now that you have absolutely no mind at all. So, this was what all the provocative dressing up was for. You were trying to seduce me into desiring you. How could you have been so foolish? And the money. Can you conceive of me accepting a gift of money from anyone, especially from you? And as for marrying you, my dear Mrs. Ryan, you've taken leave of your senses. In the last five minutes I have called you a whore, and an object, and a receptacle. Why maybe even Richie's too good for you!"

She tried to speak but her throat was dry and the tears

were beginning to form. “Enough of that Goddamn crying!” Stein said. “Stand up and look away from me.” She quickly stood and turned her back to him. “Now, take off that gown and bend over and spread the cheeks of your ass.” She brushed the tears away and did as he ordered. “That’s all Richie sees in you, a place to stick his cock. You could weigh four hundred pounds and have a hair lip and a humped back. It wouldn’t matter to him. He can’t tell the difference between a Ming vase and a common sewer. To that drooling idiot you are less than a whore, less than an object. You are only an ass he can fuck wherever he wants to.” He paused to let his words sink in. “Now,” he began again, “you know exactly what the situation is. No deception, no surprises. Tell me you don’t want to marry him and I’ll leave immediately, and I swear you will never hear from any of us again.”

As he spoke he watched her legs begin to tremble. She uttered a small cry of despair, but remained bent over exposing her anal opening to him. The inner lips of her vagina began to glisten. Stein leaned back in his chair and sighed. “Straighten up and turn around,” he said. She felt cold and a bit dizzy. Her gown lay on the floor beside her. She wanted to put it on but was afraid to reach for it. Her breasts rose and fell rapidly. “Well, Mrs. Ryan, what is your answer?” She bit her lip and shuddered. She was about to reply when he held up his hand to stop her. “Before you speak, there is one other matter which we should clarify.” He motioned for her to sit.

She glanced at her gown but sat down naked, her knees pressed close together. “I have wondered,” he said, “if pleasing me by agreeing to my propositions is what gives you the most pleasure. Your offer to marry me suggests that might be the case. Whether you wish to accommodate me or not doesn’t matter. I must admit that up till now it did. However, I want you to know that regarding Richie I’m completely indifferent as to what you do. Your decision will neither please nor displease me."

She didn't believe him. She tried once more to speak but he held up his hand again.

"Hear me out. In all honesty I can't deny that access to Richie's share of your new wealth offers interesting possibilities, but my life is comfortable enough as it is. Money is always attractive, but I don't really need any more of yours. In short, Mrs. Ryan, marry Richie or don't marry him. I simply do not care. Whatever you decide should and must be based on your desires, yours alone. Do you understand?"

She waited a moment, then looked up. "Thank you for your honesty." She took a deep breath. "You make this easier for me. I can't marry Richie. I simply cannot do it." She spoke so softly he could hardly hear her. She looked down at the floor.

He heaved himself out of his chair and gathered up his papers. "Perhaps it's just as well," he said. "Richie is not at all happy about the prospect of being your husband." He looked down at her and smiled. "Isn't that astonishing? Richie doesn't want you." At the door he turned back. She was staring at her hands which lay folded in her lap. "Goodbye, Mrs. Ryan. I suggest you go to Boston. Pack a bag and this time keep going." He opened the door.

"Please," she said, "I - I think maybe -"

He came into the room closing the door behind him. "I realize that changing one's mind is a woman's prerogative, Mrs. Ryan, but there are limits."

She stood up. "But I didn't say -" She paused. "Yes," she said.

"Yes, what?"

"Yes," she looked away, then down at the floor. "I feel I need to - no, that's not it. I want to marry Richie."

"How much?"

"What do you mean?"

"How much do you want to marry him?"

She turned away and leaned against the arm of the couch. "Very much," she said.

"Why?" Stein asked.

"I don't know. Truly I don't. I've tried to figure it out. Maybe I am losing my mind." She looked directly at him.

He shook his head. "No, you are perfectly sane. Different, but sane nonetheless."

"I wish I could believe that."

"Trust me. We will talk about it when there's time." He returned to his chair and sat down. "Now, to the business of your marriage." The words made her feel sick. "Are you serious?"

"Yes," she said, and knew she was saying it because that's what he wanted to hear. She didn't love Stein. It wasn't that at all. But she felt this unexplainable compulsion to please him and pleasing him excited her.

"As I told you, Richie is quite reluctant."

"But won't he do as you say?" she asked.

"He will, but in a matter as important as this I'd feel better if he were at least halfway convinced that a marriage to you could be in his self-interest." He paused. "Do you think you might persuade him?" He saw her back stiffen as if she'd been shot.

"When?" She turned to face him.

"Now."

"What do you mean?"

"I thought this might become a problem so I brought Richie along. He is in the cab."

She drew in her breath trying to stifle a cry of rage that was swelling in her chest like a huge bubble. He had tricked her again. Richie was here. In a moment he would be in her house. She felt the tightening in her chest and the tingling sensation in the pit of her stomach.

Stein picked up her gown and offered it to her. Quickly she put it on and fastened it. Stein had pushed the drapes aside and was rapping on the window. "The objective will be to raise his level of expectation. We must not only prove to him that you are most anxious to become his bride, but that you are eager to serve him in a variety of ways."

She heard Richie on the steps.

"You have a pretty mouth, Mrs. Ryan. You might consider using it." Richie pounded on the door. Stein motioned to her. She opened it and Richie lurched in, almost knocking her over.

"Sh-sh-shit," he said.

"Ahh, Richie!" Stein shouted warmly. "You must be half frozen. Come over here by the fire." In the firelight Richie appeared more menacing than she'd remembered. He wiped his nose and mouth on his sleeve, glaring angrily at her. She could hardly bear to look at him. Spittle hung from his chin and dropped onto the rug.

"I'm glad you're here, Richie," she said, forcing herself to take a step in his direction. Richie stared at her sullenly. "Can I get you something? A drink?" She tried to smile.

"A-a-ass," he hissed.

"He wants to see your ass," Stein said. Richie's hand was rubbing his crotch. Stein took her arm and led her over to the fireplace. "Show him," he said. She turned her back to Richie and bent over. She began to pull up her gown . "Slowly," Stein instructed. "No, Richie, leave it in your pants, at least for now." She drew the black gown up, gradually revealing her splendid legs and the firm round buttocks which, in the flickering firelight, seemed to move. Without being told, she spread her cheeks.

"Fu-fu-fuck," Richie stammered.

"No," Stein said. "Not tonight. After the wedding."

"To hell wi-wi-with a wed-wedding!" Richie drew the back of his hand across his slobbering lips. With his other hand he automatically stroked the bulge in his pants. He looked from her to Stein then at the floor. After a moment he shook his head. “N-n-nuh, won’t d-d-d-do it,” he mumbled.

“But she hasn’t proposed yet,” Stein said, smiling. “At least let her do that.” He turned to Kathy and pointed to the floor in front of Richie. She got down on her knees before him. He smelled of sweat and stale urine. His torn work shoes were thick with grease. They fit loosely around his skinny ankles. For a long while she stared at the cracked toes of his shoes. Finally she said, in a voice that was barely audible, “Will you marry me?”

Richie glanced at Stein who carefully formed a word with his mouth. “B-b-beg,” Richie said. Instantly she recalled the night in the warehouse and heard again Vinnie’s harsh demand that she moan. And now, on her knees before his slobbering son, she would not. She would not. There were other ways. In front of her Richie’s grimy hand still fingered his cock. She reached up to touch him. He jumped back cursing. She lost her balance and fell forward on her hands.

“B-b-beg, yuh fu-fu-fu-fuckin whore!” he shouted. She looked up at him. He was grinning, his broken discoloured teeth, his wet lips, the drool seeping from the corner of his mouth. In the light and shadows cast by the fire he seemed not so much a mindless idiot as a fearful incarnation of something both cruel and cunning. The sight of him sickened and frightened her. To herself she repeated, ‘I will not beg. I will not beg,’ but even as she said it she was aware that she might be able to cum simply by squeezing her legs together.

She got to her knees again and, looking once more at the tips of his shoes, tried unsuccessfully to control her voice and hold back the tears.

“Please Richie, will you marry me?”

He glared down at her. “B-b-beg muh-muh-more,” he said.

She looked at him this time. “Please Richie, don’t you see, I am begging you. Please. I will be a good wife. I will do everything you ask.”

Richie glanced at Stein who nodded his head. "I'm sure Mrs. Ryan will make you happy Richie. Won't you, Mrs. Ryan?"

"Yes, yes, I'll try very hard." She was aware of the stickiness between her thighs.

"And she no longer has any feeling at all for her late husband, do you Mrs. Ryan?"

There was a burning in her stomach and for a moment she was afraid she might be sick. She lowered her head. "No," she whispered, "none."

"And why don't you Mrs. Ryan? Is it because of Richie?"

"Yes," she replied in a monotone, "It's because of Richie."

Stein winked at Richie. "Your first husband wasn't nearly the lover Richie is. Isn't that correct, Mrs. Ryan?" She nodded her head. "Convince him," Stein demanded. "Richie needs to be persuaded."

Kathy continued to stare at the tips of Richie's shoes, forcing herself to say the words she knew Stein wanted to hear. "Mr. Stein is right, Richie. My husband could not please me the way you do. I mean the way you do it to me." The burning in her stomach had moved like hot fingers down to her crotch. "You, you are a real man, Richie."

"Say the words, Mrs. Ryan. Tell Richie how you feel about him," Stein urged. "Say the words."

Richie was grinning. She looked up at him, then bowed her head. "You have made me fall in - in love with you," she whispered.

"Show him," Stein said.

Tentatively she reached once more for his hand and, gently pushing it aside, she pulled down his zipper. The urine smell was stronger. His saliva dripped on her neck and slid down between her breasts. She took his stiff penis in her hand and pulled back the foreskin. She noticed a small scar on the dark head of his cock. It was the same as the tiny U shaped marks that branded her own nipples. Without hesitating, she touched her lips to the scar in a way that was both tender and maternal. The feeling lasted only a moment. Then the hot flood of desire spread like oil just beneath the surface of her skin. She glanced up at Richie. His lips were drawn back in a hideous grin. The sight of him nauseated her. "Please," she whispered. His cock jerked in her hand.

"Duh-duh-do it," he said.

She leaned forward and her soft lips closed over the head of his cock. Sliding her mouth down its length, she took it in. Her head moved back and forth, slowly. With her right hand, she cupped his balls and squeezed them gently. She withdrew his cock and stared at it. It twitched and glistened in the firelight. The tiny scar was now bright red. The thought that she was sucking where they once sucked excited her. She pictured a leech, perhaps the big one, stretching the length of Richie's cock, hungrily feeding.

Richie grunted and reached to pull her against him. She gripped his cock firmly at its base, her tongue circling its head. Richie made a guttural sound in his throat and grabbed for her hair, but she had already taken him in and was milking his cock with her mouth. It dripped with her saliva. Her swollen lips slid back and forth along its length until she, too, began to whimper and moan softly.

When he began to cum she jerked back, but then quickly closed her mouth over his cock and held it there, swallowing the hot spurts of his jism. With one hand she continued to squeeze his balls and with the other she held his cock in her mouth until he finished cumming.

Richie supported himself on the back of a chair, grunting and panting and slobbering. Kathy tucked his limp cock back inside his pants and zipped them up. She remained on her knees, looking down at the floor.

"Ah, Richie!" Stein said, "you're a lucky man. She never sucked off her husband like that, did you Mrs. Ryan?" Kathy didn't answer. "Speak up, Mrs. Ryan. Richie wants to know if you ever did it like that for your husband, suck like that and take all his cum in your mouth?"

Kathy didn't look up. "No," she said softly, "no, Richie, I never did it like that for my husband."

"What does that mean then, Mrs. Ryan? Tell Richie what it means."

"I don't know what it means," Kathy said.

"I'll tell you what it means." Stein leaned forward. "It means you got a taste for Richie's jism. It means you're going to be Richie's cocksucker. It means you're going to let Richie fuck your cunt any time he wants to. It means you're going to let Richie fuck your ass any time he wants to. It means your mouth and your cunt and your ass will belong to Richie. It means you're going to be Richie's woman. Isn't that true, Mrs. Ryan?"

Kathy nodded.

CHAPTER TWELVE - ARRANGEMENTS

She was sitting on the couch facing the fire. Stein had come in quietly and sat in his chair. They looked at each other for several minutes. Stein shook his head, "You should have killed me when you had the chance," he said.

"I know!"

"You're like a high-jumper. Your sexual excitement is determined by leaping over your own moral convictions. To marry Richie is a way of raising the bar." He leaned back in the chair. "In the beginning it was no more than your desire to masturbate in view of your uncle. Then came your marriage and a long period of conforming to conventional and rather boring sex. But you found this frustrating. I'd venture to say that your orgasms in front of your uncle were more intense than any you experienced with your husband." He waited for her to respond. When she didn't, he continued. "To deny a sexual appetite as voracious as yours can only lead to a powerful hunger. It doesn't go away. It gets worse."

"That might account for Wally, but what of the horrible things I've done since then? And now Richie?"

"Self-debasement is an old and familiar path to sexual excitement. History is full of examples, and, for that matter, so is the Bible. Although the erotic aspects are not explicitly defined, they are clearly there in both the Old and the New Testaments."

"But if you're right, if I need to travel this path and I have to keep putting up higher obstacles, can't I get help?"

"Possibly, but not until you are sincerely interested in returning to the kind of life you led with your former husband. My guess is you would probably discover that habit is a worse monster than Richie."

"Then Richie is not the last barrier? I can't imagine a more repulsive one."

"He could be but, from what I know of you, it's unlikely." He paused, looking at her intently. "Do you honestly want to see a psychiatrist?"

"No," she answered.

"And isn't it true that any sort of union and especially marriage between you and that ugly cretin violates not only reason but also challenges all of your moral convictions?"

"Yes," she said, "yes, just the thought of it is abhorrent."

"But isn't it also true that the memories of sexual experiences with your husband and even with Wally do nothing to stimulate you?"

"Yes," she said. "I've tried remembering, but it's no good."

"And when you think of yourself as the bride and the lawfully wedded wife of Richie, what happens?"

"I say to myself, 'I would rather die first', but I also find myself getting - getting -"

"Wet? Yes, wet. And you need that excitement, don't

you?" He leaned back, folded his hands over his belly, and closed his eyes. After a few moments he spoke. "Let me try to explain it in a slightly different way. You seem to suffer from three somewhat common maladies which are largely psychological. You embrace guilt. You seek it out and exaggerate it. Then you look for ways to expiate it. For you, atonement takes the form of intense humiliation coupled with a rather modest amount of pain. It's called, as you know, masochism. To some extent we all give ourselves over to it from time to time. But you, my dear, are an extreme case. Finally, you have a highly sensitive libido, one that needs constant attention."

"You mean by marrying Richie, by submitting to him I'll reach reach some kind of bottom and then rise up and be normal?"

"Yes, but I caution you that to be 'normal' often means to accept external desires that are not really your own. To be normal is to conduct your life in ways that are often in conflict with your true self. It is better, I think, to strip away all that is false. It is better to question every action to make sure it is truly and honestly felt."

"Then marrying Richie might be a cure?"

"No, not at all. It could be no more than a first step. Or it could destroy you. Your journey through the dark may never end."

"I might always be as I am, always looking to raise the bar?"

"Yes, but is that so bad? Think of the alternative, the 'cure' as you call it." Stein shifted his huge bulk and leaned forward. "For you, Mrs. Ryan, such a cure would be a lobotomy of your essential nature. Look at your so called 'normal' friends. Do you really want to be like them? You've been there. Do you want to go back?"

"I'm not sure," she said. "But to be the way I am, to become the wife of that beast!"

"No," Stein said, "you're too kind. To compare Richie with the beasts is to do them a severe injustice. Even the lowly reptile is more acceptable. Richie, it has always seemed to me, most closely resembles a maggot. He is cold, entirely devoid of feeling. Blindly he drags himself through life leaving behind him a trail of slime. He not only has the sensibilities of a maggot, he has the look and feel of one. Do you agree?"

"Yes." She felt a chill run through her.

"And tonight you have chosen to be the obedient bride of this human equivalent of a maggot." He studied her through half-closed eyes. "You have made that choice, haven't you?"

She looked away from him. "Yes."

"Well, it's settled then?"

"Yes," she said, "it's settled." Yet even as she said the words, she felt certain she could not go through with it. Sometime between now and Saturday, perhaps at the last moment, she would have to refuse. She looked into the fire for a moment then back at Stein. "You said you were making arrangements." She tucked her legs up under her and sat back in the corner of the couch. "I hope you're not planning on -"

"But of course," he cut her off, "a formal wedding: a gown, a cake, a reception, even an ordained priest."

The image of herself and Richie standing before an alter in a public church seemed both ludicrous and terrifying. "Where?" she asked.

"In my refurbished apartment, the warehouse. In fact, I'm sure Richie will insist on consummating the marriage immediately after the ceremony. He will want to do that for the edification and enjoyment of the assembled guests. Are you agreeable?"

"You mean -"

"I mean he will want to, as you say, take you from behind before the delighted eyes of the wedding guests."

"No!" she said sharply, "I won't agree to that." She leaned

forward, "The answer, Mr. Stein, is no."

Stein shrugged his shoulders. "Richie will be anxious to demonstrate his manhood. He will be disappointed."

"Then he'll be disappointed."

"But you did promise to be an obedient wife. Therefore you will, as they say, give yourself to your husband on your wedding night?"

The memory of Richie's shuffling gait, his grimy fingernails digging into her, his wet lips and lopsided face made her almost retch again. She looked away from Stein. "Yes," she said, "I will give myself to him, but not for the amusement of his guests."

Stein leaned back and sighed. "Oh well... I don't think it would be wise for Richie to move in with you here. Besides, as you know, he is helpful to me. Since I do not intend to share my humble dwelling with a woman, you will stay here in your own house alone during the week. If Richie behaves himself and does his chores properly, I'll let him have you on the weekends at my place. I'm sure Richie's real father will also want to fuck the new bride from time to time. And just to make things interesting, perhaps we'll have an occasional party."

She looked across at him, feeling nauseous and afraid. "Nothing as crude as a gang-fuck," he said, "but some interesting and imaginative entertainments. Both Vinnie and I have friends, and then there are the pets."

Her hands were folded in her lap. She moved them down toward her crotch. Stein shook his head. "No," he said, "none of that. None of that all week. I want you to save your orgasm. Let it build. Think of it as the first of many self-denying sacrifices you are going to make in order to please your new husband. Dwell on it constantly but save it until Saturday. Is that clear?"

"Yes." She moved her hands up. She could feel the warm wetness between her legs.

"I believe I mentioned Stella before," Stein continued. "She's Richie's mother. She and Vinnie divorced shortly after Richie was born. She's a remarkable woman in many ways. Along with her other talents, she is a fine seamstress. She has insisted on making your wedding gown. You are to arrive at four o'clock Saturday. You will need a provocative nightgown and white heels. No undergarments. Make-up, perfume, all the seductive accoutrements a young bride deems necessary."

"But," she paused, having difficulty saying Richie's name, "it's obvious he doesn't notice or care; it doesn't matter to him."

"Exactly! You will know that whatever you do, however beautiful you appear, however provocatively you dress, however seductively you speak or move, it will be wasted. That's the reason you are giving yourself to him, the only justification for such a bizarre match. Any other man in the world, except possibly me, would be overwhelmed by your beauty. Any man the least bit aware would recognize in you a genuine capacity for tenderness and love. Remember how quickly you turned Wally into a worshipful schoolboy and how you despised him for it? I think, in time, you might even conquer Vinnie. But on Richie, you are wasting yourself. As you say, he does not care. He is incapable of caring." Stein smiled at her. "Beauty and the -"

"Maggot," she said.

Stein laughed. "Yes, the maggot." He leaned back looking at the ceiling. "You must always, always appear before your new husband as provocative as you can be. Clean, meticulously groomed, carefully made-up, revealingly dressed, always the epitome of what every man desires. You must not hide. Although he will at first be reluctant, you and Richie must go out together where people can see you: restaurants, night clubs, dances, parties."

To be seen in public with Richie, she thought. Too horrible to imagine. Impossible. "Yes," she said, "I understand."

"And out among strangers or friends you will always be demonstrative, affectionate, loving. As soon as he realizes he can safely humiliate and abuse you, believe me he will. But you will return his abuse with affection, with loving words. In private and in public you will tease him, fondle him, kiss him."

"I will."

"At all times and in all places you will demonstrate to Richie and everyone else that you are a submissive and obedient wife."

"Yes." she said, "I will try very hard to be so."

They looked steadily at each other for a long time. Stein nodded. "So, Mrs. Ryan, I believe you. I am convinced that you really do want to become Mrs. Richie Sconzo, and that your desire has nothing to do with my wishes. I think we may have a surprise or two for you on your wedding day. Are you still opposed to a public consummation of the marriage vows?"

"I couldn't do it! I just couldn't!"

"Very well." He rose and crossed to the door. "Oh, I almost forgot," he said, turning back to her in the open doorway. "Bring your wedding band." She appeared confused. "This one," he said, taking her left hand. He slowly removed Jeff's ring and placed it in her palm. "One small step at a time," he said.

CHAPTER THIRTEEN - PREPARATIONS

She stood before her open closet. Only four weeks ago she was selecting an outfit to wear to Jeff's funeral. Choosing clothes for her wedding day seemed even more difficult. She decided to wear the same things she had worn then. The black suit and shoes, a white blouse, no bra or panties or stockings. She'd had the skirt and coat cleaned, but in putting them on she was reminded of that afternoon and night at the warehouse. Her clit and nipples immediately swelled and she became wet. She wanted desperately to make herself cum, but remembered Stein's admonishment to save it.

The afternoon was bright and clear, unusually warm for October. Colour blazed across the Pennsylvania countryside, and the blue sky was cloudless. She rolled down the windows of her car and drove slowly. A husband and wife were raking leaves. Three boys tossed a football the length of an expansive lawn. Several laughing children were chasing after a large collie. There was a trace of wood smoke in the air and, far off, the sound of a high school marching band. The world seemed normal and orderly and, she thought, a safe and pleasant place.

She hesitated before making the turn into the old access road. Straight ahead, the highway intersected with the Pennsylvania Turnpike. She could keep going. In her rear-view mirror she saw a car coming fast. She cut the wheel quickly and was swallowed up in the overgrown tangle of bushes and tall weeds that lined the twisting ruts that led to the warehouse.

She pulled up and stopped beside Stein's building. It looked the same. If he had made changes, nothing was visible from the outside. Standing before the heavy metal door, she considered the possibility of running back to the car and driving as far away from this place as she could. Once inside, she'd be trapped. She knew Stein was watching her on the monitor. Almost as if it had a will of its own, her hand reached out and her extended finger pressed firmly on the button. In a moment the steel mechanism sprung back with a precise click. She pushed the door and went inside. The bolts slid into place behind her. Her heels clicked on the iron stairs. She opened the door at the top and stepped through into the hall. Behind her, the door closed and locked automatically.

Stein had indeed made some improvements. The walls and doors had been panelled. On her left were hung beautifully framed abstract paintings. Under her feet the gray carpeting was thick and soft. A miniature black poodle decorated with a rhinestone collar and pink ribbons ran down the hall barking furiously, then ran back to the main living quarters as if to announce her arrival. She tried to remember which of the storage rooms on her right contained the pets and which was Richie's room.

The dog stood yapping at the end of the hall. "Muffy, stop that!" someone yelled. Then into Kathy's view stepped a tall thin woman wearing a red satin dress and shoes to match. Her short hair was bright orange and done in a 70's Afro. It looked as if a tiny sunset cloud had settled on her head.

"Kathy!" the woman shouted, rushing forward to take Kathy's bag. "I'm Stella, the groom's mother." She stood back looking at Kathy and laughing in a high screeching voice, her bony arms flying up in mock surprise. "I never in my wildest dreams expected Richie to have a wife! That imbecile son of mine is such a thoughtless boy and disgustingly dirty, and cruel. He's just like his father."

She took Kathy's small suitcase and, with her other hand, squeezed Kathy's arm. "When Mr. Stein told me, I just laughed in his face. Thought for sure it was a joke." She chuckled. Her thin lips were heavily coated with bright lipstick. The dog began to bark again. Stella reached down to pick it up. Kathy noticed the slit in her skirt, her bare legs like sticks, and her long thin feet. "My God," Stella was saying, "and here you are looking like a movie star!" She grabbed Kathy's hand and led her into the large room. "Mr. Stein!" she cried. "The bride is here!"

Stein sat at his desk, his back to them. "Ah, Mrs. Ryan," he said, swinging around to face her. "I see you've met your new mother-in-law." He smiled up at them. "Stella has been going crazy. You'd think she was the one getting married."

"Wait till you see your dress," Stella said. "Oh, Mr. Stein," she clasped her hands and rolled her eyes dramatically, "she's simply beautiful. I had no idea. But when I think about her marrying Richie - God, what a terrible waste!"

"Yes," Stein cut in quickly. "Mrs. Ryan, how do you like the changes?" He gestured around the room. Kathy hadn't been able to take it in. It was still large, but seemed much less spacious than she remembered. Along the wall to her right, the kitchen had been redone completely: new appliances, a centre cooking island, and a serving counter before which stood a long glass table containing covered trays of food, along with china, silver, and a huge wedding cake.

"While Stella locks that animal up in the pet room, I'll give you a short tour." Stein lifted his heavy bulk out of his chair. She noticed he was wearing a new black suit and shoes, a stiff white shirt and narrow black tie. "The money from the settlement has enabled me to live much more comfortably. So, you see, your husband's death wasn't a complete loss." The old game again. "Well now, as you can see, the major structural change is the addition of this partition." He led her toward what was formerly the back half of the room. A walnut panelled wall had been erected across its width. "Behind the new wall is the master bedroom, and it's a rather special one. Adjacent to it is another bedroom with a dressing area and closets. Stella will take you to these rooms in a few moments. Over there," he pointed to her right, "is the bath which has been tripled in size."

The support posts to which she had been chained were inside the new wall, but she could see small tightly fitted doors at the levels where she'd remembered the eye bolts. Since there was no visible entrance to either of the bedrooms, she assumed the only access to them was through the bathroom.

"The whole place has been completely insulated and sound-proofed, rewired, new plumbing installed, completely air conditioned, and I've added a high fidelity system that represents, as they say, the finest in the art. Concealed speakers are everywhere."

Two long modular couches covered in burgundy leather along with several matching chairs were arranged to face the wide expanse of the new wall. On a small platform was a lectern which, in turn, faced the chairs and couches. On either side of the platform were large vases of fresh-cut roses.

"Our make-shift chapel," he said, chuckling. "And here is one of my favourite toys." He led her to the centre chair in the grouping. It resembled Jeff's chair, the one he had used in his visits to her home. Next to it was a small console. He flicked a switch and the top slid open to reveal a panel containing three long rows of numbered buttons. "The wonders of computer technology puts the entire house at my fingertips," he explained. He pressed several of the buttons. Indirect lighting bathed the room in soft amber which gradually changed to red then to blue. "Any single colour you desire or any combination. I can paint the rooms with light."

His pudgy hand touched the console again and the walls exploded with the 'Ode to Joy' chorus of Beethoven's 9th which resolved into the high thin notes of a jazz flute and, finally, the room was filled with the old Peggy Lee rendition of 'Fever'.

"My little magic board controls a whole host of delightful surprises," he said, as its cover slid pneumatically into place.

Off to the side, between the dining table and the chairs for the wedding guests, was a rounded waist-high object covered now with a dark blue velvet cloth that hung to the carpeted floor. Stein noticed her staring at it. "Ah, yes," he chuckled, "we've discreetly hidden your pre-nuptual couch, the exact place where you first realized that you wanted to be Richie's woman." He winked at her. Crossing to place a hand on the covering he asked, "Would you like to see it again?"

"No!" she said quickly. "I never want to see it again."

"But both Richie and I expect that you will and, I think, so do you." He waited for her to respond. She looked away. "Oh well, time enough for that. A lifetime, in fact," he laughed again. It was clear that he enjoyed tormenting her.

Stella bustled into the room, her low hanging breasts visible in the deep wide V of her dress. "My little bitch of a dog is so excited there's just no keeping her still." She looked at Stein. "When will Richie and Vinnie be back?"

"In about an hour." Stein turned toward Kathy. "They're at the airport picking up the clergyman."

It's happening, Kathy thought. It's really happening: the clergyman, the wedding cake, the podium, the chairs for the guests, the flowers... everything was coming together for a ceremony which would soon take place. In a few hours she would be the lawfully wedded wife of Richie Sconzo. She would, as Stein had said, be Richie's woman. It was no longer a game. For the first time she began to fully realize what she had done and what was yet to come. She felt sick.

"I still can't seen why a pretty young thing like her would want to marry that ugly butt-fucking son of mine," Stella said. Once again she took Kathy's hands in hers. "Certainly you don't love him, do you dear?" Kathy couldn't be sure if the old woman was serious or putting on a private little act for Stein's amusement.

"Maybe she likes having her ass reamed?" Stein said. It was a question. They waited for Kathy to reply. She looked first at Stella, then at Stein.

"Yes," she said.

"Jesus!" Stella exclaimed, "I Goddamn hated it! That's one of the reasons I divorced Richie's father."

"She had Richie late in life," Stein interjected.

"I was thirty-eight," she said. "After the kid was born that bastard, Vinnie, wanted something tighter than my cunt. My ass just couldn't take it. He's got a cock the size of a bull moose." She shook her head. "Oh, I forgot. You already know how big it is," she said matter-of-factly.

Stein laughed again, "The way to begin a long and loving family relationship is with absolute honesty," he said.

"Oh, sure." Stella took Kathy by the arm and led her toward the bathroom. "That Goddamn Vinnie's been bragging for weeks about what a hot number you are. Ain't nothing sacred or secret around here."

"Close the door, Stella," Stein called, "and keep her there until we're ready. I don't want the groom to see his blushing bride until she walks down the aisle."

"Stein likes everything done properly," Stella explained, closing the door which Kathy noticed had no visible lock. "Ain't this something?" Stella stood back so that Kathy could get a full view of the bathroom. It was done in black tile with heavy stainless steel rings spaced evenly along the walls. Against one wall were a large stall shower, a toilet, and twin sinks. "The shower doubles as a steam room," Stella said, pushing open the door. "And here's the bath and whirlpool," she pointed to a rectangular tub which occupied half of the large room. "We managed to get Richie into the shower and we got his hair cut, but the son-of-a-bitch has an aversion to water. There's no way to get his hands clean or feet either." Kathy thought of Jeff's strong hands and manicured nails. Stella motioned for Kathy to follow her. "You haven't seen nothing yet," she said.

The room next to the bath contained a king size bed. It was an old-fashioned four poster with a canopy. There were two walk-in closets. "Stein had this made especially for you," Stella said, pointing to a dressing table with a huge lighted mirror and a blue velvet vanity bench. "This is kind of a guest room. Through here's the master bedroom, only no one's used it yet. Stein's been saving it for you and Richie's wedding night."

She opened a heavy oak door that, Kathy noticed, could be locked with the same kind of electrically controlled bolts that secured the front doors. Stella waited expectantly for Kathy's reaction. Although up until now she had succeeded in remaining passive, Kathy couldn't suppress a gasp as she stood in the doorway.

The old woman grinned. "I made some suggestions, but it was mostly Stein's ideas," she said. Except for the straight wall that separated it from the living area, the major portion of the room was round. In its centre on a circular raised platform was an enormous bed. Suspended about six feet above the bed was a polished mirror the same size as the platform. This mirror was supported by three stainless steel columns, one at either side of the bed and one at its head, leaving the bottom third of the bed which faced the flat wall unobstructed.

The columns were hollow. Near the top of each was an opening that contained a small pulley. Over the pulleys and hanging halfway down each pole were black plastic coated wires. On the end of each wire was what seemed to be some kind of heavy metal clip. The walls of the rounded portion of the room were mirror glass from floor to ceiling. The flat wall that separated this room from the living quarters was covered in black velvet. She noticed lighting recesses in the ceiling and floor. Otherwise, the room was plain. The huge bed was the only piece of furniture. There were no pictures or closets.

"It looks more like a stage than a bedroom," Kathy said.

"Come on," Stella smiled, "it's getting late. Stein wants you to have a relaxing bath and then I'm to fix you up real nice. There might be some last minute adjustments to be made on the gown, we weren't exactly sure of your measurements." She led Kathy back to the bathroom and turned on the whirlpool jets. Kathy undressed, embarrassed under the admiring gaze of Richie's mother.

"What a lovely body!" Stella exclaimed. "Skin like Dresden china. And no pussy hair! I shave mine, too."

Kathy quickly submerged herself in the hot turbulent water. She could hear Stella in the other room unpacking the suitcase and arranging things on the make-up table. Kathy tried to push the approaching ceremony from her mind. She positioned her cunt so that the powerful jet stream flowed against it. She spread her legs. Suddenly Stein's voice boomed from a speaker hidden in the ceiling, "No, Mrs. Ryan! I told you to save it!" She jumped up looking wildly around the room. "TV camera," Stein's voice said, "and out here is a large monitor." Stein sounded as if he were in the room with her.

Stella appeared in the doorway. "Come," she handed her another towel, "dry off. I'm anxious for you to try the gown." She led Kathy to the dressing table. "Stand here," she said. She began rubbing Kathy's body with the perfumed oil, her strong fingers squeezing Kathy's hard nipples and probing between her legs. "You sure are a juicy little bride," she chuckled.

Kathy felt the colour rise to her cheeks. Her skin glowed with a smooth sheen of oil and the air became heavy with the fragrance of the expensive perfume. Kathy had always applied her own make-up, but now she gave herself over completely to Stella. "Just eyes and mouth," the woman said, "no need for rouge." Stella expertly shadowed Kathy's eyes and painted her full lips bright red, coating them afterward with a glistening oil. She brushed Kathy's hair vigorously. Then she inspected the red polish on Kathy's fingers and toes.

"I did them this morning," Kathy said.

"Yes, exactly the right shade," Stella agreed. "Now," she picked up the new shoes and kneeled at Kathy's feet, "let's try these. A closed pump. Most appropriate for the bride, but such a naughty high heel!" She laughed, sliding the shoes on Kathy's feet. "Beautiful legs!" She moved her hands up the bare calf of one and rubbing Kathy's firm inner thigh. "Stand," she said. "Ah, what those heels do to your ass! Look how they push it up and out." She turned Kathy sideways to the mirror, patting the tight smooth skin of Kathy's ass. "What a waste giving this to that idiot Richie."

She opened the closet and carefully took out the wedding gown. "Now, the piece de resistance!" She held it out for Kathy's approval. "Nothing underneath, right?"

"No," Kathy said, "nothing."

"Perfect! I made the top skin tight." Although the gown seemed to be one piece, it was really two. The white satin skirt was a wrap-around that snapped at the waist and hung in graceful folds to the floor. The bodice overlapped the skirt with a few inches of scalloped lace. A row of tiny pearl buttons drew it tightly across Kathy's stomach. It buttoned up only to just below her breasts. The entire upper swell of her breasts was exposed under very shear white nylon. It was cut so low the rosy top of each nipple was clearly visible.

"Just right!" Stella cried, giving the bodice a final tug. "Stein wanted your breasts and nipples to be seen." She buttoned the satin sleeves at Kathy's wrists.

My wedding gown, Kathy thought, looking at herself in the mirror: no underclothes, spike heels, wrap-around skirt, my breasts all but naked. And this horrible painted old woman touching me, twisting my nipples, breathing her whiskey breath in my face. And out there waiting for the ceremony were the fat man, and Richie's brutal hulk of a father, and Richie himself: a mean, lopsided, slobbering, retard. And there are the guests who will be total strangers to me. And this is my wedding day. In a few minutes I will walk through that door and take my place beside my new husband. And most astonishing of all, I have elected to be here. I have said yes to all of Stein's obscene propositions. I kneeled before Richie, on my knees before that grotesque cretin and I begged him to marry me. How could it be possible?

Her thoughts were interrupted by Stella who, with a broad wink, placed before her a square box made of highly polished wood. "From Stein," she said. "He told me to give it to you when we finished with the wedding gown."

There was a tiny brass clasp on the front of the box and small brass hinges on the back of the lid. Kathy sat down and stared at it, afraid to look inside. "Go on, it won't bite you," Stella urged. Kathy's trembling hands unfastened the clasp and slowly she lifted the lid.

The box contained her four leather bracelets. gold initials had been embedded in each. The letters were K.S. - Kathy Sconzo. Under these was a fifth strap much thinner than the others, sheathed in black velvet. It was studded with what appeared to be diamond chips. On one end was a small but solid buckle and a steel ring that folded down out of sight. "It's a velvet collar," Stella said, gently lifting it out. At the bottom of the box was an envelope addressed to Kathy. Her fingers shook as she tore it open and extracted a note.

"For you," it said. "But wear them today only if you wish to submit to your husband in the way and at the time and place he requested."

She picked up the leather straps one by one and examined them. On the inside of each were faded sweat stains from the first time she'd worn them. Her new initials reflected the light.

She handed them to Stella, lifted her skirt, and held out her right foot. Quickly Stella knelt and tightened a strap around one ankle and then the other. "Stein will be pleased," she said. "We were all hoping you'd change your mind." She unbuttoned the sleeves at Kathy's wrists, folded them back, buckled a bracelet around each wrist, then covered them with the sleeve cuffs again. Kathy held up the black velvet collar.

Stella took it. "I don't know if I can hide this."

"Don't try," Kathy said. "Let it show."

Suddenly Stein's voice from the overhead speaker startled them both.

"It appears you are ready," he said.

CHAPTER FOURTEEN - WEDDING

Kathy stood up straight. The white satin gown clung to her, tight against the swell of her breasts, tight at the small circle of her waist, and tight over the flaring curve of her hips. Her dark hair contrasted with the half-veil that Stella was placing carefully on her head. She felt the heat between her legs. A moment ago her mouth was dry, but now she had to swallow the saliva that had suddenly begun to flow.

"Sweet Jesus!" Stella exclaimed, "you are truly a most beautiful woman." She stood back and shook her head. It was a sincere expression of admiration. Kathy herself was astonished by the mirror image that seemed only vaguely familiar.

Stella opened the bathroom door. A strange Gregorian chant played softly through the loudspeakers. Except for a bright spotlight above the lectern, the room was in absolute darkness. Kathy could see an old priest and, standing before him wearing a white coat, was Richie. Stella placed a small bouquet of orchids between Kathy's trembling hands.

Kathy's legs wouldn't move. She stood there shaking her head. Then she felt Stella's hand tightly gripping her arm. Together they walked slowly toward the altar.

Kathy kept her head down, staring at the floor. She did not look at the guests. She and Stella stopped in the circle of light. She sensed Richie beside her. She could see his new black shoes and the black trousers that did not quite reach his thin ankles.

The priest cleared his throat with a phlegmy cough. Kathy raised her head and found herself looking into the pale blue eyes of her uncle. She dropped the bouquet she'd been holding. Her hands flew up to her mouth too late to suppress a startled cry. Her uncle did not seem to recognize her at first, but when she withdrew her hands he leaned over the lectern, peering down at her, a puzzled frown creasing his forehead.

"They told me it would be you," his voice was high and raspy, "but I wasn't sure what they meant. Didn't I marry you already?" The tears came immediately to her eyes. She nodded, unable to speak.

Richie was staring at her, his small mean eyes looking at her now with hatred and lust. The music from the loudspeakers faded and stopped. As Stella released her arm, Kathy felt as if she might sink to the floor. The rise and fall of her breasts strained against the transparent netting. Her mouth had suddenly gone dry once more.

"Shame, Kathy, shame." The old priest shook his head. She was a little girl again and he was here to bear witness to her sins as he placed his arthritic hands on either side of the lectern and looked out over the heads of the strange couple who stood before him. "We are gathered here in the name of the Lord to join these two young people in the Holy bands of matrimony..."

Kathy became aware of Richie's hand searching for an opening in the back of her gown. Instinctively she pushed his arm away. She wanted to scream, but her uncle had asked her something and was waiting for an answer. "The ring," he said to Richie impatiently.

"Here it is," Stella said. Taking Kathy's hand, she carefully placed something in the open palm. Richie, with Stella's help, had taken her left hand and was pushing a wide black iron band on her third finger.

Then the old priest gestured to Kathy, pointing to the

familiar gold ring she held.

"The ring," Stella whispered, "give it to Richie." Stella was holding Richie's grimy hand up to her. Kathy stared at the thin fingers with their long, grease caked nails. Then she slid her ring onto the finger Stella held out to her. It was Kathy's own wedding ring, the one Jeff had given her: it fit perfectly.

"Do you, Richard Sconzo, take Katherine Ryan here to be thy lawful wedded wife?"

"I d-d-do," Richie mumbled.

"And do you Katherine Ryan take this man Richard Sconzo to thy lawful wedded husband to love, honour, and obey till death do you part?" She couldn't answer. She couldn't say the words. Thank God, she just could not go through with it. "Say I do," her uncle ordered with unexpected authority. He glared down at her.

"I do," she whispered.

Stella lifted Kathy's veil and turned her to face Richie, gently shoving them together. Richie's lips were wet with spittle. Closing her eyes, Kathy pressed her warm mouth against them. He quickly drew back, cursing, and spit on the floor.

"You will have to teach your new husband to tolerate your kisses and, perhaps, even enjoy them," Stein said from the darkness behind her. "Richie," he continued harshly, "do you want her?"

"I-i-in the ass," Richie stammered.

"Then you must let her kiss you. She's now your wife. She likes to kiss, don't you Mrs. Sconzo?"

Kathy turned her back to Richie. Gently Stella turned her around to face him. She looked at him for a long moment, then took his misshapen face between her hands. For the second time she pressed her lips to his, slowly pushing her tongue between them. Her tongue explored his mouth tasting the whisky and feeling the sharp edges of his broken teeth. Against her, she felt his cock stiffen.

"I told you she was a hot little bitch!" Vinnie shouted, rising out of his chair and moving toward her. The lights came up bathing the room in a soft amber glow.

"Not yet," Stein said, waving his hand at Vinnie, "later."

Kathy, her face scarlet, her hands visibly trembling, turned to face the guests. In addition to Stein and Vinnie there were only two others: a large florid man in his sixties and a tall, thin Japanese dressed in an expensive black suit. He wore thick eyeglasses. His bronze face was expressionless. He looked at her as if he were appraising a piece of sculpture.

"This is Mr. Satomi," Stein said, "possibly one of the wealthiest men in the world."

Kathy nodded, but the Japanese continued to study her without acknowledging the introduction. Everyone watched him, waiting. Even Richie sensed that something important was taking place. Kathy stared back at the Japanese for several moments, but under his steady gaze she lowered her lids and, finally, bowed her head. Stein smiled. The Japanese looked away from her. Everyone relaxed.

"Mr. Satomi is an acquaintance of your benefactor here," Stein nodded toward the other man.

Kathy looked up. "I'm Henry Forbes," the man said, rising and crossing to her, extending his hand. "I represented you in court against the airline. Congratulations." He bent over to kiss her on the cheek. Stella had helped the old priest down from the lectern and was leading him to a chair.

"We had a hard time finding your uncle," Stein said. "He was in a mental home, but his credentials are all in order so you and young Richie here are as legally married as anyone can be." The old priest sank wearily into a chair, shaking his head and muttering to himself. Stella poured him a shot of bourbon and held it to his lips.

Richie began to stutter.

"Later, Richie, in due time," Stein said. He turned to

Kathy. "I see you are wearing my little gift." He pointed at the collar. "And the others?" he questioned.

Kathy hesitated, then lifted the hem of her gown.

"And just why are you wearing them?"

"You know why."

"Yes, of course, I know. But our guests seem puzzled."

"Because," she looked at Forbes and the Japanese, "because Richie - because my husband wants to, to consummate the marriage here in front of you." The Japanese stared at her impassively.

"That still doesn't explain the bracelets," Stein insisted.

She turned to speak directly to Mr. Satomi. "I'm wearing these bracelets because Richie prefers," she stopped for a moment, then continued, "because Richie prefers anal intercourse. I can't do that unless I am restrained."

"My God," Forbes exclaimed, "why do you allow it, then?"

"Because, Mr. Forbes, I hope to be a good wife and I want to please my husband." She looked back at the Japanese and thought she saw a flicker of a smile cross his face.

Stella had gone over to the big table. "Come on," she shouted, "there's a cake to be cut and some drinking to be done."

"That's right," Stein said, rising. "We must toast the health and good fortune of this happy couple." He took Kathy by the arm and led her to the table. Richie, Vinnie, and Forbes followed. Mr. Satomi shifted in his chair so that he faced the gathering, but he remained seated, refusing Stella's offer of drinks with an elegant wave of his hand.

Vinnie came up behind Kathy and put his arm around her waist. "You gonna treat your new daddy good, ain't you baby?" His huge hand moved up to cup her breast. Her nipple stiffened immediately. Richie was standing off to the side scowling at them. He quickly finished the drink he was holding and lurched across to Kathy.

"K-k-kiss," he demanded.

Vinnie grabbed him roughly, pulling him away.

"It's all right," Kathy said, stepping between them. Richie grabbed her buttocks and pulled her roughly to him. His mouth pressed hard against hers. She tried to hold her lips together, but as his bony hands moved up the white satin to painfully squeeze her breasts, she opened her mouth. His fingernails dug into her swollen nipples. As if against her will, she found herself pressing her crotch against his hardening cock. Again, holding his face between her hands, she closed her eyes and slid her tongue between his wet lips. The kiss lasted a long time.

She was moaning softly when he pushed her back. She fell against the table, trembling and flushed. She felt as if in that gross embrace something had come alive in her, that some grotesque thing had begun to form in her womb and she was powerless to do anything but nurture it. It was obvious to all of them that she had experienced some kind of dramatic conversion.

She leaned over the table, her head bowed, her eyes shut, supporting herself with both hands, trying to catch her breath, afraid she might faint. But all the while she was sharply aware of the intense burning between her legs and the hot stickiness that oozed from her vagina. She lifted her head and looked across the little space that separated her from Richie. She saw in his small mean eyes that he also understood. Somewhere in the dim recesses of his brain it had become as clear to him as it was to her.

To Kathy, the transformation of all that she believed herself to be was instantaneous, complete, irreversible, and terrifying. She tried to turn away but felt compelled to continue looking at Richie. There was an exchange between them, an unspoken but clear understanding. She could read in his eyes the intuitive revelation that had also come to him in the same moment. His eyes said to her, "You are my woman." She fought against it, but my lowering her eyes she acknowledged that he had won. She said to herself, "Yes, I am now your woman." In less time than it takes to tell of it, she had given herself completely to this mindless creature who was now her husband. She felt utter revulsion and absolute terror, but at the same time a sexual passion that threatened to consume her.

Richie nodded his head. She knew that he had understood the message she had sent. She belonged to him. For the first time in his life something was his. He owned something. He could do whatever he wanted with it. He could make it tongue kiss him. He could make it get down on its knees and suck him. He could make it open its cunt for him. He could make it spread its ass cheeks for him. He could make it beg for his cock.

It would do anything he wanted it to do...

CHAPTER FIFTEEN - HONEYMOON

"Come dear, let's freshen up," Stella said, directing Kathy toward the bathroom. The older woman sat her at the dressing table. Kathy stared straight ahead, the tears rolling down her cheeks. Stella pulled up a stool and sat down facing her.

"You are, I declare, one of the most beautiful woman I've ever met, but also the most confused. You couldn't possibly care a fiddler's fuck for Richie. He's disgusting and he's vicious. For a woman with your looks, your body, your intelligence and good breeding to even speak to a sub-human half-wit like Richie is obscene. But to kiss him, kiss him in the way you did... strange. Very strange." She stood. "Well then, we can't keep our guests waiting, can we now?"

She put her hand under Kathy's chin and tilted her head up. "Beautiful," she said again. "Such delicate features, and the colour in your cheeks." She reapplied the lipstick and gloss to Kathy's mouth and brushed her hair lightly. "There is just one more thing." The old woman was holding a bright silver chain about four feet in length. On one end was a spring clip. "Stein thought it might be a nice touch."

Kathy lifted the steel ring on her collar and Stella attached the chain to it. Then looking hard into Kathy's eyes, the older woman placed both hands on Kathy's breasts. Her hands were cold and her mouth was set in a straight line. Kathy saw something of Richie in his mother. The concern Stella had professed earlier had quickly become something else.

"Watching the way you kissed that imbecile son of mine made me hot," she said, applying pressure to Kathy's nipples and bending over to examine them closely. "I see you've fed the little pets." Kathy blushed. "It's all right," Stella twisted the nipples causing Kathy to gasp, "so have I, lots of times. It looks like we have more in common than we suspect." She smiled. "If you belong to Richie and I am Richie's mother, maybe you belong to me as well?" Kathy was about to protest but the old woman tugged gently on the leash. "Shall we go now?"

Stella walked ahead, leading Kathy by the silver chain.

The room was in darkness again except for a harsh circle of light on the keg, which was still covered with the velvet cloth. A slow, bluesy jazz number with a low growling saxophone played through the speakers. The chairs had been pulled up so that they faced the keg but were about three feet beyond the circle of light. Stella paused beside the keg, but Kathy motioned her toward the assembled guests. She stopped before the Japanese and lifted the scalloped hem of her bodice. Then she offered him the bow that secured her skirt. Unsmiling, he shook his head in refusal.

She moved to stand before Richie. Again she lifted the scalloped hem. Richie hooked one finger onto the waistband of her skirt and pulled it down to reveal her stomach. He cleared his throat and spit, aiming for her belly button. His saliva was phlegmy and cold. It slid down her stomach toward her shaved cunt. She squeezed her eyes shut and swallowed. She could feel her legs grow weak and fought to keep them from trembling.

"I'll do it," Stein said. She crossed to him and he pulled the bow. The satin skirt fell to the floor with a soft whispering sound, revealing her splendid ass and legs, and the smooth roundness of her belly which glistened with the slime of Richie's spittle. They could see, too, the milky ooze that coated the pink furrow of her slit.

"Goddamn!" Vinnie gasped.

"Shame, shame," the old priest said.

Stella led Kathy back to the keg. The silver chain sparkled in the bright circle of light. As Stella pulled the velvet cover off the keg, Kathy turned to face the silent watchers. She stood straight, unsmiling, looking out into the darkness where they sat. Stella unfastened the chain. The bodice was tight at Kathy's waist, accenting the flair of her hips and the rising swell of her breasts. The extreme spike heels lengthened the long curve of her calves and elevated her buttocks. After a moment, she turned and, spreading her legs to straddle the keg, she bent over it. Stella quickly snapped the ankle cuffs to the base of the supports. Kathy placed her arms along the front supports and Stella secured the wrist cuffs.

It was then that Kathy noticed the carpet had been cut so that the keg formed the centre of a four foot circle. Stella stepped back beyond the perimeter. There was a slight humming noise and Kathy felt the platform begin to move. When her anal opening was opposite the wedding guests, the platform stopped. Both the angle of the keg and the supports served to open her, but now Stella spread Kathy's ass cheeks even wider.

"Holy Christ!" Vinnie gasped.

"Exquisite, simply exquisite," Forbes whispered aloud.

"Like a soft little mouth," Stein said, "pink and tight."

She could hear Richie from the darkness, "Fu-fu-fu-" he mumbled, his slurred speech no more than a guttural sound.

"Just a minute," Stella ordered. Kathy could feel drops of warm oil on her legs, then Stella's strong hands rubbing one leg and then the other, and smoothing the oil over her ass. Finally, the K-Y. Stella's index finger gently circled the rim of Kathy's exposed opening and then pushed into it. "Relax," she whispered, "relax." With the middle finger of her left hand, she rubbed Kathy's clitoris. Suddenly, she shoved two fingers of her right hand into Kathy's anus. Kathy moaned and stood on her tiptoes. Stella teased her, flicking the swollen clit with a sharply pointed fingernail. Kathy moaned again. "You hot, baby?" Kathy nodded her head. Abruptly, Stella withdrew her fingers and stepped outside the circle.

Kathy squirmed, trying to find the raised welt in the leather covering of the keg. It was no longer under her. She could feel it against her inner thigh. The platform moved a quarter turn so that the guests would have a view from the side.

"Tell your husband what you want," Stein said from the darkness.

Kathy struggled to find her voice. "T-take me," she said. "Take me like this, take me from behind."

"Oh my," Stein said in mock surprise, "only married half an hour and already she sounds like a demanding wife. Have you forgotten your promise, Mrs. Sconzo? Have you forgotten your vows? Have you forgotten your place?"

"I'm sorry," Kathy said softly, "please forgive me."

"Are you speaking to me?" Stein asked.

"Yes, Mr. Stein."

"But you are not my woman, Mrs. Sconzo. Whose woman are you?"

"I am Richie's woman."

"I suggest you never forget that. Now, perhaps you'd like to rephrase this rather vulgar request?"

"Yes, thank you Mr. Stein." She was still for a moment. "Richie, I truly belong to you," she began. "My only desire is to please you now and to please you always." She paused again and felt the hot flow seeping from her vagina. "My mouth is yours, dear Richie. My cunt is yours. My anal opening which I am offering you on this, our wedding day, is yours as often as you wish to take it."

"B-b-b-beg," Richie slurred.

"Please, Richie, please my dear husband, consummate our marriage here, now before our guests. See, I am open for you. I want to feel you inside me, deep inside me. Take me like this, Richie, please, I am begging you."

She heard him lurch across the room and stop behind her. Once again she felt the cold drool of Richie spittle on her back, his fingers digging into her sides, and then the searing plunge of his prick. She screamed, the pain cutting into her like a knife. But in a moment she was thrusting back against him, frantically trying to rub her clit against the edge of the keg. The light leapt along the play of muscles in her legs and along the contracting cheeks of her ass. She strained against the ankle cuffs, her heels lifting off the floor as she rubbed back and forth on the keg. It was no use. Her clit swelled and the cream flowed freely, but she could not make contact with the leather nub.

After several hard grunts, Richie came. His nails dug into her flesh. Looking back at his claw-like hands, she caught sight of her wedding band. She was the wife of this sadistic creature. Not only was she his wife, she belonged to him. Stretched over this hideous keg, her orifices open to the eyes of strangers, the pain of his anal rape burning inside of her, the terrible ache between her legs, none of that mattered. He had cum in her ass. Perhaps she had pleased him. She wanted very much to have pleased him.

"Thank you," she said softly.

"Look at this!" Vinnie was standing before her, his club-like cock inches from her face. She lifted her head. "You remember it?" She nodded her head. "Stein says you ain't cum in over a week. That right?" Again, she nodded. "You want to cum?"

"Yes, please," she managed to whisper.

"Yeah, you're a hot little cunt who's got to cum all the Goddamn time, right? Well, maybe I'll make you cum and maybe I won't." Vinnie waved his cock in front of her face.

"Please," she said, and pressed her pussy against the leather covered keg, grinding against it in a circular motion, but it did no good.

A drop of cum oozed from the gaping hole at the end of Vinnie's cock. He bent down, holding it a few inches from her mouth. She extended her tongue. He moved back just out of reach. The drop grew and glistened in the light and the tip of her tongue curled out to touch it. Finally, he leaned forward and she licked the head of his cock.

"That's a good girl," Vinnie mocked, stepping back. "You just married that retard son of mine, so I guess that makes me your new Daddy. I think you ought to ask your new Daddy real nice for what you want."

"Please," she whispered hoarsely, "please fuck me."

"No, no, girl. I said to ask your Daddy. From now on you to call me Daddy."

"I can't," Kathy said. "I just can't."

"Well then," Vinnie started to push his cock back into his pants, "Daddy ain't gonna give his big fat prick to his stubborn little girl."

"Oh, please," Kathy groaned, "please Daddy, please fuck me."

"That's better. And remember to say Daddy or you ain't never gonna cum. Besides, that's how Richie wants it."

Slowly Vinnie took his place behind her. She raised up

on her toes again to give him easy access to her pussy. "You want me to shove this hard dick up your cunt?"

"Yes, please - Daddy."

He drove into her, slamming her hard against the keg. She moaned and squirmed trying desperately to push her clit against his shaft, but the angle was such that his plunging cock filled her aching cunt but did not touch the centre of her feeling. After only six strokes, he came, came and withdrew.

"No, no, NO..." her cry became a whimper.

The platform turned in order to give the guests a view of her swollen clitoris and the glutenous stream of Richie's cum flowing from her ass to mingle with his father's cum which oozed from her open cunt.

CHAPTER SIXTEEN - STELLA

At a signal from Stein, Stella quickly unsnapped the wrist locks, pulled Kathy's hands behind her back and coupled them together. After releasing the short chains that secured Kathy's ankles, she helped Kathy to stand and supported her while hooking the silver leash to the girl's collar. Kathy bowed her head as Stella led her out of the room.

Behind her she could hear Stein proposing a toast. "To the late Jeffrey Ryan, and to the young stud who has so completely and forcefully made the former Mrs. Ryan his very own." Stella closed the bathroom door, cutting off their laughter.

The emotional strain of the last week, combined with the utter confusion about her willing subjection to Richie and the physical abuse of the last hour left Kathy in a dazed state. She followed Stella's directions, only half aware of what was happening. Stella sat her down on the velvet bench, parted her legs and wiped her thighs with the scented oil. She then reapplied the make-up and tried, unsuccessfully, to pin the netting of Kathy's bodice. It had torn loose and her bare nipples stood out, pink and hard.

Stella removed the pins and ripped the netting off and peeled the tight bodice down so that Kathy's breasts were now fully exposed. "Shoes?" Stella said, stepping back to get a full view of the seated girl, whose hands were still shackled behind her back, thrusting her breasts forward. Kathy squeezed her bare legs together. "I think we'll leave the shoes on," Stella said, bending down to push Kathy's knees apart. "Jesus, you made me hot." She pinched one of the stiff nipples whilst Kathy moaned and struggled against the cuffs that held her wrists. "And look at this," Stella said, kneeling between Kathy's parted legs and scraping a pointed fingernail against Kathy's swollen clit. "So juicy and so very ripe."

"Please!" Kathy cried, squirming.

"Patience, my dear, patience." Stella stood, taking Kathy by the arm. "Come," she said. Together they entered the mirrored bedroom. Stella closed the heavy door and heard it lock. After freeing Kathy's hands, she gently laid her back on the bed. Before Kathy could touch herself, Stella had attached each wrist cuff to one of the overhead wires. The wires retracted, raising Kathy's arms a few inches off the bed. Then each wire slid outward along its track until both arms were spread as on a crucifix. Stella attached the ankle cuffs in the same way. The wires pulled Kathy's legs up then parted them. Her anus and her cunt were completely bare and reflected in the mirrored walls that surrounded her.

Kathy became vaguely aware of a slight humming sound, and the platform which supported the bed moved a quarter turn so that her spread legs and wet orifices faced the front wall. As soon as the platform stopped, the entire wall which separated this room for the living room slowly descended into the floor, exposing her once more to the assembled guests.

Although she could not see them, she could hear their murmurs of approval and the yapping of Stella's dog. She could sense their eyes burning into her openings. She could feel the colour rise to her cheeks. Even before Richie took her, she had not been this open to them. An overhead spotlight swivelled slightly until it shone between her spread legs. Someone cursed and smacked the barking dog, but the animal continued to whine.

The platform turned again affording them, as before, a view from the side. Suddenly Stella was on the bed, naked, kneeling above her, straddling her, leering down at her. She felt Stella's hands on her breasts, kneading them, pinching her nipples, and Stella's bony knees pressed tight against her ribs. Then she felt Stella's bare cunt hot and wet against her stomach. The horrid old woman smiled lasciviously, wetting her lips and bending her face down to Kathy's.

"A kiss for Mommy," she said in a stage whisper that was meant to be heard by the guests. Kathy looked up in horror at the thin bright red lips, the crooked teeth stained with streaks of brown. The old woman's breath smelled strongly of whisky. Kathy turned her head away, clamping her mouth shut. "Little slut!" Stella shouted, and smacked Kathy hard across the face so that she cried out as much in shock as in pain.

Stella signalled someone in the audience. The barking of the dog became louder and more furious. Kathy could feel it on the bed between her spread legs. Suddenly it was lapping her swollen clit, its rough tongue jabbing into her cunt, licking her anus. She cried out again, this time thrusting her hips forward, "Oh, God yes, oh yes, yes!"

Stella took Kathy by the chin, holding her head still, forcing her to look up. "It took years to teach the dog that, years to train it how to lick pussy," she said. "I think you will learn faster." She gestured toward the audience with her hand. The dog yelped and was quickly pulled back on a leash. Kathy continued to move her hips whimpering, "Please, please..."

Stella leaned over her once again, this time extending her tongue, saliva gathering at its pointed tip. Kathy watched the painted face come closer, the tongue wiggling back and forth, the saliva glistening in the light. Slowly Kathy parted her lips. The old woman's tongue slid, snake like, between them. Kathy sucked on it.

The dog was released once more to lap Kathy's cunt. "Now these," Stella said, drawing back and offering her breasts to Kathy's mouth. They were small but surprisingly firm. Kathy lifted her head, licking, then pulling the dark brown nipples into her mouth. With a sharp click, Kathy felt her arms released. She put her hands on the old woman's buttocks. Stella moved up until her cunt was poised above Kathy's mouth.

Kathy stared into the gaping slash. It opened above her like some deadly purple flower, but breathing, alive. Oozing from its dark centre was a thick secretion that shone in the bright light. Kathy inhaled the musky, sweet odour. She looked up into Stella's gray eyes. "Yes," she whispered, hardly aware now of the dog between her legs.

Stella lowered herself onto Kathy's open mouth. "Make Mommy cum," she said softly. "Make Mommy cum good." Kathy swallowed the old woman's juices while she licked her slowly and tenderly. When Stella came, Kathy came, too, but the pleasure of her own long delayed orgasm was not equal to the pleasure she felt in making Stella come.

Before the wall rose up out of the floor shutting them off from the men, Kathy heard a phlegmy cough followed by the familiar raspy voice.

"Shame, Katherine, shame."

CHAPTER SEVENTEEN - CORDELIA

Kathy woke up at home, naked. It was almost noon. She must have been dreaming of the past because she awakened remembering how, as a little girl, she was fascinated by the books her uncle kept on the high shelves of his study. When he was out of the house, she'd stand on a chair and take them down. They were old books, large and heavy. In some the pages were yellowing and cracked. In them were paintings, and ink drawings, and descriptions of martyrs, of long lines of flagellants whipping themselves, their eyes gleaming, their faces looking much like Stella's face just after she'd cum.

The religious histories Kathy thumbed through as a child contained detailed scenes of torture and humiliation. But in them, the victims appeared not to mind. Often they appeared to be in a trance, and sometimes they seemed to be actually experiencing pleasure in their suffering.

Kathy remembered how these pictures stimulated her and how quickly she would cum as she rubbed against the pole in her uncle's basement, especially when she imagined the stern priest whipping her. Then, how disappointed she'd be when he stepped out of the shadows to do no more than admonish her with his "Shame, Katherine, shame."

Suddenly, on this late morning the day after her wedding, the image of the Japanese came to her - what was his name? - Satomi? Yes, Mr. Satomi. She recalled his cold calculating appraisal of her, his curt refusal to pull the bow of her skirt, the thin flicker of a smile that crossed his face when she said that her only desire was to please her husband.

Stein was imaginative and clever. Richie was dull-witted and cruel, but the Japanese... she felt he was much more clever than Stein and could be unmercifully abusive. He had looked at her as if her only reason for being was to debase herself for his amusement. Although she was frightened of both Stein and Richie, the memory of the impassive face and hard bright eyes of Satomi frightened her even more. Was he in the car that brought her home? Did he follow in the car behind them? Had he come into her house?

The ringing of the telephone interrupted her thoughts. It would be Stein, she was certain. She let it ring, debating whether or not to answer it. She'd had enough of Stein's erotic carnival, enough of her new husband, at least for awhile. But it might not be Stein. It might be the austere Japanese. She picked up the receiver.

"Ah, Mrs. Sconzo." She shut her eyes and bit her lip. She hated her married name and Stein knew it. "I trust you've had a restful morning?"

"Yes, Mr. Stein, it's been pleasant."

"You mean you haven't missed your new husband?"

"No, I haven't missed him at all. I truly wish I never had to see him again."

"I'm sorry to hear it. You've awakened the beast in the boy. All day he's been drooling on my new carpeting, and pulling at his cock, and asking me when he can have you again." She didn't answer. "Well?" Stein asked.

"Richie's my husband," she said quietly. "He can have me whenever he wants me. He shouldn't have to ask." Although she tried to remain calm, she couldn't keep the tremor from her voice. Even before saying the words, she felt a wave of heat wash over her body.

"Well said, Mrs. Sconzo, well said. But if I let Richie have his way, you would get precious little rest. He entertains but one thought in his empty head." She did not respond. "However," Stein continued, "that is Richie's problem. I'm really calling to apologize. In the excitement of the wedding both Stella and I neglected to tell you about the dinner party."

"Dinner party? Oh no! Richie..."

"It has been arranged. Do you remember the list of people

you provided me with when we were planning the wedding?"

"Yes." She shook her head trying not to believe what he was suggesting.

"We wanted to make it a rather intimate dinner party so we sent out invitations to just four couples. But on such short notice only two couples will be able to attend. I took the liberty of inviting them to your house tomorrow, 7:00 PM, for dinner and, of course, to meet your husband."

"Who - who accepted?"

"Let me see, I have the names somewhere." She could hear him rustle through papers. "Ah, here it is," he said. "Alice and Tim Butler and a Cordelia and Brian Anderson."

"No!" she exclaimed. "Absolutely not Cordelia!"

There was a pause. She knew he had caught the urgency in her voice and could tell how upset she was. "Ah, Mrs. Sconzo. Why does Cordelia bring such a negative reaction? She was most enthusiastic in her response to the invitation. I take it you don't care for her?"

"Her husband and I, well, we went together for a little while before I met Jeff. In fact, Brian introduced me to Jeff."

"But you and this friend of your late husband's never..."

"No. Jeff and I were virgins."

"Very well, if you say so." He paused. "Now, this man Anderson was in love with you, perhaps is still in love with you, and his wife Cordelia is jealous?"

"Yes," Kathy said, "she always has been."

"Without cause?"

"Yes, without cause. You know how I loved Jeff. There was never anyone else for me."

"Until now?" You love Richie now?"

"No, of course not. No, no, it's not love."

"But a feeling as powerful as love?"

"I don't know." She wanted to slam down the receiver. "Yes, is suppose in a way it is."

"So, when you told Richie that he excited you, excited

you sexually, more than any other man ever had, that was the truth. Well then, you should be proud to introduce this remarkable new husband to your friends?"

"Yes," she said evenly. "I'll be proud."

"Good. It's settled. I wish I could attend. Cordelia sounds like an interesting woman."

"You're not coming?" She couldn't hide her disappointment.

"No, but Stella will be there. She will bring Richie, and she's promised to give me a full report."

Kathy went to bed early, slept soundly, and woke up refreshed. Remembering last night's conversation with Stein, imagining what today would bring, she thought again of escaping back into a normal life by driving off to Boston. Maybe staying a few weeks, then flying to London. She could spend the winter there with Jeff's lovely young sister, Mary Margaret. Perhaps stay for the rest of her life.

Instead, she went about preparing for the guests in an almost mechanical way. She did the necessary shopping, baked a ham, made a casserole of vegetables and another of potatoes, set the table with her best China and silver, arranged bouquets of flowers, and laid a fire.

As she began the careful preparation of her body, she started to feel the familiar curl of excitement and fear in the pit of her stomach. Tonight she would play in another of Stein's little entertainments. She wished he were coming. Perhaps he wanted to discover if she could be trusted to perform well without his pudgy fingers pulling all the strings? It was all part of his plan, she thought - to isolate her, make her entirely dependent upon him.

The weather had turned cold. They would be dressed in new fall outfits: corduroy, suede, leather, sensible shoes, warm wool tweeds. She selected a tight rust coloured skirt that buttoned up the side. From her closet, she picked out a peasant blouse. It had puffy sleeves with elastic at the wrists. Elastic was also woven into the scooped neckline. The green silk clung to her bare breasts and it gathered at her waist before flaring slightly at her hips. She chose green heels which were little more than crisscrossing laces which tied at her ankles. Her bright red painted toenails caught the light and winked up at her.

She stood before the full-length mirror. Stein would have approved. The curve of her breasts was clearly visible. The skirt stretched tight against her round buttocks. The high heels accentuated her tiny ankles and firm calves. She wore no stockings, panties, or bra. She unbuttoned the bottom three buttons of her skirt. Yes, she looked like a whore, perhaps, but a very, very expensive one.

Closing the drawer of her make-up table, she noticed the tube of K-Y jelly Stella had packed with her wedding gown. Surely Richie wouldn't - no, of course not. However, after the guests were gone, he would take her in the way he liked and he would want her as soon as the front door closed behind them. There might not be time to prepare herself. She unbuttoned her skirt, lifted it and, bending over, applied the jelly to her anus. The touch of her fingers against that sensitive spot excited her, but the thought of Richie's cock entering her there caused her legs to tremble as the fear and dread of him washed over her.

Her guests, Brian and Cordelia and Tim and Alice, came in separate cars but arrived at the same time. They had obviously met somewhere for drinks.

"Well!" Cordelia exclaimed, after Kathy had put away their coats, "what are you dressed for? My God, you look like - what does she look like, Brian?" She turned to her husband who had not taken his eyes off Kathy.

"Good," he said quickly, "she looks real good."

"She sure does." Tim laughed and kissed her lightly on

the cheek. Tim had roomed with Jeff in college and was his best friend.

"I don't think 'good' is quite the word," Cordelia said, stepping forward to take Kathy's hands in hers. "For a recent widow and a new bride she looks absolutely decadent. Does your husband buy your clothes?" Cordelia's hands were cold, the fingers long and slender.

"No, but -"

"Where is he?" Alice interrupted. "We're anxious to meet him."

"He's on the way," Kathy said, moving to the bar.

"Here, I'll mix the drinks," Brian stepped in front of her and began setting up glasses.

"Yes, Brian, you do that," Cordelia said. She lit a cigarette. Leather, wool, and suede. Cordelia wore dark brown slacks, a yellow turtle neck, and a tweed jacket. On her feet were suede boots. "Just what does this new husband of yours do for a living?" she asked, taking the martini Brian held out to her.

"He works for his father, cars, an agency near Crafton."

"His father must be a slave driver," Alice said. "You two should be honeymooning." She gave Kathy a little hug. "You didn't say why he's not here."

Kathy passed Tim a drink. "Richie's picking up his mother," she said. "They should be along shortly."

"Oh, Mommy's coming?" Cordelia said sarcastically.

"Which car agency?" Tim asked quickly. "Maybe we can throw some business his way."

"Sure," Brian added, placing a vodka and tonic in Kathy's hand. "We' re thinking about a new car ourselves. What kind of agency is it?"

"I'm not certain," Kathy said. "Chryslers, I think."

"We want a BMW," Cordelia said.

Brian poured himself a straight Scotch. "What about the Club?" he asked. "You two are joining, right? Does he play golf?"

"I - I don't know, Brian."

"Brian," Cordelia said, "they're newlyweds. They've got more on their minds than golf and tennis. I mean after collecting the airline's settlement, our little Kathy here certainly didn't marry him for money."

"Now, Cordelia -" Brian began.

Cordelia swung around and glared at him. Then, smiling, turned back to Kathy, "He must have something, this stud of yours. I mean, well, Kathy you have to admit it was a very short engagement. Why poor Jeff was hardly -"

"Cordelia!" Tim said sharply.

"All right, all right, it's what we've all been thinking, but I'm the only one with guts enough to say it." She glanced out of the window, "Well, it looks like we're getting company."

Kathy wanted to run, but her legs felt rubbery and her stomach seemed to be filled with concrete. Quickly, she drained her glass and crossed to open the door.

"Ah, my dear, dear girl!" Stella cried, embracing her warmly. Then, stepping back, she held Kathy at arm's length. "My, my, just look at you! So beautiful and sexy!" She nodded at the others as if acknowledging their unspoken agreement with her compliment.

"This is Stella," Kathy said, forcing a little smile. Richie was standing in the shadows, his back against the door. Kathy took his arm trying to lead him into the room, "and this is Richie." She looked at her guests, who were staring, dumbfounded. "My husband," she added softly. Violently, Richie pushed her hand away and lurched over to the fire, turning his back on them.

"Now Richie!" Stella shouted, "that's no way to behave. These are Kathy's friends. They've come to meet you."

"Fu-fu-fuck 'em," Richie grunted.

"Richie, whatever's got into you?" Stella said lamely.

"Now behave yourself or I'll have to take you home."

Kathy bit her lip and could feel Alice reach out to squeeze her hand. "Oh, my God, Kathy," she whispered, "what have you done?"

Cordelia burst out laughing. "Well, well, well, it looks as if our sweet little Kathy's got herself a real man!"

Richie turned around scowling, his lopsided face red in the firelight, his bony fingers clenched into tight fists. Brian stepped over to Kathy's side. "Kathy, surely you didn't... I mean this is some kind of a game or joke, right?"

Cordelia laughed again, high and shrill. "Can't you see, Brian dear, it's no joke. Kathy's got herself a superstud!"

"But Kathy," Tim began, "I can't believe..."

"Cordelia's right." Kathy tried to keep the quiver out of her voice. "I am Richie's wife, his lawfully wedded wife. No games. No jokes."

"And does this lawfully wedded wife take her marriage vows seriously?" Cordelia directed her question to Richie, whose right hand had automatically begun to rub his cock through his trousers. "These nice little Catholic girls usually do." She took a step toward him, smiling. "Does she do what you tell her, Richie? Does she love, honour, and obey?"

The image of his wedding night flashed into Richie's mind: a group of strangers holding up their glasses to him, telling him he was a man, saying he should fuck his bride. He felt his cock begin to stiffen under his hand. "K-k-kiss," he stuttered, spraying his chin and shirt with saliva.

Kathy hesitated, then walked over to him and, closing her eyes, pressed her lips to his slobbering mouth. His tongue quickly darted between her lips and she felt his hands roughly pulling her ass into him so that her pussy rubbed against his cock. She fought against it, but moaned again just as she had on their wedding night. She could taste the whiskey he had drunk earlier.

"Jesus, Kathy!" Brian shouted, moving forward to separate them. As Brian grabbed her arm, Kathy spun around. Richie cowered behind her. She looked up flushed and angry. "Take your hands off me," she said. Tim had also stepped toward them. "Don't either of you touch him," she said. There was a long pause. Cordelia smiled and sipped her drink. Richie, sensing he was safe, slid out to stand next to Kathy.

"God, she's perfect!" Cordelia screeched. "The perfect wife, just like always. The perfect wife for Jeff and now the perfect wife for this - this -" she gestured toward Richie. "But never the perfect wife for you, Brian, never for you!" She laughed again. Richie had taken Kathy's hand and placed it on his cock. She left it there and felt him begin to stiffen once more. "Look at them," Cordelia continued, "someone should take a picture and put it on one of those sweet Hallmark cards."

"It's disgusting," Tim said, turning away. Alice was taking their coats from the closet.

"Please stay," Stella insisted. "Kathy's prepared such a nice dinner."

"Certainly we'll stay!" Cordelia cried. "But it looks as if the lovebirds can't wait. Isn't that right, Richie?" The bulge in his pants twitched under Kathy's small hand. "Tell her, Richie," Cordelia urged, "tell her what you want." Cordelia had quickly discovered how she could manipulate the witless creature.

"Fu-fu-fuck," Richie said, and slid his fingers up under Kathy's blouse.

She let go of his cock and turned to face him, "No, Richie," she said. "No, not now." His hand was damp and cold against her bare skin.

Cordelia crossed to stand beside them. "She's your wife, Richie. She promised, didn't she?"

"Nuh-nuh-now!" Richie said, unbuckling his belt.

"Goddamn you!" Brian shouted, and started toward him. Kathy slipped between them, and before Brian could react she slapped him hard across the face. He stood there for a moment looking stunned. They heard the door close behind Tim and Alice. Kathy was vaguely aware of Stella easing herself into the big leather chair. She heard Richie moving behind her, zipping down his fly. She continued to stare up at Brian as she bent to unbutton her skirt.

"Look, Brian," Cordelia rasped, "that's the perfect little wife you've been in love with all these years!"

Brian could not take his eyes off Kathy's fingers as she undid the buttons. She stood up straight, still staring at him, then deliberately she let her skirt drop. Brian stepped back breathing hard. Kathy's shaved pussy was wet with cum. "No," Brian said, shaking his head, "please, Kathy, don't."

"Shut up, you fool!" Cordelia whirled on him. "She wants it, can't you seen that? The little bitch is hot for it!"

Behind her Kathy heard Richie's pants drop to the floor. Richie, confident now, continued to pull at his hard cock.

Still looking directly at Brian, Kathy said, "Yes, Richie, I am your wife." The hurt look on Brian's face turned to revulsion. She got down on all fours, then, lifting her buttocks high, she pressed her face against the rug and reached back to spread her bottom cheeks.

"There, Brian!" Cordelia hissed. "There's the woman you've been dreaming about all these years. Do you want her now Brian? Do you?" Kathy heard Brian groan like a struck animal, and a moment later the door slammed.

"He'll wait in the car," Cordelia said.

Kathy, her face turned sideways on the carpet, was aware of the firelight casting a wavering shadow of Cordelia who stood over her and of the tips of Cordelia's suede boots just inches away. "Make her show her tits, Richie," Cordelia said hoarsely. "I want to see them."

"Yeah, d-d-do it," Richie commanded. Without hesitating, or looking at Cordelia, Kathy pushed her blouse down to uncover her breasts.

"Richie, you're a real man," Cordelia laughed. "She does whatever you tell her."

Richie had positioned his cock against Kathy's anus. She concentrated on relaxing the muscle, but it was no good. He shoved brutally and the pain was as severe as it had ever been. She winced, and her nails dug into the carpet, but she didn't cry out.

After the first thrust, the pain became even worse. In spite of it, Kathy could feel the cum begin to ooze from her cunt. Behind her Richie was panting like a dog. "Masturbate," Cordelia demanded. "I want to watch you finger yourself." Kathy shook her head. "Tell her, Richie, make her do it."

Richie, only aware that Cordelia had asked him to make Kathy do something, grunted, "D-d-do it."

Obediently Kathy spread her legs wider and with the fingers of one hand began to rub her swollen clitoris. She was sure she would cum quickly, but was determined not to let Cordelia know it.

"You slut! You filthy slut!" Cordelia's voice rose on the verge of hysteria. "Look at me when I'm talking to you, look at me!" Kathy kept her cheek pressed against the floor. "Tell her, Richie, tell her!" Cordelia shouted.

"D-d-do it!" Richie was slamming into her. The burning pain increased, yet she pushed back to meet his thrusts.

"Look at me!" Cordelia yelled. "I want to see you cum."

Kathy lifted her head. Above her Cordelia stood, legs parted, hands on hips, the thin slash of her red mouth twisted, intense anger and hatred clearly visible in her eyes. "Make yourself cum, Goddamn it, make yourself cum! I want to see you cum!"

Kathy could feel Richie's thrusts quicken and heard him groan behind her. Then she came. The hot electric intensity spread in waves through her quivering body. Try as she might, she could not contain a scream of pleasure or the writhing convolutions that continued even after Richie's thin brown cock slid from her ass.

Finally she collapsed on the floor between Cordelia's suede boots. "What a pathetic woman you are," Cordelia whispered, "meekly submitting to that cretin. Oh, how I'd love to have you in service to me, even for a little while!" Kathy began to sob. After several minutes, she heard the front door close. She lay there exhausted, the searing pain even worse now that she had cum.

"Very good, my dear, Stein will be pleased," Stella said softly.

Across the room next to the fireplace, Stella sat back in the big chair and smiled. Her dress was bunched up around her waist. Her long bare legs were spread revealing her glistening open cunt. She crooked her finger and motioned Kathy toward her. Kathy, too tired to stand, crawled across the distance that separated them. Her head and her body ached. She wanted desperately to sleep, to wake in the morning and find this had been a terrible dream, to find Jeff beside her, the sun shining, the woods across the street undisturbed.

Stella opened her legs wider and leaned forward. Kathy crawled between them and Stella reached down to cup her face. "Poor baby, you're tired, aren't you?" Kathy nodded and forced a little smile. "But not too tired?" Stella stared down into Kathy's eyes waiting for an answer.

"No, not too tired," Kathy whispered. Stella released her and sank back into the chair. Kathy lowered her face between the older woman's legs and gently began to lick her cunt.

"Ah!" Stella sighed, "that's my girl. Slowly, slowly, make mama last." Kathy licked for a long time, teasing, bringing the woman to the edge of one orgasm after another. At last Stella pushed Kathy's head down against her clitoris, grinding hard, bruising Kathy's lips. "Suck!" she gasped, "suck, suck, suck!"

Afterwards, she lay back again and Kathy rested her head on her thigh. Stella stroked Kathy's hair. "Come, let's go to bed. Baby's had enough for one night." She helped Kathy to her feet and held her as they crossed the room together.

Richie was wide awake, lying on the couch, pulling indifferently at his limp cock. "M-m-more," he said, looking up at Kathy.

"Go back to sleep," Stella ordered harshly. "The girl's exhausted."

Kathy stopped in front of him, unsteady on her high heels, her legs trembling. "You want me?" she asked.

"In-in-ass," he muttered.

"You've had enough -" Stella began.

Kathy took Stella's hands in hers. "He's my husband," she said.

Kathy looked at Richie whose mouth stretched into an evil grin. "D-d-do what I tell you," he slurred, his chin wet with saliva.

"Yes," Kathy said quietly, "you know that now, don't you? You know that I will do whatever you say." She got to her knees beside the couch and took his cock in her hand. Bending over it, she noticed the U shaped scar. She closed her swollen lips over the head of his cock and sucked slowly, until he was hard again. She desperately wanted to make him cum this way. She was exhausted and her head ached. Her anal opening was raw and pain throbbed deep into the passage.

Suddenly Richie sat up and grabbed her by the hair, yanking her head back. He leaned close to her face, his eyes burning into hers.

"I said i-i-in your ass, Goddamn it!"

"Please, Richie, it hurts, it really hurts. Please, cum this way, Richie, cum in my mouth."

Still holding her head back, his face red with anger, he sprayed her with spittle, "You fu-fu-fuckin do what I say!"

Not letting go of her hair, he rolled off the couch and pushed her face down against the rug. Then he stumbled to his feet and stood in front of her, his dark cock wet with her saliva.

She looked up at him, tears filling her eyes. "I'm sorry," she whispered. "I belong to you." She lifted her buttocks. "Please, my dear husband, forgive me. I am grateful to be here like this." She stared at his cock for a moment then reached back and spread her cheeks for him.

He wasn't listening. It didn't matter. He knew. He had known, perhaps better than she, since that time right after the wedding ceremony. This woman was his. This tight little hole she was offering him was his. He drove his prick into it.

CHAPTER EIGHTEEN - PUBLIC OFFERING

Kathy did not wake up until eleven the next morning. Everyone had gone. By noon she had done the dishes, vacuumed, showered, applied her make-up, and dressed: short tight blue cotton shift, bare legs, and black heels. She set a fire, opened a bottle of wine, and placed a platter of cheese and crackers on the coffee table.

Stein arrived by cab and greeted her warmly. "Well, well, Mrs. Sconzo, your little party went even better than I had expected. Stella is still talking about it." Kathy had trouble with compliments from Stein. She felt like a schoolgirl being praised by a teacher she admired and feared. The effect was not lost on Stein. "My, how prettily you blush." He sank down into his big chair, and Kathy sat across from him and poured wine for each of them.

"I'm flattered that you've come for a visit, Mr. Stein. I know how you dislike leaving your home."

"I was going to phone you but decided the matter I wish to discuss requires direct contact. In addition, I wanted to congratulate you personally on last night's performance."

She filled their wine glasses hoping to delay talking about the matters Stein had come to discuss. "Well, whatever the reasons for my bizarre behaviour, it's certain I have descended as far as I can go. Or to use your analogy, I have jumped over the highest possible bar."

"Ah!" Stein put down his glass and studied her. "Do you remember our conversation here in this room right after Richie had reluctantly agreed to your proposal of marriage?"

"I'm not sure. We spoke of a lot of things."

"Yes, and among them was a pledge you made. You promised that after the marriage you would feel obliged to demonstrate your devotion to your husband in public."

"But I've done all that -"

Stein lifted a hand to cut her off. "A few friends in my house or yours do not constitute a public." She felt her heart sink, the old fear returning. "I mean," Stein continued, "I've arranged for you and Richie to spend a night on the town: dining, drinking, dancing, a special romantic evening shared by two young lovers."

"But Richie wouldn't agree. He doesn't know how to, to behave in public."

"You're right about that. But Richie doesn't much care. He has only one thing on his mind... I would advise you not to sell Richie short. He is capable of learning. It takes awhile, but he can do it."

"You've been teaching him?" she asked.

"In a way, yes. As you might expect, Richie has a very poor opinion of who he is. I've been trying to boost his self-image."

"Why?"

"Because, Mrs. Sconzo, until he understands that it is in his self interest to expand his sexual horizons, he cannot fully appreciate the possibilities in owning you. Are you taking that back? Do you now wish to redefine the relationship? Do you now wish to say you are not Richie's woman?"

She looked up and stared at him for several moments, then looked away. "No," she said feeling the heat between her legs, "No, I am his now and I don't want to change that."

"I thought so," Stein said, "therefore I have taken it upon myself to instruct your half-witted husband as to what it means. Richie has been learning that there's more than one way to enjoy his lovely bride. I believe he's beginning to realize that in order to be the man he wants to be, he must become both more demanding and more articulate. We've made some progress teaching him to be more demanding. However, I'm not so sure he's becoming more articulate."

"How can he demand more than I've already given?"

"Let's just say that I have made suggestions to the poor boy as to a variety of things he might require of you. Let us say that I have indicated if you were made to obey these demands in public places, it would show others what a man he is. He really enjoys this new found approval of others. In order to keep this approval he must prove that you are indeed his woman. As much as Richie enjoys the sexual access you open up to him, he has discovered that the respect of others derives from your willingness to do what he tells you to do. He wants to look like a big man. He realizes that for the first time in his life other men envy him. He believes he looks like a big man because he possesses a beautiful woman other men would give anything for. He knows that he can show how totally you belong to him by verbally and physically humiliating you."

"In public, you mean?"

"I mean, Mrs. Sconzo, that tomorrow afternoon a package will arrive for you. In it will be a new gown created by your mother-in-law. The package will also contain a few other things." He paused to sip his wine. She sat silently watching him. "At nine o'clock a limousine will be in your driveway. It will be yours and Richie's for the night. The driver is in the employ of Mr. Satomi - you remember him from the wedding?"

"Yes." She felt a clutch of fear and, again, the hot rush of excitement. "He's the wealthy Japanese. I remember him."

"The driver's name is Abul. He claims to be an old-line Pakistani. He has absolutely no regard for women, especially American women."

"What must I do?"

"The driver has instructions. You need only dress provocatively and go wherever the driver takes you." He smiled across at her. "When you meet your husband you must do what you promised - to obey - to be seen with Richie, to subject herself to his abuse in public places, to watch the expressions on the faces of strangers, to see their initial shock change to disgust - be assured Richie will want continuing and absolute proof that you are what you have said you are."

"His woman!"

"Yes, his woman." Stein sat thoughtfully for a moment looking across at her. "Something happened just after the wedding ceremony didn't it?"

She finished what was left in her glass before answering. "Yes, you're right. You seem always to be right. I don't know how or what, but something terrible happened. I thought - I hoped and prayed it was temporary, but it isn't. I truly am his woman and he knows that."

"Completely his, not like it was between you and me?"

"In our relationship there has always been a way out for me. I knew I could say no. I had a choice. When Richie grabbed me after the ceremony I realized that with him there would never be a choice."

"You are afraid?"

"Yes, more than you can imagine, and I hate myself. I hate what I do and what I have become, but I have surrendered unconditionally to Richie and that's just the way it is."

Stein leaned back and looked at her for a long time. "You

should never have invited me here that first time," he said. "Or you should have killed me when you had the chance."

The next afternoon, as Stein had promised, a package was delivered. She took it into her bedroom and spread its contents out on the bed. The ankle length skirt was made of gray silk. As she had expected, it was slit up the front almost to her crotch. She realized that with each step she took the full length of her bare legs would be revealed. Next, she lifted from the box a tailored shirt of pale peach nylon. She held it up and was not surprised to see that it was sheer enough to be almost transparent. In the box,under the shirt was a wide leather belt and a pair of gray leather pumps with what appeared to be five inch heels. She also removed a gray silk cape that fastened at the neck with a silver clasp. She held it up and saw that it would hang in graceful folds to the floor. At the bottom of the box she found her velvet covered leather collar. There was also a note from Stella.

Kathy had made appointments to have her hair cut and styled, her pubic area shaved and waxed, her nails done, and a pedicure. In the past, preparations like these were undertaken because she not only wanted to please herself but also to please Jeff and recently, perhaps, to win a compliment from Stein. But Richie, as Stein so often reminded her, was oblivious to her looks. He knew that because she belonged to him others regarded him differently. He also understood that his only way to prove she was his woman was to humiliate her.

She blackened and extended the thin line of her eyebrows and used a black mascara on her long lashes. Meticulously, she applied a violet eye shadow feathering it out under the arch of her brows. She touched her pale cheeks lightly with rouge and rubbed a darker colour on nipples which stiffened under her touch. She took particular care with her mouth, first exaggerating the fullness of her lips with a bright red lipstick, then coating them with a shiny gloss. Finally, she rubbed her body with perfumed oil and applied the K-Y. She was sure that the night would once more end with Richie's spittle spraying her naked back, his dirty fingernails digging into her hips, and his filthy cock deep inside her anus. She forced the thought out of her mind.

The clothes Stella had made fit perfectly. Although under the transparent shirt Kathy's breasts were clearly visible, she found that the cape would cover them. However, the cape, which clasped at her neck, was open to the floor. Slipping her feet into the impossibly high heels, she took a few unsteady steps before her full length mirror and saw that it would be impossible to cover her bare legs. With each step they could be seen almost to the tops of her thighs. The floor length skirt was cut in such a way so that if she sat down even a slight spreading of her knees would reveal her shaved pussy. In the mirror she could see that it was already moist. She buckled the collar around her neck.

At precisely nine o'clock a long white limousine glided into Kathy's driveway. The chauffeur did not get out to open the door for her. She was still unsteady on the high heels. The weather had turned colder, and the wind flared both the cape and her skirt. Although the driver had been watching her, the glimpse of his face she got showed no emotion. She was grateful for the warmth of the car and sank back in the soft leather seat, careful to keep her knees together. Without turning around or saying anything, the driver reached back over his shoulder to hand her an envelope. He touched a switch on the dashboard and a light came on above her head. Stein's instructions had been typed but were not signed.

'Abul is taking you to the Triangle Club. No doubt you've been there before, elegant and sophisticated as it is. Go to the bar. Interest a single man or, perhaps, even two. Richie will arrive soon.'

Abul was watching her in the rear-view mirror. She folded Stein's note and put it in the pocket of her cape.

"What are you waiting for?" she asked somewhat annoyed.

"Spread knees," he said.

"No," she answered. "You are very much out of line."

"A mistake!" he said. When they pulled in front of the canopy of the Triangle Club she had to let herself out. Holding the cape together against the wind, she walked the short distance to the entrance where the doorman opened the heavy door for her.

The long, dark bar was to the right of the softly lit dining room, separated from it by an oak partition and etched glass panels. Surprisingly, the bar was almost empty. A couple who appeared to be in their sixties sat at the far end. Near the middle was a tall distinguished looking gentleman with greying hair. Several stools down from him sat a well dressed man closer to her own age.

He reminded her of Jeff. In the past, she and Jeff would sometimes meet here. They would have a drink at this bar and then linger over a romantic dinner, comfortable with each other and happy. Perhaps over dinner they might start planning a winter vacation: Key West, Saint Barts, Puerta Vallarta? Then home to bed, and tomorrow would be a lazy Sunday watching football in the afternoon, maybe guests for dinner...

She hesitated and turned back toward the entrance. Reaching down to pull the front of her cape together, she noticed the black iron band on the finger where she'd so recently worn Jeff's ring. She felt her cheeks grow warm and a wave of heat flow downward to her cunt. She stepped into the bar area.

She slid up onto the padded bar stool next to the older gentleman. When she let go of the cape, it parted revealing her thighs and the fact that her legs were bare. She kept her knees tightly pressed together, and hooked her high heels over the bottom rung of the stool. Both men as well as the bartender and the old couple had been watching her. She ordered a glass of Chardonnay.

The tall man next to her smiled. "I'm glad you changed your mind," he said.

"Changed my mind?"

"Yes, you came in here like a splendid vision from some other world and for a moment it seemed as if you'd decided to go back to it again."

Kathy laughed. "That's true. I mean the part about almost leaving." He was deeply tanned and ruggedly handsome, looking, she thought, a bit like Clint Eastwood.

The younger man lifted his glass in their direction. "We are both glad you changed your mind," he said.

Kathy nodded to him. "Thank you." She turned to the man on her left. "And thank you, too."

"I'm Roger," the man next to her said, and held out his hand.

The younger man quickly moved down to sit on her right. "And I'm Glenn."

"And you are?" Roger asked.

"Kathy," she said.

"Well, Kathy," he smiled down at her, "you certainly add a large measure of grace and beauty to the stuffy old Triangle Club."

"I'll second that," Glenn said. "You are without a doubt the prettiest sight I've seen today."

Kathy blushed. For a moment she felt good about being here, about being attractive to these handsome men, about the quick and easy way the conversation had begun. She felt good about being in the company of familiars. "You gentlemen are very kind," she said.

"And what is such a lovely, refined young lady like you doing out alone on a Saturday night?" Roger questioned.

“Well, I might ask what are two handsome gentlemen like you doing out alone on a Saturday night.” She crossed her ankles, the tip of her shoe brushing against Roger’s trousers. He glanced down. She pointed her toe and smiled at him.

“I’m from New York,” he said. “Just a lonely business man with a comfortable suite of rooms in the Sheraton overlooking Pittsburgh’s Golden Triangle.”

Glenn signalled the bartender to bring them another round even though Kathy’s glass was still almost full. “And I’m recently divorced,” he said, “and rattling around in a big beautiful Victorian house in Forest Hills.”

Roger shifted so his leg pressed lightly against hers. “I don’t suppose you would grant myself and Glenn here the privilege of treating you to dinner?”

“And afterwards,” Glenn laughed, “maybe, just maybe helping one of us be a little less lonely on this lonely Saturday night?”

Kathy sipped her wine. Then carefully putting down her glass, she looked up at them. “Maybe both,” she said, smiling. Her cape had parted enough so that the outline of her breasts could be seen through the shear blouse. She was aware that Roger had noticed. However, she made no effort to pull the cape together. Here, Kathy thought, are two good men: handsome, articulate, interesting, rich, available, and she knew she could have her pick, not just for tonight but possibly for a relationship that would become permanent. Maybe marriage, a normal life. If she didn’t acknowledge Richie when he arrived, if she pretended not to know him, they would throw him out...

...just on cue came Richie appeared.

He made his way along the bar, dragging his left foot and muttering to himself. She saw that under a shabby raincoat several sizes too big for him, he was wearing the same clothes he’d worn at their wedding. The bartender put down the glass he'd been drying and started toward him.

Kathy caught Richie's eye and felt the familiar sinking sensation, then the sudden rush of heat. She glanced at the iron ring on her finger which bound her to him in ways she could not understand but realized were irrevocable. "No," Kathy said quickly, "it's all right. Please don't." She slid off the stool and looked directly at Richie, forcing a tight smile.

He glared at her for a moment then reached out a grimy hand to tug at her cape. "T-t-take it off," he grunted. The two men had turned around to watch. The bartender still appeared as if he were ready to throw Richie out. The old couple whispered to each other. Kathy, her back to the men, undid the clasp at her neck. The cape slid down, and she draped it over her arm.

"There, Richie," she said.

"S-s-show your fu-fu-fuckin tits."

Kathy felt the colour rise to her cheeks and felt her nipples stiffen. Keeping her eyes lowered, she turned to face the men.

"Jesus, she's wearing a collar," Glenn said.

Roger stood up. "Kathy, if you need help -"

She shook her head, still looking down at the floor.

Glenn had taken a step toward them, "This asshole can't be your date?" he asked.

"He's my husband," Kathy said quietly.

"Yeah," Richie sneered, "th-th-this cockteaser be-be-be-longs to m-m-me." His mouth was wet with spittle. He gripped Kathy's arm. "Ain't that right?"

"Yes, Richie. I belong to you."

"Sh-sh-show your sha-sha-shaved cunt!"

She turned to him. "Please Richie -"

"G-g-goddamn it, do what I fu-fu-fuckin say," he spat at her.

She nodded and turned back to face the three men. With her head still bowed, she reached down and parted the split skirt and inched it up to reveal her pussy. The men stared for a moment in shocked silence, then the bartender, angry and red faced, pointed to the door. "Out, both of you, and don't come back!" he yelled.

Richie fished in his coat pocket and withdrew a thin silver leash which he gave to Kathy. She clipped it to the small ring in the collar and handed the other end to him aware, once more, of the warm wetness between her legs.

Richie glared that the bartender. "Fu-fu-fuck you!" he said.

Kathy followed three steps behind her husband. Richie permitted himself a sly grin. Things were looking up. Stein had been right. She would do whatever he told her. He thought back to all the years before this one. He'd been neglected and abused by his parents, shunned and ridiculed by boys and girls his age. He'd been in special classes until he dropped out of school. Then there was that thing with the girls at the mall and afterwards reform school Even there they laughed at him and smacked him around. But now it was different. He'd seen the look on the faces of the men at the bar when he told Kathy to show her tits and her cunt. He remembered how everyone applauded when he fucked his bride's ass at the wedding. He thought about the night at Kathy's fancy house and that skinny woman telling him what a man he was. 'When people see that your wife does exactly what you tell her, they'll respect you,' Stein had said. Stein was always right about things like that.

He realized that the men at the bar were angry, but because his woman did what she was told, they were also jealous. It was a good start to the evening. He knew that things were going to get better, a lot better.

Instead of turning toward the dining room, he led Kathy to the heavy glass entrance doors. Behind him, he heard the sharp tap of her heels on the marble floor. Ahead, through the doors, he saw the limousine parked at the curb just as Stein said it would be.

CHAPTER NINETEEN - ABUL

Kathy, expecting to be paraded through the elegant dining room on a leash behind Richie, almost shouted for joy when she realized he was heading toward the entrance. Stein must have altered the plan or Richie's muddled brain forgot it. The doorman and passers-by stared at the bizarre couple. Kathy's cape was still draped over her arm. The silver chain linking her to Richie glinted in the glare of headlights. Richie stumbled, and muttered, and stopped to spit on the sidewalk. The weather had turned colder, and the wind tore at Kathy's split skirt. She felt it through the thin blouse and against her bare legs.

Abul remained behind the wheel. Richie opened the limo door and entered, giving a hard jerk on the chain which snapped Kathy's head forward. She quickly slid in beside him. Before starting the car, Abul looked back at them. "This woman," he said, pointing a finger at Kathy, "is much too proud for her own good. She don't do what I tell her."

"T-t-tell her again," Richie grunted.

"Spread," Abul demanded. He turned on the dome light above her. Kathy, her hands gripping the seat on either side glanced at Richie, then slowly parted her knees. "More." She opened wider until her shaved pussy was fully exposed. She knew he could see that her slit was wet. Abul looked at Richie, who nodded. The Pakistani leaned over the back seat. "You like showing me your cunt?" he asked.

"No," Kathy said, "I hate being made to do this for you. You're supposed to drive the car. You have no business trying to give me orders."

"Wrong answer!" Abul wiggled a long dirty finger at her. Richie quickly turned toward her and twisting her nipple dug his fingernail into it. She cried out but made no move to resist.

"Now," Abul ordered, "give right answer."

"Yes," she said, "yes, I like showing myself to you."

Abul smiled. "Now, say to me that you would like very much for me to fuck your hot cunt."

Turning to look out of the window, she remained silent, until Richie applied pressure to her sore nipple. "I-I would like you to do it to me," she said.

"Not correct," Abul glared at her.

"I would like for you to fuck my hot cunt," she whispered, just loud enough for him to hear.

Abul turned around and, leaving the dome light on, started the car. He glanced back at her. "Maybe instead, if you ask nice, I let you suck my dick." Richie released her nipple. The limo pulled out into the traffic.

After a few minutes, she drew her knees together. Abul looked at her through the rear-view mirror. "Open up, bitch," he said.

"D-d-do what he says." Richie raised his hand but did not slap her. Slowly, she spread her legs. The arrogant Pakistani disgusted her. He was ugly and smelled bad. He should be working in some shabby gas station, washing her windows, and tipping his hat, and saying 'thank you, mam'.

"You need to train her better," Abul said. "She don't know her place." They drove on in silence for several minutes. Abul glanced over his shoulder at Richie. "Tell her to fingerfuck herself."

"Please, no!" She touched Richie's arm. "Please Richie, not for this man."

"Do it," Richie said.

Tentatively, she placed her right hand over her exposed pussy. Abul looked up at the mirror. "I don't see no action," he said. She slipped her middle finger into her vagina which was now oozing. Against her palm she felt the hard button of her clitoris and the first tingling surges of pleasure. She closed her eyes, her breasts rising and falling rapidly. She began to rotate her hips. A small moan escaped from her parted lips. Both men laughed. "That's enough," Abul commanded. "Little bitch ain't supposed to cum." She placed her hand back on the seat, keeping her eyes closed and her legs spread.

Beside her she felt Richie move and heard him unzip his pants. He poked her with his elbow. She hesitated for a moment, then slid her left hand inside his trousers. His thin cock was hard. Very gently she began to stroke him. She had not opened her eyes. She cupped his balls and drew her fingernails over them.

Now she squeezed his cock and wanted desperately to touch her clit. The cock she now held in her small hand had been caressed by her mouth. She had swallowed its jism. Four times it had pushed brutally into her anal opening and had spurted deep inside her. Almost as if he'd read her mind, Richie said, "N-n-no more." He brushed her hand away and zipped up his fly. "G-g-got to save it for later," he said. "Fu-fu-fuck your ass."

Kathy opened her eyes. Abul was watching her in the mirror. "You like a stiff cock up your ass?"

She looked out of the window, "Yes," she said, "my husband's."

"Yeah, her ass b-b-belongs to m-m-me," Richie said. "S-s-she belongs to me."

"What if you told the rich American bitch to suck me off?"

"She w-w-would."

"Is he right?" Abul asked. "You do what he says?"

Kathy continued to look out of the window. "Yes, I'm his woman," she said. They rode in silence for a long while. The thought that Richie might demand that she satisfy Abul sickened her. She loathed the Pakistani. He was contemptible and repulsive. He reeked of perspiration. It was clear he hated her. She wondered why she was here in this car with these two men who, in the past, she would not have hired to carry away her garbage.

She sat with her knees spread wide, obediently exposing herself to Abul who still kept glancing up at the rear-view mirror. Next to her, Richie wiped the drool from his mouth with the back of his hand. Before long she knew he would stutter 'K-k-kiss" and she would press her parted lips against his and accept his tongue. She was sure the night would end with the fierce pain of another anal - could it be called rape when she was his woman?

Abul tilted his head back and turned slightly toward them. "Richie - that chain you're holding - make her pull it tight into her slit."

Richie nodded. He handed Kathy the chain. "D-d-do it!" One end of the thin chain was still attached to her leather collar. The end Richie had released hung down to the floor.

"Now," Abul said, "pull it up and back so the chain is between your cunt lips."

Kathy centered the chain between her breasts and carefully pushed it between the folds of her shaved pussy. Abul watched her through the rear-view mirror. "Tighter," he said. "Lift up, reach under, and pull it tight between your ass cheeks. Keep your legs spread."

Kathy raised her hips and guided the chain along the crease of her pussy and between her buttocks. Abul grinned. "Richie, it ain't tight enough," he said. "Reach around her and yank it."

Kathy looked at Richie, pleading. "Don't Richie, don't listen to him. He's only the driver."

"Sh-sh-shut the fu-fu-fuck up," Richie said. He slid his hand under her until he was able to grab the chain.

"Yank it," Abul yelled, "make it hurt."

Richie pulled hard. Kathy cried out as the chain cut against the sensitive flesh of her vagina. Both men laughed.

"Say something nice to me and maybe I can get Richie to let go," Abul scowled at her in the mirror.

"You stink," Kathy said.

Abul's face reddened in anger. "Pull it, Richie, pull it hard!" This time the slicing pain caused her to double over. "You want more?" Abul asked. He waited for Kathy to catch her breath.

"No!" she whispered. "I - I'm sorry for what I said. I - I -like you."

"Not good enough." She saw that he was about to tell Richie to pull again. "No, wait!" she cried. "Please!"

"How much you like me?"

"Very much."

"What you like to do for me? Put my hands on your tits and ask me to squeeze them?"

She shuddered at the thought of this man touching her. "Yes," she said.

"Tongue kiss?"

"Yes," she said quickly. "Tongue kiss you."

"How about you get on your knees for me?"

"No!"

Richie yanked on the chain once more, causing her to cry out. He held the chain tight until she nodded her head. After he relaxed it and she caught her breath she whispered, "Yes, I would get on my knees."

"You want me to fuck your mouth with my prick?"

She felt sick and cold and thought she might vomit. "Yes," she said, fighting to control her voice, "You can fuck my mouth."

"Your mouth be hot - and you lick my balls?"

"Yes, yes, whatever you say."

"Later," he said. "You can count on it."

CHAPTER TWENTY - HARRY'S, ACT ONE

Oh God! - they were turning into Harry's Bar!

There were several cars, a motorcycle, and a pick-up truck in the lot. Drapes had been pulled across the windows and a 'closed' sign hung on one of them.

She was surprised to find that Abul was very tall and thin as a post. His long bony face and bulging eyes made him almost as ugly as Richie. He tapped on the entrance door and someone she couldn't see swung it open. The barroom was dimly lit and empty. She noticed their three shadowy reflections in the bar mirror. They made a strange procession: the Pakistani driver leading, her husband shuffling along behind him, and, at the end of the chain he held, she saw herself, Richie's woman.

At the far end of the bar was a heavy oak door which Abul pushed open. When she stepped into the large room, her heart sank and her legs trembled so much she had to hold onto the door frame for support. The room was brightly lit with floodlights which hung from pipes near the ceiling. Projecting out from the far wall was a raised stage. In front of it were several small formica tables and metal folding chairs in which slouched a small group of grinning men who turned to look at her.

At one table, Stein sat alone. At another she saw Vinnie, and Wally, and Harry, the owner of the bar. She recognized Cliff, the angry black who had offered ten dollars for her panties. With him was a huge man, bigger even than Vinnie. He wore an Army undershirt and Army fatigues, and his powerful arms were covered with tattoos. Next to him, staring not at her but off into space, was a grinning old man with long white hair and a scraggly beard.

Abul had gone over to a table in a far corner which was out of the glare of the lights. There was a figure at a remote table there. She drew in her breath when she saw that it was

Satomi, the impassive Japanese.

She looked for Stella, but she was not there.

Kathy took an unsteady step into the room, and Vinnie stood up and yelled above the catcalls from the others, "Come on over to your Daddy," he said. "I got what you want right in here!" He grabbed his crotch, and the others laughed.

"You mean to tell me this hot lookin bitch is married to the Goddamn loony?" shouted out the big man with the tattoos.

"That's right, Harley," Wally said. "And Frank tells me she jumps through every fuckin hoop the retard holds up. She'll get down on her knees and suck your fat dick if he tells her to. Ain't that right, Richie?"

"R-r-right!" Richie lifted his hand that held the chain. "Sh-sh-she d-d-does what I say."

"Like a dog?" Cliff asked.

"L-l-like a fu-fu-fuckin dog!" Richie shouted.

Stein motioned to Richie, who crossed the room to his table. Kathy, her head bowed, her eyes lowered followed and sat next to Stein. Richie took the chair across from them. The men continued to shout obscenities, and joke among themselves, and drink. She noticed pitchers of beer on each table along with whiskey and vodka bottles. A skinny young boy kept filling the pitchers from the bar and bringing bowls of potato chips and pretzels.

"Well, Mrs. Sconzo," Stein smiled, "how are you enjoying your night on the town?" He filled her empty glass from the beer pitcher.

"Please, Mr. Stein," she said, her voice trembling, "I can't do this. Please, I beg you, let me go home."

Stein pushed the whiskey bottle across the table. "Drink up Richie," he said. "Your bride here wants to go home."

"Fu-fuck that," said Richie.

"Please, Richie," she reached to touch his hand, "take me home. You can do whatever you want to me at home."

There was a commotion at the entrance to the barroom. Kathy, who was facing the door, cried out "No, oh no!"

Cordelia stood in the doorway for a moment. She wore a long suede skirt which buttoned down the front, dark leather boots, and an open suede jacket over a white man-tailored shirt. Her thin mouth was a bright red slash, and her eyes were heavily made up. The men yelled and applauded. Someone shouted, "Hey, maybe we get two for the price of one!"

Cordelia laughed, "No, boys. I'm not the entertainment. Mr. Stein and that super-stud Richie," she pointed at Richie who stood up grinning and waving his arms, "have invited me to be the mistress of ceremonies. I'm going to direct the entertainment!" She stood behind Kathy's chair and quickly unclasped Kathy's cape and, twirling it over her head with one hand, grabbed the silver chain with the other.

Kathy gripped the edge of the table shaking her head. "No, no, no," she whispered.

Richie grunted and, staring across the table at Kathy, said, "You d-d-do what you're fu-fu-fuckin told."

The men were getting restless. "Cut the fuckin' conference. Let's party!" someone yelled.

"Yeah, let's party with Richie's wife!"

Cordelia raised her arms, calling for quiet, "Gentlemen, please. We aren't going to party with Richie's wife. Richie's wife is the Goddamn party!" The men laughed and cheered. Cordelia tapped Kathy's full glass of beer with a pointed fingernail. "Drink it," she said, "all of it." When Kathy had finished, Cordelia refilled the glass, "Again," she said. Kathy had trouble, but she emptied the second glass.

The men watched and joked. "Yeah, loosen her up!"

"Look at that sweet fuckin mouth!"

"And them tits. You can almost see right through her top."

When Kathy put the second glass down, Cordelia tugged on the chain. "Stand up. The boys want to see your perky tits." Stein pushed a low stool over to the base of the stage.

Cordelia nodded. Kathy rose and Cordelia, holding the chain, led her to the stool which would serve as a step up to the stage. "There," Cordelia said, pointing to the stool. She unhooked the chain from Kathy's collar. Still unsteady in the high heels, Kathy mounted the stage. Blushing furiously, she looked out at the men who were yelling and grabbing their crotches.

"Take it off!" Harley yelled.

"Yeah, make her strip!" Kathy recognized Wally's voice.

"Right, a striptease," Harry called out. "A little dance music." He lifted a big boom box up onto the stage and turned it on. From the speakers came the low growl of a saxophone and the heavy beat of a bass drum, then the sultry voice of Shirley Horn singing 'Love for Sale'.

"You heard them," Cordelia said. "You can dance. Brian says you're the best. Give the boys a striptease."

Kathy looked down at Stein, hoping he might take pity on her and stop this, but he shook his head. The men started to chant and clap. Slowly, Kathy began to move to the beat, awkward in the heels. She was a good dancer, grace and rhythm came naturally to her. Often, alone in her house, she would dance just for the fun of it. She concentrated on the music, trying to pretend she was by herself at home and safe.

"Let's see them bare titties!" someone shouted.

"Yeah, strip!" Wally looked around at the excited men. "She can dance and strip. She did it for me in her Goddamn house."

Kathy glanced down at Cordelia, who stood at the edge of the stage. Cordelia mouthed the word, 'Strip'. Her hands shaking, Kathy fumbled with the buttons of her blouse. She knew the men would see that her nipples were hard. The colour rose to her cheeks. When the last button had been unfastened, she stopped for a moment in the centre of the stage. "Off, off!" the men were yelling. Tears welled in her eyes as, very slowly, she reached up to her shoulders and pushed the material back, letting it slide from her arms and drop behind her to the floor.

"Push them tits out, baby!"

"Keep movin', move that cute ass."

Kathy picked a spot on the far wall above their heads and tried to focus on it. She swayed her hips to the music and cupped her breasts with her hands. "That's it, baby, shake them!"

"Yeah, jump down here and shake my dick!"

"Wheee, look at that. She painted her nipples! You do that just for us?"

Kathy was moving across the stage to the wailing saxophone, trying to hear nothing but the music, hoping desperately that this agonizing night would soon end. The sultry voice was singing 'appetizing young love for sale, love that's fresh and still unspoiled.'

"Now, the skirt," Wally yelled. "Take off the fuckin skirt!"

"Let's see some pussy!" someone else shouted.

Not able to hold back the tears, Kathy began to unfasten the clasps at her waist. There were four, the last just a few inches below her crotch. Still moving back and fourth across the front of the stage in time with the music, she started with that one. As she unhooked each clasp, the men pounded on their tables and cheered. Just when the final mournful phrases of 'Love for Sale' ended, Kathy's skirt settled to the floor. She stopped and, brushing the tears from her cheeks, bowed her head.

"Look at that pretty shaved cunt!"

"She must of shaved her pussy hair so as to turn us on!"

"Them fuckin tears is just an act. The little bitch wants fucked."

"Let's see your rosy asshole."

"Yeah, show us where old Richie shoves his puny prick!"

Kathy didn't look up or move. Cordelia quickly handed Richie the chain and urged him to the stage. Grinning and slobbering, and dragging his left foot, he climbed onto the stage and clipped one end of the chain to Kathy's collar. Kathy had not raised her head. "T-t-turn around." Kathy did as he ordered. "B-b-bend over." Obediently Kathy placed her hands on her knees and bent over. Again the men whistled and shouted.

"Oh, shit, that is some lovely ass!"

"Look at them baby cheeks! Smooth! Round as apples!"

"Richie, you really been fuckin that sweet ass?"

Richie, still grinning foolishly, nodded his head. "All the fu-fu-fuckin time!"

"Hey, Richie, show us where you put it in!"

"Yeah, make her show her asshole."

Richie jerked the chain. "Spread!"

Despising herself, her hands trembling, she reached back and pulled her ass cheeks apart. Some of the men crowded up against the stage for a closer look. Her dance and exposing herself to them in this way had fired them up.

"N-n-nobody fu-fu-fucks her ass but me," Richie said.

"Yeah, but what about that little baby-girl cunt?"

"And them juicy lips?"

"Hey, Richie, how about she wrap them lips around my stiff prick and suck it?"

"In good time, gentlemen, all in good time," Cordelia laughed. She handed Kathy the cape. "Put this on," she said. "Leave the other stuff where it is." The cape fastened only at the neck. Kathy tried to hold the front together. "Don't touch it," Cordelia said in a loud voice. "The boys want to see your tits and your bald pussy."

Kathy shot a terrified look at Richie, who stood beside her still holding the chain. Cordelia stepped onto the stage lifting up her hand to quiet the men. "Patience, boys, patience," she laughed. She turned to Kathy, "I bet doing your little dance made you nervous, right?"

Kathy bowed her head. "Yes," she said.

"And you had two big glasses of beer didn't you?" Kathy nodded. "Well then," Cordelia took the chain from Richie's hand, "you would probably like to use the bathroom?"

To get away, even for a few minutes, from these drunken foul-mouthed animals would be a godsend. Kathy looked up, "Yes, Cordelia, please."

Cordelia smiled at her, then pointed to Wally. "Sir, would you be kind enough to hand us that empty potato chip bowl?"

Kathy's eyes widened and she stepped back. "No! No, you can't make me do that!"

Cordelia let go of the chain and grabbed Kathy's wrists, pulled her close. "Listen to me you little slut!" She spoke in a fierce whisper. "You are not to refuse or even object. Richie has told you that. Stein has told you that and, if I'm not mistaken, Mr. Satomi has told you that."

Kathy couldn't speak. She nodded and quickly looked away from Cordelia. Wally had brought a big stainless steel bowl to the edge of the stage. Richie took it and handed it to Cordelia. Holding the bowl up to the derisive cheers of the audience Cordelia shouted, "Now the little whore is going to make pee pee for us." She turned to look at Kathy, "Isn't that right, little whore?"

Again Kathy nodded. After placing the bowl at the edge of the stage, Cordelia took Richie's arm and they both stepped down to the floor. The men had pushed several tables back and crowded around that part of the stage where the bowl had been placed. Her head bowed and her eyes lowered, Kathy straddled the bowl. The men had suddenly grown quiet. Her cheeks burning with shame, Kathy bent her knees to squat. Although the pressure to urinate had been strong, it seemed now she couldn't. She strained. No one spoke or moved. She could feel the men staring at her shaved pussy. She shut her eyes and imagined herself in her own white tiled bathroom. She relaxed and the first trickle splashed into the bowl followed by a steady forceful stream. The men yelled and pounded each other and the stage.

"You can get up now," Cordelia said. Kathy stood, her trembling legs still straddling the bowl. "Let's have a round of applause for the little whore!" Cordelia shouted. The men clapped and cheered. "She got us all worked up so what's she gonna do about that?" someone yelled.

"Yeah, how about you tell her to lay down and we take turns?"

Kathy looked at Cordelia, "Please, please, Cordelia, I'm begging you, please don't let them!"

"There, there," Cordelia said, "a lot depends on how good you do me." She led Kathy back several steps so the men could not hear. "I want you to ask to be allowed to lick my cunt!" Kathy shook her head. "You are to go up to the edge of the stage and announce that you want very much to pleasure me, to pleasure me right here for their enjoyment."

"Oh no!"

Cordelia grabbed Kathy's arms, her fingernails digging into the flesh. "Listen to me, you bitch. Those men out there are half drunk and they want to fuck you. All that's between you and a savage gang rape is me. Now, what's it to be?"

"I'll do what you want."

Cordelia led her to the edge of the stage. The men were drinking at the tables. They stared up at Kathy. She could see the lust and the anger in their eyes. They would not hesitate to rape her, she was sure. She looked out over their heads fighting the impulse to cover her exposed pussy with her hands. She started to speak, "I - I want very much to -"

"Louder! We can't hear," someone yelled.

Kathy took a deep breath and began once more. "I want very much to satisfy Cordelia."

"What?" someone asked.

"To - to satisfy Cordelia - to please her." Kathy felt her cheeks burning with shame.

"You mean eat her pussy?"

"Yes."

Cordelia pointed to a leather sling-back chair by the far wall. Harry quickly brought it to the centre of the stage. "Side view or front view?" Cordelia asked.

"Front!" several men called.

"Yeah," Harley said, "while she's sucking your cunt we want to look at her sweet ass." The men were shouting and laughing again.

Cordelia sat back in the chair and, sliding her hips forward, pulled her skirt up until the black patch of pubic hair appeared. She crooked a finger toward Kathy and pointed to the floor between her parted thighs. Once more, the tears welled up in Kathy's eyes. "Take off the cape," Cordelia said. "They want to see your ass." Kathy opened the clasp at her neck and the cape dropped to the floor. The men cheered. Wearing only the spike heels and the collar, Kathy crossed to stand before Cordelia. The men were silent as Kathy got to her knees. She looked up and could see the hatred in Cordelia's eyes. "Ask for it," Cordelia ordered. "Say please."

Kathy bowed her head and shut her eyes. "Please - please," she paused and started again. "Please let me lick your cunt until you - until you cum."

"Lift your ass up and wiggle it for the boys," Cordelia demanded. Kathy crouched down until her mouth was almost touching Cordelia's musky slit. She bent her back and raised her hips. "Tease them," Cordelia hissed. Kathy shook her ass. The men laughed and shouted obscenities. Cordelia pushed Kathy's head tight against her gaping cunt. Kathy had never felt so ashamed, so degraded, so terribly weak. But she also felt the warm secretions oozing from her vagina and knew that the men could see how wet she was becoming.

With the fingers of one hand, Cordelia parted her pussy lips. With her other hand she grabbed Kathy's hair jerking her head back so that Kathy had to look up at her.

"Wiggle your ass!" Cordelia grinned. "Now, tell me that's where you belong, down there on your knees wanting to service my cunt. Say it!"

Kathy fought the impulse to rise up and put her hands around Cordelia's neck and twist until she could feel the small bones break. Instead, still looking up at the face that mocked her, she said, "This is where I belong, on my knees wanting to service your cunt."

Cordelia smiled and released her grip on Kathy's hair. "Then do it, little whore. And don't forget to shake your ass for the boys." She spread her legs wider and pulled Kathy's head down between them. Soon, Kathy's face was wet with Cordelia's juices. Behind her, she could hear the men yelling as she wiggled her hips.

"Hey, Richie, you fuck that beautiful ass?" someone shouted.

"You cum in her ass, Richie?"

"Fu-fu-fuckin right," Richie stuttered.

"She like your prick in her tight ass, Richie?"

"I m-make her b-b-beg for it." Richie could see that the men believed him. He knew that for the first time in his life he had something they wanted. He knocked down a shot of whiskey and it felt good. The woman up there on the stage was his. He knew it was true. He knew it that night right after the wedding. She had looked across at him and he knew it. She would do anything he told her to do. He'd show these men who's woman she was. He would make her beg him to fuck her ass tonight. He'd make her beg him from right up there on the stage. Then, he would do it and they would be down here looking up at him as he shoved his stiff dick into her little asshole.

Kathy shut out the sounds of the men's catcalls and laughter. She concentrated on trying to make Cordelia cum. She felt that her ordeal would be over when Cordelia had an orgasm. Unlike Stella's pussy, Cordelia's tasted sour and her juices were watery. She smelled fetid as if she hadn't bathed. Kathy felt nauseous.

Cordelia thrust her pelvis forward and held Kathy's head tight against it. "Lick, little whore, lick. Tongue fuck me till I cum!" she shouted. The men cheered and applauded. Cordelia began to moan and cry out as she gyrated her hips and bucked, still pressing Kathy's face into her sharp pelvic bone. Finally, she fell back releasing Kathy, exhausted, dropping her arms over the sides of the chair. Kathy, still on her knees, backed away. Her face was covered with Cordelia's cum and her lips were swollen and bruised. She tried to stand, but her legs would not support her. She collapsed and lay naked on the stage, sobbing.

Stein gestured to the black man, Cliff, who jumped onto the stage and lifted Kathy up in his arms. "Follow me," Cordelia directed and, picking up the cape, led Cliff out into the bar then to the ladies' room. Cliff stayed far enough behind Cordelia so that she couldn't hear him whisper to Kathy. "Look," Cliff said, "if you want out of here just let me know. Even later, just say my name, 'Cliff', and you'll be outside and on your way home in two minutes. I carry a razor, and they know not to mess with me."

Inside the ladies' room, Cliff lowered her gently to a chair which faced a dirty sink and mirror. "You OK now?"

"Yes," Kathy said looking up at him and trying to smile, "I'm OK. Thank you very much."

"You can go now." Cordelia held the door open for Cliff.

After Kathy had washed and dried her face, Cordelia placed on the shelf a new lipstick, gloss, mascara, eye shadow, and rouge. Kathy shook her head, "No," she said, "no more. I've had enough." She turned away from the mirror and from Cordelia. "I won't subject myself again to those mindless drunks out there. I hate them. I hate Richie and Stein. Most of all, I hate you Cordelia!" She stood up, grabbed the cape and fastened it around her neck. "I'm leaving," she said.

Cordelia quickly reached into her handbag and withdrew a small envelope. "Before you go, I suggest you read this."

Kathy's first impulse was to ignore it. She was sure it would be another trap. But she was also determined to call for Cliff's help and walk out, go home, be free of them all. She sat down, opened the envelope, unfolded the typewritten page, signed S - S or Satomi!: 'I have instructed that you receive this if at any time during your trial you showed signs of terminating the vow of obedience you made to your husband. You are obviously considering such a betrayal or you would not have been given this note.

'I remind you that it was inconvenient for me to attend your wedding. It is even more inconvenient to be here tonight. If you break your vow of obedience, you not only dishonour your marriage contract you dishonour and disappoint me as well. However, if you truly wish to leave this place, you may go immediately. I guarantee your safety. No one will harm you now or in the future. I will no longer have the slightest interest in you.'

First Cliff and now the powerful Japanese, lurking there in the shadows. Within three minutes she had been given two opportunities to leave and, once again, the choice was hers. Kathy's hands trembled as she folded the note and slid it back into its envelope. She looked up at Cordelia. "I'm very sorry for what I was about to do. I belong to you just as I belong to Richie."

"Right! Now, I want you paint your face like the little whore you are." Cordelia handed Kathy the lipstick. It was plum coloured, a very dark red. "Put it on thick and use plenty of that gloss. I want you to look like a slut, like a cheap cocksucking slut. And rouge your nipples, rub it in and use lots of it."

When she had finished, Kathy stared at the image in the mirror. The face that looked back at her was not her own. She looked like a painted slut, beautiful, but a slut nonetheless. Her swollen lips were exaggerated, the dark colour shining with oily gloss. The heavy mascara and eye shadow contrasted sharply with her pale cheeks. Her rouged nipples seemed much larger and were pointed and hard.

CHAPTER TWENTY-ONE - HARRY'S, ACT TWO

Cordelia stepped onto the stage still leading Kathy with the leash, and as soon as the men saw them they started yelling and applauding. Once more Cordelia raised her arms and asked for quiet. When the men settled down she announced, "OK, boys, are you ready for Act Two?"

"Yeah!" they shouted, "Ready! Ready!"

"Right, then. First, we're going to warm her up." Kathy shot a quick glance at Cordelia, then bowed her head again. Cordelia pushed a bar stool to the front of the stage and directed Kathy to sit on it. "Now, little whore, take off the cape." Kathy unsnapped the clasp and the cape fell to the floor. The men cheered. "Put your hands behind your neck and arch your back. Push those titties out."

"She painted her nipples again!" Vinnie yelled.

"Now," Cordelia tapped Kathy's knee, "spread your legs and show the boys how wet the little whore's pussy has become."

"Look at that sweet juicy cunt!" Harley yelled.

The barboy had come in and placed a bowl on the stage. The bowl was so hot it had been wrapped in a towel. "Now," Cordelia looked out over the audience, "is there any man here who can't get it up?"

"Mine's been up all night!" Harley shouted.

"How about old Gummy? He ain't had a hard-on in twenty-five years," Vinnie said.

"Get him up here," Cordelia stepped forward. "Let's give

old Gummy something to play with."

"He's almost fuckin blind. He'll have to feel his way," Harry said.

"All the better." Cordelia came to the edge of the stage and took the old man's hand as they lifted him onto it.

"How long has it been since you felt a woman?" Cordelia asked. Kathy brought her knees together.

"Don't remember," he said.

Cordelia turned to Kathy, "Tell him to touch you, tell him to feel you and say please."

Kathy said quietly, "Feel me, please."

"Shout," Cordelia ordered, "he can't hear."

Kathy, still not looking at him, said in a loud voice which threatened to break, "Please, I want you to feel me." The men jeered.

Cordelia placed the old man's trembling hands on Kathy's thighs. "That's it," she directed, "touch her, feel her legs, rub her ass. You can squeeze her tits if you want." The old man grunted as he moved his hands over Kathy's belly then around to the firm cheeks of her ass. "Tell him to play with your nipples, and speak up," Cordelia commanded. Kathy, her eyes still closed, said nothing. "Damn you!" Cordelia whispered, "tell him!"

"Play with my nipples," Kathy said. Again the men catcalled and shouted obscene remarks. Very slowly the old man moved his hands along Kathy's ribs until he cupped each breast. Immediately, her nipples stiffened.

"Look at that," someone said. "She likes it."

Cordelia directed Gummy's head to Kathy's breasts. "Bite her nipples," she said. Kathy quickly lowered her arms to cover her breasts. "Put your hands back where they were, little whore!" Cordelia commanded. Slowly, Kathy raised her arms and clasped her fingers behind her neck. "Now, tell him to suck your nipples, and say please."

Kathy lifted her chin and looked out into the dark corner

where she knew the Japanese was sitting, "Please, mister, suck my nipples." The men shouted and laughed. The old man nuzzled his head between her breasts and made low growling sounds. Then, he moved his slobbering mouth to the nipple of her left breast and drew it in. Clamping it between his gums, he sucked hard. Kathy had to fight to keep from moaning. He sucked for a long time, then took her right nipple into his mouth. His drool ran down her breasts and over her stomach.

"Gum them, Gummy!" Wally shouted.

Kathy's nipples had become hard and pointed. She could feel the stickiness between her legs.

"Hey!" Harley yelled, "the old fuck is turning her on!"

Cordelia picked up the bowl and directed Gummy to dip his hands in it. "It's hot oil," she said, leaning over so that he could hear. "Start at her ankles and rub her body."

"Do it Gummy, you horny old bastard, do it!" someone shouted.

Kneeling at her feet, his hands shaking, the old man spread hot oil up one leg then the other. "Spread, little whore," Cordelia said. Cum oozed along the outer lips of Kathy;s pussy. "That's it," Cordelia encouraged, "rub the little slut's wet cunt." The men jeered and laughed. Cordelia moved behind Kathy, "Lean back against me," she said, "and lift your legs so he can grease your asshole." Obediently, Kathy leaned back and raised her legs. When Gummy's rough fingers touched her anal opening, she gasped.

"Th-th-that b-b-belongs to me," Richie stuttered.

Cordelia reached around Kathy's shoulder and tilted the bowl over her breasts then down her back. Gummy continued to make unintelligible sounds as he rubbed the oil over Kathy's stomach, breasts, and back. When he finished, her naked body gleamed under the harsh lights. Cordelia led the old man to the edge of the stage where Harley lifted him down. Cordelia then turned back to Kathy who still had her hands clasped behind her neck, however she had drawn her legs together.

"Open," Cordelia ordered. Kathy parted her knees. "Put your hands down and spread your pussy lips." Kathy did as she was told. Her pink vagina was slick with her secretions and glistened. The nub of her clitoris was swollen and bright red. "Masturbate for the boys. Show them how you play with yourself." Kathy felt the colour flush her cheeks and neck. Hesitantly, she slid her finger along the crease. As she began to rub her clitoris she tilted her head back and closed her eyes. Her breathing quickened and she began to moan softly.

"That's enough," Cordelia said. "On your knees, now." She positioned Kathy near the edge of the stage and parallel to it. "Now put your head on the floor and turn to face the boys." Kathy, holding back the tears, turned her head to face the men who had once more lined up against the front of the stage. "Raise you ass higher and wiggle it for the boys." Kathy shifted her knees and bent her back and shook her buttocks. The men kept shouting and laughing. "Spread your cheeks," Cordelia ordered, "and tell your husband what you want."

Kathy reached back and pulled her ass cheeks apart, exposing the pink bud of her tiny anal opening. "Richie," she began, "I want you to - to fuck my ass." The men hollered and banged their glasses on the tables and the stage. Richie looked around at them smiling slyly. Remembering what Kathy had done on the night she proposed and on their wedding night, he looked up at her. "B-b-beg me," he said.

Tears formed in Kathy's eyes. Cordelia stooped down, "Keep wiggling your ass," she whispered. "Make him want it. Tell him it's hot and tight. Do like he says, beg for it."

After a moment, Kathy bent her back lower and raised her hips. She wet her lips. "Please, Richie, please," she shook her buttocks, "My - my ass is tight, Richie, and its hot for you. My ass is yours, Richie. It belongs to you." She moved her buttocks in a circular motion. “Please, Richie, I want to feel your cock in my ass. Richie, please.” She pulled her ass cheeks wider apart and wiggled her ass lasciviously. “Fuck my ass. I’m begging you Richie.”

Richie climbed up onto the stage. The men cheered. Quickly he shuffled across to stand behind Kathy. He dropped his trousers. Some of the men laughed at his short, skinny cock. Kathy felt his cold fingers grip her buttocks and the familiar slime of his drool on the small of her back. Without waiting for her to relax, he shoved his hard brown prick into her. Kathy cried out and pressed her hands flat against the floor to keep from sliding forward. She was still very sore from the last time he had taken her, so now the burning pain increased with each thrust.

“That’s it, Richie, fuck her!” several of the men yelled.

“Go, Richie, go! Give it to her!”

Kathy squeezed her eyes shut and clenched her teeth to hold back screams of rage and pain, yet she felt a new surge of heat and cum flow down to her crotch. She could sense the swelling of her nipples and knew her clitoris was engorged. Rich held off as long as he could then, with a loud grunt, came deep inside her. The men cheered until they were hoarse. After a moment, Richie’s limp cock slid out of Kathy’s opening. He held up his arms grinning out at the men who were now laughing at him.

Slowly, Kathy got to her knees and looked toward Cordelia expecting to be given the cape and told she could leave. “No,” Cordelia said, “not yet.” She pushed the stool out of the way and dragged the chair forward to replace it. “Stand up, right here beside me.”

Kathy rose painfully. Her legs were shaking. She could feel Richie’s cum seeping from her anus and running down the back of her leg. Cordelia took her by the arm and made her face the men who quickly quieted down. “I have a few questions for our little whore,” Cordelia said.

"Ask her is she going to fuck one of us!" Harley yelled.

"The little whore is so hot she'll cum if she gets fucked," Cordelia announced.

"Who the hell cares!" Vinnie yelled.

"Yeah!" Harley shouted, "I'm hot too. The bitch has been teasin' us all night."

"We want some of that!" Wally was mad and the other men were becoming angry as well.

Kathy tried to step back, but Cordelia held tight to her arm. "Seems we have a problem," Cordelia said. "The little whore has been doing things since she got here to make you guys all hot and horney, but she's not allowed to cum."

There were catcalls at this.

"Not allowed to cum!" Cordelia repeated, more loudly. She turned to Kathy. "Tell us, little whore, what do you think all your vulgar teasing has been doing to the boys here?" She gestured to the audience. The men had been listening intently to her interrogation.

"Maybe it got them excited."

"That's right, it did! They're hot and they're frustrated, and now they're getting angry. It's your fault because you're a cheap cockteaser. So, what are you going to do about it?"

"I - I don't know..."

Cordelia held up Kathy's leash, "She can't fuck and her ass belongs to Richie. So, boys, what's left?"

"Her mouth!" someone yelled.

"Them juicy red lips!"

"A blow job!" Vinnie shouted.

"How about five, maybe six blow jobs?" Cordelia laughed. "How about if the little whore sucks off everybody who can get it up?" The men cheered. "Not only that, I think she owes it to you guys to take your cum, all of it."

"No!" Kathy cried. "No! I can't! I won't!"

She was about to call out Cliff's name. Quickly, Cordelia yanked on the leash pulling Kathy to her. "You can, Goddamn it, and you will!" Fiercely she whispered into Kathy's ear. "Mr. Satomi's idea. He wants you to do it."

Kathy looked into the dark corner where the shadowy forms of Abul and Satomi were sitting. Once more she felt the rush of heat between her legs. She glanced at the sling back chair, then at Cordelia. Cordelia nodded and let go of the leash. Her legs trembling, tears flowing down her cheeks, Kathy crossed to the chair and got down on her knees before it. The men cheered wildly.

Cordelia smiled at them waiting until they quieted. "Ah, yes, gentleman," she laughed, pointing to Kathy, "there she is, our very own little whore, right where she belongs, on her knees waiting to take your hard cocks between those soft lips and suck you dry. Isn't that right, little whore?"

Kathy, a sinking sensation in her stomach, her heart pounding, stared straight ahead at the empty chair. She nodded. "Yes," she said.

Cordelia crossed to stand behind the kneeling Kathy. "Did your first husband stick it up your butt?" she asked.

It was a moment before Kathy could answer. "No," she said.

"But you love it when your new husband fucks your ass?"

Without raising her head, Kathy said softly, "Yes, I love Richie to do it to me."

"You love being Richie's woman?"

"Yes, I love being Richie's woman."

"You will always, always do whatever he tells you to do?"

"Yes, I will always do whatever Richie tells me to do."

"Good. Now, tell us did you ever kiss your first husband's balls? Did you ever give him a blow job?"

"No, never."

"But tonight you're going to lick the balls of every man here, and you're going to take their cocks in your mouth and suck till they cum? And then swallow it?"

"Yes."

"What do you think that makes you?"

"A whore," Kathy answered.

"That's right," Cordelia said harshly, "a cheap whore. I hope they drown you in jism!" She turned back to the audience, "They'll be talking about this for years: the night of the cocksucking marathon at Harry's!" The men whooped and hollered. Kathy tried to hold back the tears but couldn't.

"Who's first?" Wally asked.

"She already had her fun with old Gummy, so let's start with the youngest," Cordelia looked toward the far wall where the barboy was standing. She crooked a finger at him, gesturing for him to come forward.

"How about it Jimmy, you want to lose your cherry in the former Mrs. Ryan's pretty mouth?"

His face beet red, the youth moved between the tables of laughing men until he stood at the edge of the stage looking up at Cordelia. "Yes mam!" he said.

"Then come on up here," Cordelia said. Two of the men lifted him onto the stage. Cordelia led him over to the chair.

"No," Kathy said, "it isn't right. I can't do it."

Cordelia turned and called out to Richie, "Your wife still hasn't learned, Richie. Will you tell her that she is to perform?"

Richie stood up, "D-d-do it, you fu-fu-fuckin' bitch!" he shouted.

The boy had seated himself. Cordelia indicated that Kathy was to crawl forward until she was kneeling between his spread legs. "Now," Cordelia whispered, "open his fly, pull out his prick, and ask him if you may please kiss his balls and take his cock into your hot mouth."

With trembling fingers, Kathy unbuckled his belt and pulled his pants and his shorts down past his knees. His young cock was as red as his face and as hard as it could possibly get. Kathy held it and felt it twitching in her hand. She stared at it for several moments, then turned away.

"D-d-do it!" Richie yelled again.

Kathy inched forward and, cupping the boy's testicles in her hand, bent over to kiss them softly. The men were absolutely silent. No one drank or even moved. After a few moments, Kathy ran her tongue along the underside of his cock and then closed her warm lips over its head. The boy jerked back and came immediately, filling Kathy's mouth with sweet tasting spurts of his hot cum. She sucked until she felt him begin to soften and shrink in her mouth.

As the men yelled and applauded, Kathy backed away still on her knees. Cordelia handed her a lipstick and a small mirror. Kathy coated her lips. Cordelia gave her the oily gloss. Kathy spread it over the dark red until her lips glistened. She bowed her head and waited.

During the next hour Kathy tried to empty her mind of all thought and shut her senses off from all feeling. She had truly become what Stein had once called her, a receptacle. Her tongue licked their cocks. Her mouth opened to receive them. She swallowed their spunk. Between one man and the next, Cordelia handed her the lipstick and gloss and held the mirror while Kathy coated her swollen lips.

When Cliff sat down in the sling-back chair, she couldn't look at him. She was aware that he had learned to despise her. "The time to call on me is long past," he said. "This woman, Cordelia, has it right. You ain't nothin but a honky whore."

His cock was so massive that she could take no more than the head into her mouth. She licked his huge balls for a long time and tongued and nibbled the underside of his cockhead. She almost did drown in his jism which came so thick and powerfully she couldn't swallow fast enough. It ran from the sides of her mouth and hung in glutenous strands from her chin. Cordelia laughed and handed her a paper towel.

Wally was last. He ordered her to lock her hands behind her back. Then, grabbing her hair, he viciously fucked her mouth shoving his cock as far back into her throat as he could. She gagged and choked. "You fuckin cocksucker," he said, "I'll teach you to put down Wally Wallowitz. I'll teach you to break your word, to act high and mighty and treat me like I'm a piece of worthless shit!" His face was crimson with rage. "You're the one who's a worthless piece of shit. After you take every Goddamn drop of my cum, I want you to tell me you loved the way I fucked your mouth and to thank me for shooting my load in it."

He held off longer than any of the others. His jism was bitter and tasted of urine. He made her keep his cock in her mouth long after it had gone soft. When he finally released her, he put his finger under her chin forcing her to continue looking up at him.

"Well?"

"I - I loved it, the way you fucked my mouth," she whispered, her voice hoarse and raspy. "Thank you, Wally, for letting me have your cum."

Wally still glared down at her. "I'm gonna get Richie to give you to me some weekend. I'm gonna keep you naked and on a chain, and I'm gonna train you like a fuckin' dog." He rose and let himself down off the stage.

She felt as if she might pass out. Her knees were sore, her legs cramped, her face ached, and she wanted to vomit. How many had there been? The boy, Harry, Vinnie, Harley, Cliff, and Wally... six. Stein had chosen to watch as had the Japanese. Thank God, Mr. Satomi had not let Abul have her. She struggled to her feet, holding onto the chair. Cordelia handed her the cape. She took it and, with shaking hands, fastened the clasp at her neck.

"You aren't worth the steam from my piss," Cordelia said.

"Yes," Kathy nodded, "I'm not worth even that." Unsteadily she climbed down off the stage. Some of the men had left, Harry, Wally, and Harley were at the bar. Stein sat beside Richie and smiled up at her. Richie had either passed out or fallen asleep, his arms and head on the table.

"Well, Mrs. Sconzo," Stein said, "I trust you enjoyed your first night on the town with your new husband. I'm sure he will want to celebrate like this quite often. You will accompany him?"

"I'm his wife," she said softly.

"His obedient wife?"

"Yes, Mr. Stein, as you have seen, I do whatever my husband orders me to do."

"Always?"

"Always," she answered. She looked at them both for a moment. "I hate him," she said, her voice rising. "I wish to God he was dead! I hate all of you!"

"Wish he were dead! Oh dear, my dear, don't say such things. You're just tired. You will feel differently in the morning."

"Never!" She watched as the Japanese left. He didn't even glance in her direction. With a wave of her hand, Cordelia followed him.

"Abul has been instructed to drive you home," Stein said. "He's in the car warming it up so you don't catch cold."

"My clothes?" Kathy asked.

"Gone," Stein chuckled. "You will have to go home just as you are."

"I don't want to go with Abul. I don't ever want to see him. I"m afraid of him. Can't you take me home?"

"I have to tend to Richie, here. It looks as if you either ride with Abul or walk."

Sick to her stomach, her legs trembling, Kathy made her way through the bar to the front door. She stepped out into a bitterly cold wind wearing only the cape and heels. The limousine was parked at the front door, Abul behind the wheel. She collapsed in the back seat, shut her eyes, and woke up with Abul shaking her knee. "Get up, whore," he said. Slowly she dragged herself out of the car and into the house. She kicked off the painful shoes and went straight to the bathroom. Leaning over the toilet bowl, she threw up until nothing was left. She brushed her teeth and gargled. Then, she brushed her teeth a second time. Her black silk robe was hanging from the bathroom door. She removed the cape, splashed cold water on her face and, too tired to shower, slipped into the robe.

The lights were still on in the living room. As she entered, her hands went up to her mouth to stifle a cry. Abul was sprawled out in the big leather chair watching her. She stepped back, staring at him. The floor lamp next to the chair gave her the first opportunity to really look at his face. It was gaunt, a high forehead, sunken cheeks, large hooked nose, almost no chin, thin lips and the rotting teeth she had noticed earlier. His heavily lidded eyes were bulbous and protruding, the white was a yellow phlegmy colour, the pupils, black. His black hair was cut short and parted in the middle. He was unshaven. He continued to stare at her. She took another step back and steadied herself against the door frame. Slowly, he sat up and, placing his hands on his knees, leaned forward. "Now," he said, "it's my turn. Now you suck my cock."

Quickly Kathy crossed behind him and into the kitchen. She took the receiver off the wall phone and, standing in the doorway, fought to keep the fear out of her voice. "Get out," she said quietly, "or I'll call the police. Of all the men I've ever met, you are the most despicable, the most vile. You are a hundred times more disgusting than Richie." Her voice steadied, anger replacing the fear. "Me suck your filthy cock? You must be insane. I wouldn't touch you with a ten foot pole. You stink. You're stinking up my house. Now, get out!"

His face was twisted with hatred. He stood up quickly and spit on the floor. She put down the phone as he went to the front door and opened it. He turned toward her. "This is a big mistake!" he hissed.

CHAPTER TWENTY-TWO

Halfway between waking and sleeping, Kathy drifted into a dream. It was of Satomi. In it she saw only his smooth chiselled face in profile. Still asleep, she slid her hand between her legs. Her middle finger found the hard nub of her clitoris. As Satomi turned his head to stare, unblinking, into her eyes, she experienced a series of orgasms that caused her to wake and cry out, and buck and thrash against her hand. After the intense pleasure subsided, she rolled over and fell asleep again.

She was awakened by the ringing of the phone. She let it continue. After a few minutes, it stopped, but almost immediately began once more. She picked up the receiver. "Ah, Mrs. Sconzo." It was, Stein. "I hope I haven't disturbed a well earned rest?"

"No." Her voice was a raspy whisper. "I was just getting up."

"Good. I must congratulate you once again. Your performance last night was worthy of a standing ovation." She closed eyes and said nothing. Her entire body ached. She smelled of cigarette smoke, stale sweat, perfume, and her own secretions. Her lips were still swollen, and when she turned in the bed she felt a sharp burning in her anus. More than anything she wanted a hot shower, then, a huge breakfast. After that, some time to pack and escape for good.

"Mrs. Sconzo, are you there?"

"Yes but -"

Stein interrupted, "Ah, as splendid as you were last night, it seems you ended the evening by being less than hospitable to Mr. Abul."

"I hate him! I'm afraid of that man. I swear I will never

let him near me again."

"Yes, well, I can sympathize. I get the impression he is much more clever than he appears and is capable of any manner of violence. I've noticed he has a pronounced contempt for women and, in your case, I believe it's coupled with a good deal of anger. You would be well advised to steer clear of Mr. Abul."

"I fully intend to. Now, Mr. Stein, please..."

"Right. Forget Abul. I'm calling to tell you that you got your wish."

Kathy was puzzled. "What wish?"

"The one you made just before leaving last night."

"I don't remember any wish...."

"How could you have forgotten? You wished that Richie would die and so he has. You are once more a widow, my dear."

"Oh, God, no!"

"Do you recall telling me that your parents went out to buy you a Christmas present and were killed in an accident?" He didn't wait for her to respond. "And you sent your husband away so that you could spend an evening with me and poor Jeffrey returned home in a coffin. Now, in the presence of a very very powerful man who has expressed some interest in you, you wished your new husband were dead. Guilt, Mrs Sconzo - guilt and penance seem to be your lot in life."

"But Richie was asleep at the table in Harry's..." In a daze, Kathy placed the receiver back in its cradle. She sat on the edge of the bed, letting the realization of Stein's news sink in. She began to cry, not because Richie was dead, but because Stein had reminded her of those other deaths and suggested she was responsible for this one.

She remembered saying that she wished Richie would die and she vaguely recalled Satomi passing near the table at that moment. Did the Japanese have Richie killed because of her careless remark? Stein had it right. She was Death's hand-maiden: her mother and father, Jeff, and now Richie.

Although she seemed all but crushed under the terrible burden of guilt, she also felt an exhilarating lightness. Richie's death freed her. For the first time since she was awakened by the sound of Wally's grader, she felt free - free of Stein, free of Stella, free of Vinnie, free of Cordelia, free of the men at Harry's.

And, best of all, free of Richie! Sooner or later the hold he had on her would have destroyed her. She was certain of that. Perhaps her wishing him dead in the presence of Satomi was neither innocent nor accidental?

After a long hot shower she dressed in slacks, a sweatshirt, heavy wool socks and loafers. Even though it was late in the afternoon, she made herself a substantial breakfast. She thought about driving off to Boston again, but decided she needed time alone in a place far away from everyone she knew. She called the airlines and booked a flight to San Francisco for tomorrow night.

Shortly after six, a cab pulled into her driveway. She watched Stein get out and was relieved to see that he instructed the driver to wait for him. He wore a new overcoat and carried a new briefcase. He lumbered up to the front door which she held open for him. "Ah, Mrs. Sconzo," he smiled, "I feared you might be dressed in mourning."

"I'm not trying to be anything except comfortable." Kathy took his coat and together they went into the living room. She had lit a fire in the fireplace and now she poured each of them a beer.

"Yes," Stein sighed as he sank back into the leather chair, "comfort. But I must say you look fresh, and young, and absolutely glowing with good health."

"Well, actually, I am emotionally and physically exhausted. And now what you told me on the phone -"

"Ah, yes, poor Richie... it seems that shortly after you left he went back into Pittsburgh and got himself a room at the Crosley. It's a cheap hotel down on Penn Avenue frequented by low-lifes and prostitutes. Richie fell out of his window, apparently." Stein shook his head in mock sadness. "Unfortunately, the room was on the twelfth floor."

"Apparently?"

"Well, no one actually saw him fall. The desk clerk remembers that Richie came in alone. Next thing, he is lying in the middle of the street. Dead."

"But you implied that because I wished -"

"Mrs. Sconzo, no one actually saw your husband fall from the window, and no one except you, Mr. Satomi, perhaps Abul, and myself heard you wish that Richie would die." He smiled up at her. "Now, the police are calling it an accident. However, the Japanese has an interest in you and the Japanese is an extremely rich and powerful man. Would you believe that, thanks to Mr. Satomi, there is now not even a record of your marriage to Richie? The police don't know you were his devoted bride who wished him dead... anyway, you are now the widow Sconzo."

Stein smiled at her and Kathy shook her head, "Poor Richie." They sat in silence for a few moments. "Tell me," Stein leaned forward, "suppose Richie had lived? Would you have continued as his wife? I mean as his absolutely loving wife, obedient, submissive, anxious to serve him in any way he demanded?"

She thought for a long time before replying. "Yes, I think I probably might have. In an unexplainable and frightening way I belonged to him. I truly did." She smiled across at Stein. "But I'm glad, terribly glad, to be free of him."

"Yes," Stein said, "Richie will not be missed."

"What about his father? What about Stella?"

"Richie was never anything but trouble to them. They're relieved. You, more than anyone else, know what a pathetic but vicious animal he was. The world is a better place without him. You and your oriental master did us all a favour."

"Oriental master?"

"Ah, a slip of the tongue. I'm getting ahead of myself." Stein grunted as he reached for the briefcase. He placed it on the coffee table and snapped it open. "I come not only with the news of your husband's accident, but also as an emissary from your benefactor." Out of the briefcase he took several folders.

"I don't want to hear it," Kathy said. "I don't want to hear anything. I'm going far away. I leave tomorrow night."

"Please," Stein said, "sit down. If I go back without explaining Satomi's offer, I might very well be the next one to fall out of a window!"

Reluctantly, Kathy sat. She folded her hands in her lap. "I'll listen," she said, "but I won't change my mind."

"Simply stated, the Japanese wants you to become his concubine."

"I would belong to him? Be his woman, his whore?"

"Something like that," Stein said.

"You both must be out of your minds."

"Mrs. Sconzo, we are not talking about Richie here. He was a retard, an imbecile. Satomi is, as I've observed you to notice, a very handsome man." Kathy felt her cheeks flush. "He is also one of the world's most intelligent, ruthless, and wealthy men. There are only about ten men like him on the planet. Believe me, Mrs. Sconzo, he gets whatever he wants. And what he wants is you. You are free of Richie because he wants you. He spent valuable time at your wedding and again last night observing you. He's decided he wants you."

"I don't care!"

"Let me give you some history. A few hours after my first visit here, he was informed of our evening with my pets, a complete description, all the details. That attracted his interest. From then on, everything you've done has been a series of tests. He has designed all of them. I repeat, all that has happened since your encounter with the leeches has been carefully orchestrated, not by me, but by Satomi."

"Surely not Jeff's death?"

"Even that." He leaned forward, his hands on his knees. "I'm saying Satomi is an absolutely ruthless man. He gets what he wants."

"But Jeff died of salmonella poisoning, the autopsy proved that."

"There are several poisons that, in fatal doses, give the appearance of salmonella. Like most of us, flight attendants can be bought or terrified. A single mother with small children is extremely vulnerable... Satomi gets what he wants."

"Oh, my God!" Kathy buried her head in her hands. "Even Jeff! If I had refused. I mean if I had not fed -"

"Satomi would never have heard of you."

"He still doesn't even know me. How could he love me?"

Stein sat up and laughed. "Love! You, of all people, still babble about love! Ah, my dear, when will you learn? Satomi's view of you isn't much different than Richie's. Satomi sees you as an object. Something to own, like a very valuable painting. Something that will make other powerful men envious. Something he might lend to associates as a favour or to adversaries as a bribe. He sees you as a useful commodity. Unique, yes, but a commodity all the same. The man is incapable of what you call love. If the truth be known, most men are."

"My answer is no."

"He could arrange it so that you would be disfigured, even killed."

"Is that a threat?"

"No, not a threat. I mention it only as a possibility."

"Kindly finish what you have to say, Mr. Stein. I have much to do tomorrow before I leave."

"Very well, then. First, if you agree to his proposition, your service as his concubine would last only fourteen months. If you perform satisfactorily, at the end of that time you will be given fifteen million tax free dollars and a five million dollar home anywhere in the world that you chose. The contract would have been fulfilled and you, my dear, would be an extremely rich woman and entirely free."

"I still can't do it..."

"I have here," he interrupted, indicated the folders, "all of the necessary legal documents. If you sign, then everything you own will go into a trust that cannot be accessed during your period of service. In other words, during that time you will be penniless, completely dependent upon Mr. Satomi." He picked up a second folder. "In here are letters addressed to your friends and relatives. You will inform them you've gone on a world tour and expect to be away for fourteen months. At various intervals these letters, apparently from you, will be mailed from different cities around the world."

"He's thought of everything, hasn't he?"

"He is a very through man. Power is in the details."

"And just what are the duties of a concubine?"

"I was coming to that. He wanted me to explain exactly what would be expected of you."

"It's not going to happen, but tell me anyway. I don't want to read in tomorrow's newspaper that you've fallen out of a window."

Stein smiled. "Thank you. As his concubine, you will in every sense of the word, belong to him. You will obey without hesitation or question every order he gives you. In that regard you will function much as you did with Richie only I expect his requirements will exceed anything either you or I can imagine. Occasionally you will accompany him at important political, business, and social functions. Often, as I said, he will lend you to acquaintances or business associates or others when he feels it is in his interest to do so. You will be expected to service both men and women. As long as you perform satisfactorily, you will live in luxurious quarters and will be perfectly groomed and richly adorned. However, except for special occasions when you serve as his paramour, you will be treated not as an equal but as a concubine."

"A whore," Kathy said.

"Yes, I suppose so. But a very special whore." Stein smiled across at her. "Another thing to consider. Mr. Satomi is not monogamous. You would be one of several concubines in his service."

"What's in this for you?"

"Well, my dear, if I fail to persuade you, I'm afraid someone else will have to tend to the pets. With a man like Satomi there's no place to hide."

"And if I should agree?"

"Then my fondest wish will come true, just as yours did last night. I will have earned a five million dollar finder's fee!" He laughed as he gathered the folders together and pushed them across the table toward her.

"He'll have you killed if I refuse?"

"That's the impression I got." He leaned back in the chair and closed his eyes. "Don't allow my possible passing to enter into your decision. I've had a long and rather useless life. Of course, I'd like to live a few more years, especially as a rich man, but if I don't - well, like Richie, it would be no great loss."

She reached out to touch his hand but drew back. They sat in silence for several minutes. "I can't! I simply can't! Richie was enough!"

"I remind you once more, Satomi is not Richie. With Satomi the bar will be raised as far as it can go."

"I can't, Mr. Stein. You will have to take your chances. I'm sorry."

He sighed and heaved his bulk out of the chair. "Very well." He closed the briefcase and pointed to the folders on the table. "I'll leave these just in case." She helped him with his coat and walked with him to the door. "Should you change your mind," he added, "there would be one more test."

It had started to snow. She watched his slow progress down the walk. At the door of the cab he turned and waved to her. As she waved back the thought occurred to her that he was old enough to be her father. She stood in the open doorway, the swirling snow lightly brushing her face, until the cab was out of sight.

CHAPTER TWENTY-THREE - COMPLIANCE

Even before she fell asleep, Kathy had begun to change her mind. She remembered a line from her high school Macbeth, 'I am in blood stepped in so far that, should I wade no more, returning were as tedious as to go o'er'. Like poor Macbeth, she thought, I am so far into this river of depravity, it would be as hard to go back as to go on. In the morning she would probably sign the papers and become whatever the Japanese wanted her to become.

It was not because she was afraid of what might happen to her if she didn't. Satomi, she was sure, would not harm her if she refused. Stein had been wrong. Not that the Japanese would hesitate out of moral convictions. He had no sense of morality, and he was so powerful he could either ignore the law or buy its practitioners. Pride would prevent him from threatening her. Compelling her to do his will would diminish him. By forcing her, he would have lost. To have her freely consent to serve him as a concubine was another matter entirely.

However, she did consider the threat to Stein as a real possibility. In spite of the incomprehensible turn her life had taken because of Stein, in spite of the unimaginable humiliations she had suffered at his hands, a mutual respect had developed. She genuinely liked him and was sure he had grown to like her. Their's, she thought, had become a kind of symbiotic relationship, two lunatics adrift on a sea of excrement. In an indirect way, she had been responsible for the murders of Jeff and Richie. She did not want Stein's death on her conscience.

Then there was Mr. Satomi. She recalled the fear and excitement she felt when she first saw him on the night of her marriage. She had begun, she realized, to consider his apparent indifference to her as a challenge. She wanted to change that stoic, imperial look of his. She wanted to prove, if only to herself, that the man of marble was only a man after all. She wanted him to want her in the way other men had. For the past two months she had been at the center of a ring around which they all cavorted: Wally, Stein, Vinnie, Richie, her uncle, Cordelia, and the rest. She seemed, of course, to be the submissive Mrs. Sconzo, but in a very real sense it had been she who controlled them.

Only Satomi had remained outside the circle and, if Stein was right, Satomi had been cracking the whip. All of them, especially her, had been jumping through the hoops he held up. She wondered if she could draw him in, cause him to put away his hoops and his whip?

It was decided. She would start tomorrow night. There was this final test. She was certain the Japanese would administer it himself. He would come here to her house, and she would prove that she was worthy to be the most prized of his concubines. She dropped off into an untroubled sleep and didn't awaken until eleven o'clock the next morning.

She retrieved the folders Stein had left, skimmed through them, and signed her name next to the x's he had marked. The papers were simply legal documents listing the conditions Stein had described. She also signed the letters which were to be mailed from the various countries on her supposed world tour. She was surprised to see that letters were addressed to Jeff's parents, and to her friends, Tim and Alice. There were even letters for Mary Margaret, Jeff's younger sister, who was now studying in London. She wondered how Satomi knew about Mary Margaret and why he had gone to all this trouble. Stein had been right. The Japanese was certainly attentive to details.

She had just finished returning the legal papers and letters to their folders when the phone rang. "I'm calling to inform you of the arrangements for Richie's cremation," Stein said. "Your refusal of Mr. Satomi's offer last night sounded so final, I'm not even going to ask you to about it. In fact, I'm rather glad you declined, even though your doing so puts me in a rather disheartening position."

"But -" she began.

Stein, either not hearing or deliberately ignoring her, continued. "I shudder to think what would happen to you if you were to agree to his terms. The man is obsessed with his own importance. He is without conscience and knows nothing of pity."

Kathy smiled, remembering she once would have described Stein in the same terms. "Why, Mr. Stein," she laughed, "I think you are genuinely worried about me?"

"I would be if you had accepted. But since you refused - "

"I've done it again," she interrupted. "I've changed my mind."

There was a long silence before Stein spoke. She heard him sigh. "I wish you would reconsider, truly I do."

"I thought it all through after you left last night. I expected you to be pleased. Your life is no longer in danger and, with the finder's fee, you will become a rich man."

"Yes, but -"

"It's done. I must admit to being terribly fearful, but I'm trying to compose myself for the final test. I think you said it would occur tonight?"

"The test? Oh, yes, the test," Stein seemed distracted. She heard him shuffle some papers. "Here are the instructions," he said. "At four o'clock this afternoon two Japanese servants of Mr. Satomi will arrive at your house, a man and a woman. I believe they are husband and wife. They will examine the legal documents and, if everything is in order, they will begin to prepare you for, ah, for tonight's test."

"And the test itself?".

"It is to determine if you are capable of becoming a worthy concubine, to see how quickly and completely you obey."

"I thought I demonstrated that last night."

"You did, my dear, you certainly did. But apparently Mr. Satomi requires additional proof."

"And he will want to prove that himself. He's coming here tonight. I'm sure he is!" She couldn't hide the excitement in her voice.

"I cannot say because I do not know."

"What if I fail?"

"I don't know what would happen. However, if you insist on going through with this, I strongly advise that you not fail. Please, get out now while you can."

"I won't fail!"

"Very well. I suppose your success depends on how much you desire to serve the Japanese."

"Yes," she said, "it comes down to that, doesn't it?"

"I'll inform him of your decision. You needn't concern yourself with Richie. Stella and I are attending to that... good luck, then. I'm going to miss you." He hung up before she could say goodbye. She replaced the receiver. Inside her, there was a long sinking like going down fast and alone in the elevator of a tall building. She made herself lunch, showered, applied a light make-up, put on jeans, a loose fitting sweatshirt, and slipped into her penny loafers.

At exactly four o'clock, a black Toyota Camry pulled into

her driveway. She watched as the Japanese couple removed two large suitcases from the trunk and struggled up the walk with them. She opened the door. The couple nodded, unsmiling, as they paused in front of her. She pointed toward the living room. The man went first, the woman behind him, and Kathy followed. They put down the cases and turned to face her. Both were short and thin and, Kathy thought, quite homely. She guessed they were in their mid-forties. The man reached inside his coat pocket and withdrew an envelope which he handed to her. Like the other messages from Mr. Satomi, it was typed and unsigned.

'This will introduce Mr. Naka and his wife, Miko. They are my personal servants. Miko will prepare you for your trial. She has her orders from me. You must follow her instructions. Mr. Naka will first examine the papers you were given. If they are properly signed, he will take them. He has been instructed to make a video tape of your trial. He is an accomplished professional and will be unobtrusive.'

That was all: direct, concise, impersonal. Compared to Satomi, Stein had been a chatterbox. But Satomi would come here tonight, of that she was sure. She knew he himself would want to participate in the final trial. She was free of the fat old voyeur, free of the demented Richie, free even of poor Jeff. She was at last involved with a man who was not only extraordinarily powerful and wealthy, but he was also intelligent, perceptive, exacting, handsome, demanding, self-assured, and, she had to admit, frightening. Two men had died because he wanted her. Tonight he would tell her what he wanted. She would see him naked, taste his mouth, feel him inside her. She would be equal to whatever the trial required. Nothing could be worse than what she had endured in Harry's Bar.

"You eat?" Miko asked.

"Yes, before you came."

"Good. Now, sleep for three hours." Miko shook two pills

from a container she had taken from one of the cases.

"But I don't need..," Kathy began to protest.

"You sleep," Miko said sternly.

Kathy took the pills and went into her bathroom for a glass of water. Miko followed her and watched to see that she swallowed them. The two women returned to Kathy's bedroom. Kathy fell onto the bed and was asleep almost immediately.

Three hours later she awoke, not knowing, at first, where she was. Then she saw Miko impassively sitting on a chair next to the bed. Under the single sheet that covered her, Kathy was naked. The Japanese woman must have undressed her. She wondered if the woman's husband had helped. Gradually, she became aware of a burning pain in her anus. Reaching behind her, she felt the smooth circular base of an anal plug tight against her opening.

"Leave it," Miko said. "You too small. Stretch little bit."

Kathy opened her mouth to object, but Miko held up her hand, palm side out, "Stop," she said, frowning. "You do what I tell you. No back talk. Mr. Satomi does not permit... now, we clean inside and out." She stood and pointed to the bathroom. Kathy, not wanting to be seen naked by this stranger, tried to cover herself with the sheet as she got out of bed. "No," Miko said, "leave it." She followed Kathy into the bathroom but did not close the door. Kathy noticed an elongated plastic bag hanging from the shower bar. It was obviously filled with liquid. Attached to its base was a thin hose which ended in a hard rubber nozzle.

Kathy turned quickly to face the Japanese woman. "No, I won't let you."

"Every time you object, I write down in report. That was number two. Bend over toilet."

Blushing with shame, Kathy did as she was told. Carefully, the Japanese woman removed the anal plug and then slowly inserted the nozzle. As she released the closure valve,

Kathy felt the warm liquid flow up into her rectal passage. She looked behind her and was shocked to see that Miko's husband had set up his video camera in the doorway. "Please don't!" Kathy cried out.

"Objection number three," Miko said evenly.

Kathy heard the slight whirr of the video camera. Soon her belly began to swell with the liquid. She glanced at the plastic bag which was still half full. "I can't take any more," she said.

"Take all," Miko answered.

The pain increased as her distended belly stretched. Her legs trembled, and she thought she might faint. When she looked up again, the bag was empty. "Hold in," Miko said as she withdrew the nozzle and quickly replaced it with the anal plug. Kathy fought to keep from screaming. The pressure intensified, and something had been mixed with the liquid that burned her insides. "Must get accustomed," Miko said. "Concubine must do enema every day, some days two times."

After a few minutes, Miko directed Kathy to turn around and sit on the toilet. Deftly she reached between Kathy's legs and, with a twist, removed the plug. Mr. Naka's camera had not stopped, but Kathy's relief was so great she was almost oblivious to it.

"One more," Miko said as she poured a small amount of a thick colourless substance into the enema bag. "Only a little bit this time. Feel good. Make passage slippery. Smell nice." Without protesting, Kathy again positioned herself over the bowl so that Miko could insert the nozzle. The thick fluid tingled as it drained into her rectum. When the tingling sensation subsided, she felt a warmth in the passage that was not at all uncomfortable.

"Feel hot twelve hours, maybe more," Miko said. "Now, empty."

Kathy turned around and sat on the toilet bowl facing

Mr. Naka's video camera. The liquid had been heavily perfumed. Her bathroom now smelled of sandalwood and cinnamon.

Miko reached into her bag and took out a leather case which she snapped open. From it she withdrew another anal plug and held it up before Kathy. "Little bit bigger," she said. "Need to stretch more." She indicated that Kathy was to get up and bend over. Slowly, the woman inserted the plug. The pain caused Kathy to gasp. "Need to learn to open hole like you open mouth," Miko said. "Hole be used many, many times. Must learn to make open, then make tight to give man pleasure. Must always be clean, smell good."

"Yes," Kathy said.

"Now shower first, then special bath."

After Kathy had showered and dried, Miko once more instructed her to sit on the toilet. The Japanese had laid out, next to the sink, an old-fashioned shaving brush, soap, and a straight razor. "No hair anywhere except on head," she announced. Expertly she shaved Kathy's pubis. "Soon get treatment so no hair ever grow again. Smooth everywhere all time."

When Miko had finished, she filled the tub with very hot water. From her bag she took several small bottles and poured their oily contents into it. The room was suddenly rich with the fragrance of tropical flowers. "Now, soak for half hour. Let skin take in oils." Mr. Naka filmed Kathy getting into the water, then turned off his camera. Both he and his wife left the room and closed the door behind them.

The warmth in her rectal passage and the pressure of the plug were constant reminders that Satomi's preferred orifice would be her anus. She wanted desperately for him to take her in the natural way. He would, she thought, have a beautiful, thick, very hard cock. He would cum deep inside her. They would cum together. She would make him hard again and once more they would cum together. She longed to feel his cock pumping her; feel it sliding up and down against her sensitive clitoris. But if, like Richie, he wanted to take her the other way, then he would do so.

Her nipples had stiffened. Inside the folds of her pussy she could feel the slick ooze of her secretions. She was tempted to bring herself to an orgasm but withdrew her hand from between her legs. She knew she was required to wait. The thought that she would never cum again unless Satomi gave her permission excited her.

After exactly half an hour, Miko returned. "Dry yourself and come to bedroom," she said.

The pillows were gone from Kathy's bed. It had been covered with a plastic sheet. On a folding table next to the bed was what looked like a fondue pot. A tiny flame burned under it warming a clear sweet smelling oil that halfway filled the container. Miko pointed to the bed. "First on stomach. I give special massage."

The Japanese woman began at Kathy's small feet: rubbing them with the hot oil; probing, gently twisting, heel, arch, toes one-by-one then together. She took a very long time, slowly and expertly massaging Kathy's ankles, calves, the backs of her thighs. When she began to squeeze the cheeks of Kathy's ass, she said,

"Is good. Smooth, hard. Men like."

Kathy gave herself over to the ministrations of Miko's strong fingers. She was instructed to lie on her left side, then on her back. Miko spent fifteen minutes massaging Kathy's pubic area: rubbing and pinching the labial lips. Kathy blushed as she felt her clitoris swell and her vagina moisten. Her breasts also received a long and attentive massage that left her nipples hard and her breath coming rapidly. She was told to move to her right side. Again, starting at Kathy's feet, the Japanese woman worked tirelessly and silently along the entire length of Kathy's body. The fragrant oil warmed her skin and made it gleam under the soft light. When Miko finished, Kathy felt both completely relaxed and intensely aroused.

"You want sex now. Want bad." Miko stated it as a fact rather than a question.

"Yes," Kathy said, "very much."

"Preparation of concubine for sex is like tea ceremony, exact, never change, always successful. Concubine is only to give pleasure. First pleasure to look at. Pleasure to smell. Pleasure to taste and feel. Must be quiet. Must never speak unless asked question. Always bow head. Always agree in soft voice. Say what master, man or woman, want to hear. Understand?"

"Yes, I understand."

Miko indicated that Kathy was to sit in the chair beside the dressing table. "Fingers and toes now," Miko said. From her case she took several small bottles, nail clippers, and a file. "Must let nails on fingers grow very long. On toes little bit long." Carefully, she first gave Kathy a pedicure, then a manicure. The lacquer was a dark red. A second coat of a special clear polish added a high gloss and seemed to give the colour a rich depth. "Like enema, nails done every day you to be used," Miko said as she finished.

"Used?"

Miko looked across at her impassively, "Concubine is only instrument of pleasure, like lute, only a thing. To everybody you only a thing. Lower than the lowest of servants who serve meals, who wash sheets, who sweep floors, who scrub toilets. People like me who prepare you to serve are higher than you, much higher. To us and to all you are like the silverware that must be polish to look good. We make you look good for master's pleasure. To us you not deserve any more respect than silver spoon or fork. You are only pleasure instrument. We are your betters. Do not forget that."

Kathy looked away from the woman, "A thing," she said

half aloud.

"Yes," Miko nodded, "like silver pitcher, beautiful to look at and made to be used. A thing." She stood, "Come," she started back to the bedroom, "make up face now and dress. You not concubine yet, far from it," she muttered.

Yes, Kathy thought, one more test to pass before I'm given the privilege of being a pleasure instrument, a thing. Still, the idea of becoming less than she was excited her. As Mr. Satomi's personal 'pleasure instrument' she might eventually cause the powerful Japanese to dance to her tune. He couldn't be that much different from other men.

Miko was exceptionally skilled in applying Kathy's make up. When she finished, Kathy was startled as she looked in the mirror to see the transformation. She appeared slightly Asian or more precisely Eurasian. Her eyebrows were arched high and extended in a long thin black line. Blue eye shadow was feathered out to where her straight black hair framed her face. Black mascara seemed to lengthen her lashes. Through the artistic application of a variety of cosmetics, Miko had given Kathy's eyes a slightly slanted look. She then exaggerated the natural fullness of Kathy's mouth with a red lipstick that matched the colour of her nails. Finally she brushed Kathy's lips with a sweet smelling gloss that made them glisten.

She directed Kathy to stand while she placed around her waist a corset of dark red velvet trimmed in black leather. The corset began under Kathy's breasts and was cut in such a way that it pushed them up and out. It ended just above the swell of Kathy's hips. It laced in the back. With each hook, Miko pulled it tighter until Kathy's waist was smaller than she would ever have thought possible.

"A robe?" Kathy asked.

"No, nothing more except shoes." From her suitcase she took a pair of heels the same shade of red as the corset. They were exactly the right size. Kathy slid her tiny feet into them.

Two velvet covered leather straps crossed at the base of her toes and thin ribbons tied around her ankles. The heels were as high as those on the pumps she had worn last night. Again, Kathy had difficulty walking in them. "Take small steps. Concubine must learn always take small steps, keep eyes lowered, not look at anyone," Miko instructed.

"Yes, I'll try to remember," Kathy smiled up at her.

"Not try," Miko said sternly, "must do, or punish. No more questions. Just do what told." Holding Kathy's arm, she led her into the living room. Taking small steps, Kathy felt the painful stretching of her anus and hoped Miko would soon remove the plug. Mr. Naka filmed their entrance. He had built a fire in the fireplace and positioned the leather hassock in the center of the living room facing the couch. The coffee table had been pushed to the side. "Sit," Miko said, pointing to the hassock. "Hands behind back." Quickly Miko clipped thumb-cuffs to Kathy's thumbs and locked them together.

Then she placed a heavy black leather mask over Kathy's eyes and buckled it tightly. "Spread legs, always spread legs, show cunt. Cunt is for pleasure. Must show like flower." Kathy parted her knees. She heard the camera whirr. "Now, we wait for master."

Kathy thought of Satomi. She imagined his lean hard body, his finely chiselled face, the cold indifferent glance. She imagined his cock. Beautiful like marble but pulsing with hot blood, perfectly formed, swelling under her touch, the smooth texture of its skin, the dark head, the heavy testicles, the smell of him perhaps like the sea or freshly turned earth, the taste of him... clean, yet not like any other taste. She could feel her cunt become wet with her own juices and knew that Mr. Naka was filming her.

It was a very long time before she heard a car pull into the driveway. Miko went to the door. There was a murmured conversation then she heard Miko and another person enter the living room. Someone sat down on the couch opposite her. She was sure it was Satomi. His presence was almost palpable. She knew he was staring at her. She wanted to spread her legs wider. She wanted him to see how wet she had become. However, she was afraid to move. Her breasts rose and fell rapidly. Her nipples swelled and stiffened. She had to fight in order to keep from moaning. Her need for him was like nothing she had ever felt before. She remained still, her head bowed. The room was silent for several minutes.

Then, she heard Miko step behind her. Miko began to remove the blindfold. "Do not look up," she cautioned. Kathy wanted desperately to look at her master, but kept her head down.

It was a long time before he spoke.

"In certain places and at certain times you will be called Katherine," he said. "At other times you will answer to other names. You have signed the necessary documents and arrangements for your training have been made. I think you will be acceptable for service, but it depends on your absolute unconditional obedience tonight. Is that understood?"

The sound of his voice caused Kathy to tremble. Her vaginal lips were slick with her secretions. She felt in her stomach the terrifying sinking sensation.

"Yes," she whispered.

She heard him rise and cross over to her.

"Look up," he said.

She lifted her head and looked directly into his eyes. It was the first time she had seen him close without the dark glasses. His eyes were ice blue and hard. Impossible! she thought, a Japanese with blue eyes...

His classically formed face was as impassive as she had remembered it. He was dressed in black. A black silk shirt, black trousers, black shoes, a black dress coat. He was quite tall, his broad shoulders tapering to a narrow waist. But it was his face that startled and excited her, the penetrating eyes, so unexpected in their piercing colour, the high cheek-bones, the smooth brown skin, the full lips. There was about him the unmistakable sense of power, of authority. This, finally, was the man she needed. She knew she would do anything he required. She felt she had known it from the first time she saw him at Stein's on her wedding night.

She took a breath and was about to speak when he raised his hand to stop her. "The trial will begin in a few minutes," he said. "I have appointed a surrogate for myself." She felt her heart sink and struggled to keep from protesting. "I want you to obey him as if he were myself, unconditionally and without hesitation or question. I want you to pleasure him in every way that you can and make him believe that you want nothing more than to give him pleasure. You will show him with spoken words and with your body the kind of complete and absolute devotion I expect you to give to me. As a concubine it will be your duty to serve others as you would serve me. Tonight you will prove or fail to prove that you are capable of that. Your only desire in this test will be to please me through your total submission to the person who comes here in my place."

As she bowed her head again she heard him rise and, in a few moments, the front door opened and closed.

Miko covered her eyes with the blindfold and tightened it, and the waiting began.

CHAPTER TWENTY FOUR - ABUSED

The front door opened. Someone entered the room. "Kneel," Miko said. Kathy slid off the hassock to her knees. "Keep legs spread." Kathy felt someone approach and stand before her. Close. The odour was strong and unmistakable.

ABUL!

Kathy fought against the impulse to scream, to stand and order them all out of her house. The tears welled up in her eyes and ran down under the blindfold. She couldn't contain a small whimpering cry.

"Open mouth," Miko said.

Kathy hesitated, then obeyed. Slowly a long finger pushed between her parted lips. She felt the ragged fingernail against her tongue and tasted the grit and sweat. She began to gag. "Suck," Miko demanded. Kathy sucked the finger. After several minutes the finger was withdrawn and another inserted. She sucked it clean.

She heard Abul unzip his pants and step between her spread legs. The reek of his crotch made her ill. "Beg to suck it, arrogant American bitch," he said.

Again she felt waves of heat wash over her body. Her nipples swelled and stiffened. She could feel her juices ooze along the lips of her pussy. But her situation made her want to vomit.

"Please let me s-suck your cock," she said.

"You suck it good! Make love to it!"

She couldn't accommodate the thought of Abul here in her house, the realization that she was on her knees before him, that she had agreed to obey him, and that she could not escape him or expect help. "Yes," she said meekly, "I'll make love to it."

He moved forward. She felt the uncircumcised tip of his cock brush her lips. She extended her tongue and licked the bunched skin which covered the end of his prick. Gradually his cockhead emerged like a dark purple plum. Instinctively she pulled back from the repulsive odour. Then her red lips glistened as she opened them ever so reluctantly to receive him. She sucked slowly for a long time, then licked the underside of his thick penis and lowered her head to lick his huge testicles, laving them with her saliva. He pulled her back to the tip of his cock where a large drop of cum had formed.

"Taste," he said.

She extended her tongue and licked up the bitter drop. He held her head away from him. Behind her Miko removed the blindfold. His frightful face was more repugnant than she'd remembered. His eyes burned into her so she had to look away. "You want my cum?" he asked. She glanced at his cock. The purple veins were prominent and thick, like fat dark growths under a skin which was almost black.

"Yes," she said, forcing herself to look at him, "I want it." She moved forward and opened her mouth to take him in. He pushed her back and tilted her head up. She understood what he was waiting for. "Please," she said. He continued to stare down at her. "Please - I wish only to give you pleasure."

He released her and she took as much of his cock as she could and sucked until he exploded thick hot gobs of sour tasting jism in her mouth. She swallowed it. He kept her head over his cock. "Milk it," he said, "suck it dry." This was worse than Wally, worse than the leeches, worse than Stein, worse than Vinnie, worse than all the men at Harry's, worse, by far, than the humiliation and pain she suffered on her knees before Richie. In her thoughts she held onto the words of the Japanese. This filthy excuse for a man who stood sneering down at her was, for tonight, Mr. Satomi's surrogate.

She looked up at Abul. Some of his jism clung to her lips. She licked it off. The tight corset thrust her small breasts up toward him. Her thumbs locked together behind her back also made it appear that she was offering them to him. Her rouged nipples were stiff and he could see the wetness between her legs. "You want me to play with your tits?" He grinned down at her, the broken stubs of his yellow teeth clearly visible. She nodded. He rolled her nipples between his thumbs and forefingers. She closed her eyes and parted her lips and moaned softly.

Suddenly, he dug his long fingernails into her, cutting the sensitive skin. She cried out and jerked back. He let go of her. "You said your only wish was to give me pleasure," he hissed. "Remember, last night you treated me like shit." He paused. "You say you want to give me pleasure. I say that hurting you gives me much pleasure."

Slowly she inched back to him on her knees and lifted her breasts toward him. "I wish to please you," she said. Once more he viciously twisted her nipples but this time she closed her eyes and directed the pain down to her center where in some curious way it flowed hot between her legs and intensified her need.

"Stand up," Abul said. Since her hands were bound behind her back, she struggled to get to her feet. Miko took her by the arms and steadied her. "I heard you beg that miserable Richie to stick his little cock in your tight hole. You beg me to put my big Pakistani prick up your rich American lady ass?"

She was sure even after the stretching, he would split her...

"Yes, I'll beg for it."

"And will you invite me into your bed, the bed you shared with your rich husband?"

She hesitated. "Yes," she said at last, repulsed at the thought of this pig in their bed.

"Make love to me like on your first wedding night? Tongue kiss?"

"Yes."

"Right." He gestured to Miko who turned Kathy around and led her to the bedroom and closed the door behind them.

"Now we fix make-up and dress you in white gown just like on wedding night." Miko unfastened the thumb locks and unlaced the corset. "Plug stays in," she said. She sat Kathy down at the small table and once more skilfully painted her lips and spread them with gloss. She rouged Kathy's sore nipples and also coated them with a sweet smelling oil. From her suitcase she took a beautiful white silk gown which she held up. It was so sheer that Kathy could see the figure of Miko behind it as if she were looking at her through a window. She stood and slipped her arms through the wide sleeves. The gown tied loosely at her waist.

Miko pointed to the bed. "Sit," she said. "Some things you must learn first. You still want to be concubine?" she asked.

"Yes," Kathy answered, "Mr. Satomi's concubine. I want that very much."

"Mr Satomi and Mr Abul way of love not like American way. Not at all like American way." Kathy nodded. "In America man does things. Man tries to please woman. Tries to make her cum. Does what she say so that she can cum. American way, man is active in love making. This way just opposite. Man not do anything. Expect you to do all. Man don't care if you cum. Most times will not permit you to cum. You understand?"

"I think so."

"You must be the active one. You must imagine what he wants you to say and do. Must use mouth and body to excite him but always in servant kind of way. Shy, humble, not look up. Must not speak. Sneak look to see if he approve. Must feel honoured to pleasure him with tongue, everywhere, even most private parts." Kathy bit her lip and looked away. Miko frowned, "Honoured, you understand? And grateful. You are instrument of pleasure, not mistress, not lover, not wife. Only instrument to give pleasure."

"Yes." Kathy tried to smile. "An instrument of pleasure."

"To serve Mr. Abul you must learn quickly what he likes, but must not ask. Never bold. Always humble. Never thinking of self. Thinking only how to serve him. In time it will come about that your biggest happiness will be in serving him well even if doing so causes you much pain... now, kneel at foot of bed. Head bowed. Do not look up. Do not speak. You must remember after giving service you back away on knees, head down, never turn back on master. Must learn to serve completely, to be grateful, and, most important, to show high respect. You, nothing. Master, everything."

Kathy got to her knees and bowed her head as Miko had instructed. This was not like any of the humiliations she had subjected herself to in the past. No matter how much control Stein, and Cordelia, and Richie seemed to have over her, she always knew that if things got too bad she could walk away. Occasionally she had been a bit afraid, but the fear she felt now was, she thought, like that of a small trapped animal waiting for something even more terrifying and more painful than the trap.

The sight, and smell, and touch, and taste of Abul were all abhorrent, but it was in his voice she felt his undisguised hatred of her, his desire to make her suffer. His commanding voice told her that he knew with absolute certainty she could not leave, and that now, tonight at least, she was his. He knew she would serve him in every way he wished.

In the mirror she saw herself dressed as a bride on her wedding night, here in her own bedroom, the place where she and Jeff had first made tender and innocent love. Now, she was kneeling at the foot of their bridal bed waiting for a man she feared and hated, waiting to give him pleasure with her tongue and soft warm lips, waiting for him to remove the anal plug and make her beg him to take her in that opening. Waiting and desperately hoping he would also bury his cock in her wet pussy and allow her to cum. And knowing even if she were not permitted to have an orgasm, she would profess her gratitude and, crawling backward head bowed, she would demonstrate her unconditional servility and her clear acknowledgement of him as her master. And thinking these thoughts, her terrible fear and self-loathing intensified, but at the same time the heat of her desire became almost unbearable.

The door opened and closed. Someone was behind her. Footsteps. Someone was crossing to the bed, lying down on it. Miko was still there too. "Master ready now," came her whisper. The camera whirred.

Kathy crawled up onto the bed between Abul's spread legs. Slowly she licked his inner thighs which smelled and tasted of stale sweat. His crotch was matted with wiry black hair. Carefully, she moved up to kiss and lick his testicles which were huge and swollen. The thick veins of his black cock felt like fat earthworms, twisted and ugly. The purple skin bunched at his cockhead sickened her. Even though she had cleaned him with her tongue a little while ago, the fetid odour had returned, almost making her gag.

After a long while, his cock began to stiffen. "Enough," he said, and pulled her up across his naked body. He wore only a black silk robe which he had untied. Afraid to look into his eyes, she stared into the dark hole of his mouth. His discoloured teeth were evil in the candle light. His breath smelled of red wine and garlic. His wide mouth was wet with spittle. As he reached up once more to twist her nipples, she pressed her parted lips to his and, after a moment, traced with her tongue the ridges and hollows of his gums and the stubs of his teeth.

She pushed her pelvis against his cock. She felt his sharp fingernails dig into the sensitive flesh of her breasts. She moaned and drove her tongue deep into his mouth and then moved her warm wet lips back and forth over his, inviting his tongue to enter her mouth. She kissed him like that for a very long time, sometimes holding his face between her hands and softly kissing his cheeks and his closed eyes, the hollows of his neck, his chin, and then his mouth, gentle teasing kisses, then pressing her open mouth over his again and sucking his tongue. She had never made love like this to anyone.

She inched down to kiss and lick his chest and dark nipples. Suddenly he rolled her off him and looked down at her. She saw the lust in his eyes, but also the anger. Nothing she could do would ever diminish that black hatred. He took both of her wrists in one hand and pulled her arms up and back above her head. Leaning over her he asked, "You like my spit?"

Staring up at him, afraid to say anything else, she whispered "Yes."

"Open mouth," he demanded. She parted her lips. "More." Unsure of what he intended, she opened her mouth wider. "I give you what you like," he said and leaned closer to her open mouth and spit a long stringy gob of saliva into it. Then he held her mouth closed. "Drink," he said. After she had swallowed, he grinned down her her. "Thank me for honouring you with my spit."

Feeling her stomach turn and the hot rush between her legs, she closed her eyes and said the words, "Thank you for honouring me with your spit."

He nodded. "Yes," he said. "Spit is easy. Later maybe I will honour you with things not so easy. And you will thank me. Yes?"

"Yes, I will thank you."

"My prick is stiff again. You didn't cum last night so you must want much to cum?"

"Yes, please, I would be very grateful if you would let me cum."

"You should be grateful for whatever I do, make you cum or not make you cum."

"Yes, I am grateful to be allowed to give you pleasure. To be permitted to give you pleasure is all that I want and need."

"You like me to fuck your cunt or your ass?"

"My cunt. Please fuck my cunt."

"But it would give me more pleasure to fuck your ass." He still held her wrists over her head and continued to look down at her.

Kathy could not answer right away. After a moment she whispered, "Then, please, fuck my ass. Let me beg you on my knees."

He released her and she quickly slid off the bed and kneeled beside it. He turned to sit facing her, putting both feet on the floor and spreading his legs. She inched between them and bowed her head. "Please, please, Mr. Abul, I beg you, I beg you with all my heart, I am begging you please to fuck my ass."

"Is your passage clean?"

"Yes, I have carefully prepared my passage. It is clean and lubricated with perfumed oil for the honour of serving you."

"And you have widened it?"

"Yes, so it will better accept you."

"I hate American woman, especially rich American women who act high and mighty but are no better than goat shit. I truly hate you for the things you said to me last night." His face was dark with anger. "I will take pleasure, much pleasure, in hurting you. You are nothing! Nothing!"

Now Abul was pointing to his long, dirty toes.

"Kiss!"

Kathy crawled backward and, remembering the afternoon at Stein's when she knelt at his bare feet, she lowered her head and pressed her lips to his feet. She continued to kneel there with her head bowed while he lifted his legs and, pulling his knees back against his chest, presented her with the black puckered hole of his anus. There was a strong smell of faecal matter in the thick hairs.

"Kiss," he said again. She looked up and uttered a small

cry, bringing her hands to her mouth. "Kiss!" he repeated.

She crawled forward and closed her eyes and leaned toward the opening he offered her. Hesitantly, she pressed her lips against it. "Tongue," he said. Gently, she probed his anus with the tip of her tongue. He pushed her away and sat back on the bed, his feet once more on the floor. She knelt before him, her breath coming quickly, her face flushed, her nipples and clit swollen. "What is other English name for shit?" he asked.

"Faeces," she said.

"Thank me for what I just permitted you to taste."

"I thank you, Mr. Abul, for allowing me to taste your - your faeces."

"Last night you say I stink. Asshole stink worse, yes?" She nodded, fighting to keep from retching.

"And now you want me to put my big prick up your hot ass?"

"I wish for you to take whatever pleasure my body can give you. What pleases you is what I want."

"Even when you cry out with the pain of it, you will make your ass try to hold me in. You will move against my big prick in your tight passage. And you will take my jism deep inside of you. And afterward you will be honoured to know that my cum is in you. You will want more and beg me to take my pleasure again even if your opening is raw and feels like fire. You will do this because my pleasure is the only thing on this earth that matters to you. Is that not right?"

"Yes," Kathy whispered, "I give my body to you to use as you will. I live only for your pleasure. I'm beginning to understand that now." She leaned forward and taking his huge prick in her hands lowered her head over it and sucked until he was hard again.

"Enough," he said, rolling away from her and directing her to kneel facing the headboard of the bed. She closed her eyes and turned her head sideways, pressing her cheek against the mattress. She curved her back and lifted her hips as he positioned himself on his knees behind her. She was aware that her own secretions had begun to ooze down her thighs.

Kathy raised her hips higher and reached back with both hands as she removed the anal plug and spread her ass cheeks for him. She could not bring herself to call him master. "Please, Mr. Abul, take this opening I have prepared for you. Pleasure yourself in it, I beg you."

Abul positioned the huge dark head of his cock against the tiny anal ring of her opening. Then he slowly but unrelentingly pushed until its entire length had disappeared into her. The thickness of his long penis stretched her painfully, but it was not nearly as bad as she'd expected. Perhaps the lubricant contained something that slightly anaesthetized her passage.

He waited, unmoving, his cock buried in her, his huge testicles pressing against her ass cheeks. After a few moments she began, almost instinctively, to contract her sphincter muscles so that they squeezed his cock. "Aggh," he grunted, and dug his fingernails into her flesh. For a long time he knelt behind her perfectly still while she milked his cock in this way.

Suddenly he grunted and, grabbing the cheeks of her ass, he began to fuck her hard, pulling completely free of her opening and driving his prick back in until his testicles slapped against her. The burning pain of his thrusts seared through her. Tears flowed from her eyes, but she did not cry out.

Soon the pain became less intense. She found herself pushing back toward him when he withdrew his cock. After fucking her hard again, he slid his cock out and teased her opening with its head. As he rubbed the tip of his cock around the rim of her anal opening, she pulled her ass cheeks wider and uttered little sounds over and over, "please, please, please," until he drove his glistening prick into her again.

After a long time, he began to fuck her hard and quick again like an animal. Sweating and grunting he came inside her and immediately pushed her onto her back. He kneeled over her face, his cock slick with his cum. Obediently, she opened her mouth to suck him clean. After a while his cock became soft in her mouth but he didn't withdraw it. Looking up at him she sucked and swallowed. She swirled her tongue around the ridges of his cockhead and nibbled at the bunch of uncircumcised skin which slowly closed back over it. Finally, he slid his prick from between her swollen lips.

He pointed to the floor. She eased out of the bed and once more got to her knees beside it, bowing her head.

She felt Miko step up behind her. The Japanese woman leaned over. "Now, must thank master," she whispered. "Must thank for each thing he allow you to give him pleasure. Must list. Must call him master." Kathy had trouble collecting her thoughts. The pain in her anus throbbed. She was sure he had torn her and she was bleeding. "Speak," Miko ordered.

Her head still bowed, Kathy began in a quiet voice, "I wish to thank you Mr. Abul..."

Miko stamped her foot and Kathy began again.

"I wish, Master, to thank you for honouring me in so many ways. Thank you for allowing me to caress your penis with my mouth. Thank you, Master, for allowing me to swallow your cum. Thank you, Master, for allowing me to pay homage to your testicles with my lips and tongue. Thank you, Master, for permitting me to make love to you on this my wedding bed. Giving myself here to you has erased all past memories. Until this night nothing had purpose or meaning. Now, to be worthy of serving you is everything to me."

She paused, feeling her nipples swell and the hot desire pulse in her vagina. "I thank you, Master," she continued, "for allowing me to kiss your lips and taste the inside your mouth. I thank you for permitting me to suck your tongue. I thank you, Master, for your gift of spit. I thank you for letting me kneel at your feet and kiss them. I thank you, Master, for permitting me to press my lips to your anal opening and to taste with my tongue that private place. Most of all, Master, I thank you for the honour of being allowed to receive your penis in my ass. I know it gives you pleasure to cause me pain. The sharp pain I feel now is more bearable since it pleases you. If I dared, I would beg you once more to fill my anal passage with your cock, to tear my rectum, to shoot your semen deep into me."

Kathy glanced up.

Abul was asleep!

CHAPTER TWENTY FIVE - MIKO

Miko had come up behind her again and placed on the floor a bowl of warm and sweetly scented water.

"Bend and spread cheeks of ass," she said. Kathy did as she was told. Miko bathed her anal crack with a soft cloth and immediately the soreness subsided. Gently, Miko dried her. "Take shower now."

After a hot shower Kathy found Miko patiently waiting for her beside the make-up table. For the third time that evening, Miko carefully applied the lipstick, the gloss and eye shadow. She then massaged Kathy's sore nipples with the healing rouge. From her suitcase she took a dark red silk robe and held it out for Kathy to slip into. It tied at the waist. "No shoes," Miko said, sitting Kathy down again but turning her away from the mirror. Miko had a small jar in her hand and kneeled between Kathy's parted legs. With one hand she spread Kathy's labial lips and with the other she rubbed the colourless salve along the slit and into Kathy's vagina. Whatever it was seemed to draw the blood to Kathy's cunt and sensitize the nerves and stimulate the flow of secretion.

Kathy felt a flood of heat rise from her cunt and spread through her body. She hadn't been allowed to cum last night or tonight, and now this. She put her fingers on her clit. Miko slapped them away. "No!" she said. "Must not. Think only of giving. Forget American way of thinking. Must give everything, body and mind. Body easy, mind is harder. When body and mind truly belong to master, then spirit is not only broken, but is gone. No more spirit. That is goal. Banish spirit. When spirit is gone you not think of self, think only of service. You have much to learn."

She reached into her bag and took out a number of short silver needles. "Acupuncture," Miko said. "Not hurt. Make easy for clearing mind of everything but what I say for you to think."

"I don't know if I want..." Kathy began.

"How many times I tell you? Must forget what you want. What you want not important. What master want all that matters. You understand?"

"Yes," Kathy said, "but it's hard."

"Acupuncture and my words make easier."

"All right. But Miko I'm so - so much in a state. I need to cum."

"Stop. Wrong way. You need to obey and to serve and to forget self. That what you need." Deftly Miko inserted the first needle beneath Kathy's right breast then another under her left breast. Before placing the next four needles in the back of Kathy's neck under each ear, Miko dipped their tips in a vial of bright green liquid. In a few minutes there were twenty-three thin silver needles placed at different points in Kathy's body, including four in her feet. Miko had been right. There was no pain other than a slight pinch as each needle broke the skin and, now, an almost imperceptible buzzing at her temples.

When Miko was finished, she stood behind Kathy and in

a low monotone began to speak as she rubbed Kathy's forehead.

"Tonight master is Abul. He sleep maybe two three hours. You kneel in worship looking only at his body, then lean forward and let your eyes see only his penis. You fill mind with sight, touch, smell, and taste of it. It becomes for you most beautiful, most sacred thing in entire world. You see all shades of its colour. You remember taste and feel of it in mouth. You desire to smell and taste again. You desire to feel it up deep inside anus. You willing to suffer anything, to sacrifice anything in worship of his body. You nothing. Master, everything. It is great honour to be allowed to touch any part of him. Empty head of all but this."

She took Kathy by the hand and led her back to the foot of the bed. Carefully, she removed the needles. Once more she spread the heat inducing salve along Kathy's crevice and into her vagina. Kathy crawled up on the bed and kneeled between the legs of the snoring Pakistani. She stared at his naked body and discovered that her mind contained nothing but the suggestions Miko had put there.

Kathy had no sense of time. She felt nothing but the overwhelming obsessive desire to please this man. She focused, as Miko had instructed, on his penis. The bunched foreskin which so disgusted her had become a lovely purple flower which she longed to smell, and kiss, and part with her tongue until the purple head of his cock emerged like a thick deadly snake which she would lovingly caress between her parted lips. She remembered how he had offered his foul smelling anus to her and ordered her to kiss it. If now he said 'lick it with your tongue. Make love to my asshole with your mouth, and afterward thank me for granting you this honour,' she would gladly do it... Miko's needles and hypnotic suggestions had pushed her in a direction she embraced even as it repulsed her.

It must have been three hours before Abul stirred. She had lost all sense of time. Now he looked up. She quickly bowed her head.

"American whore, make me hard," he ordered.

Quickly she leaned over his limp cock and immediately began to moan as she tenderly kissed the wrinkled foreskin, teasing the swollen plum of his penis from its fleshy cover. Gently she sucked it into her hot mouth while pulling back the skin. She licked the underside of his cock and pressed her wet lips to the place where it met his heavy testicles. Then, lowering her head, she caressed his balls with her soft lips and tongue. Holding them up, she licked the place between his scrotum and anus.

"Please," she whispered.

He raised his legs and she buried her head between the rancid smelling cheeks of his ass where her tongue found his hole which she licked and probed. He pulled his ass cheeks apart and she pressed her lips tightly over the wrinkled rim of his opening and sucked at it. She pushed her tongue into it, savouring the foul smell and the bitter taste.

"This is your place, rich American lady," he said harshly. "Here is your place, in your big house on your wedding bed sucking the dried shit from my ass. Am I not right?"

For an answer she spread his cheeks wider and drove her tongue as deep into his dark hole as she could and fucked his ass with her tongue and sucked at the hole which opened wider under her lips which she pressed even tighter against it. He grabbed her hair roughly and pulled her head up so that she had to face him.

"Miko has done well. You are learning how to show respect."

Quickly she got to her knees and bowed her head. "Thank you, Master, for letting me suck at your opening. Thank you for permitting me to push my tongue into your passage. Thank you, Master, for once more allowing me to taste your excrement."

He waited a moment, staring down at her. She could sense his hatred and bowed her head still lower. "There is something you can do that would show even more respect."

The sound of his voice seemed to becoming from a spacious empty place like a cathedral. "You can clean me with your mouth and tongue right after I shit. You can suck at my asshole."

"Yes, on my knees I beg you to let me honour you in this way." The words came before she could think of them. It was as if she heard them spoken by someone else who sounded much like her.

"I will invite many friends to watch the rich American lady service me."

She felt herself trembling.

The buzzing in her head grew not exactly louder but reached, it seemed, a higher pitch. She saw herself on a circular rug in the middle of a large room. Beside her was a bowl into which Abul had just defecated. It steamed with the foul odour of his shit. Around the edge of the carpet stood many men dressed in white caftans. She lay, naked, in the center of the circle. Over her face, Abul began to squat, using both hands to spread his ass cheeks. All along his crack the light brown faeces was runny and glistening. It completely covered his anal ring. The stench was unbearable. Slowly, he lowered himself until she could feel the warmth coming from his excrement. He stopped a few inched above her mouth. She parted her lips and extended her tongue and licked the first of it which had begun to form a strand. She heard herself groan in shame, and terror. He lowered himself further and she licked his crack clean, and then sucked at his anus, and pushed her tongue deep into his hole. Afterwards, Miko wiped her face with hot towels. Then Kathy was on her knees before Abul who wore a white caftan like the others. "Thank you, Master, for honouring me with this most precious gift," she said. She bowed her head to his bare feet and, parting her lips, she kissed them and touched her tongue to his toes...

The vision was gone as quickly as it had come. She became aware that he was waiting for her to respond.

"I will show my respect for you in this way before your many friends." Hearing these words made her want to retch. She knew she could not have said them, and yet it was her own voice that had spoken.

He grunted his approval of this answer. "Now, I suppose you want fucked, want to cum?"

Still kneeling before him, she spread her knees. "As you can see, master, I am ready, but my only need is to please you."

"You are a dog. You like the smell and taste of shit. You should be fucked like a dog." He sat up and, taking her by the back of the neck, pushed her head down on the mattress. Immediately, she raised her hips. He positioned himself behind her and quickly plunged his huge prick once more into her ass. She uttered a small cry of pain as his cock tore her a second time. He fucked her brutally. She felt a warm trickle run down the inside of her thigh and wondered whether it was blood or her own secretions. Although there was much pain, she worked her sphincter to squeeze his cock and pushed back with each of his thrusts so that he could bury his prick deeper in her anal passage.

He came as before, grunting and sweating, digging his fingernails into the cheeks of her ass. When he finished she dutifully rolled over on her back and parted her lips to receive his cock and lick it clean.

As he climbed off the bed she turned on her side and put her hands between her legs. Miko was there to stop her. "No. You never cum until Master permits." Quickly Miko cuffed Kathy's wrists together and pulled her arms up over her head and secured the cuffs to the headboard with a short piece of rope.

Abul stood beside the bed. “So, you wish to cum?” Kathy was afraid to speak. She looked up at him, pleading with her eyes. He turned toward Miko. “Make her cum,” he hissed. “Make her cum, and cum, and cum.”

Miko smiled for the first time since Kathy had met her as she dragged her suitcase over the the bed and took from it a variety of restraints. She cuffed each of Kathy’s ankles and, threading a nylon cord through the ‘D’ rings on the cuffs, she spread Kathy’s legs and tied the cords to the bottom corners of the bedspring.

She wrapped each of Kathy’s thighs with a wide band of velcro and in the same way, running cords through the rings, she secured the ends to the bedspring. Next, an even wider velcro restraint was tightened around Kathy’s waist and the cords attached to the rings were looped under the bedsprings and pulled tight and tied.

Finally, a ball gag was placed in Kathy’s mouth and the leather strap was buckled behind her head. She could neither move nor cry out. Once more Miko spread the salve between Kathy’s labial lips, over her clitoris, into her vagina and her anal opening. Her pink membranes darkened and her clitoris swelled.

Behind the gag, Kathy groaned. She turned her head, looking for Abul. He stood in the doorway impassively watching. Kathy glanced at Miko, then looked again for several moments at Abul. A shudder went through her. She closed her eyes and nodded in agreement. When she opened them, the doorway was empty.

All that mattered now was the growing heat between her legs and in her anus.

Her eyes widened as she saw Miko take from the suitcase a battery to which were attached three wires. At the ends of the two long wires were metal clamps which looked like little alligator heads, the teeth pointed and sharp. Attached to the short wire was a kind of calibrated dial. Miko coated the spring clamps with the same salve she had used before and then attached one to each of Kathy's nipples. The small teeth of the clamps bit into her skin but did not puncture it. The clamps and the ointment caused her nipples to burn and swell.

From the case, Miko withdrew what appeared to be two very large vibrating dildos and a small plastic suction cup. These were then attached to another battery. There was also a dial of some sort on each of the wires leading to the battery. Miko held the inverted suction cup up before Kathy's eyes. It contained what appeared to be a series of very small lubricated brushes. Miko demonstrated that they could move horizontally, vertically, and in a circular motion.

She pressed this cup tightly over Kathy's clitoris. The rim of the cup was coated with an adhesive that held it securely in place. Miko then demonstrated the two mechanized dildos. Each could lengthen and contract as well as thicken. They were capable of twisting slightly and of vibrating at an infinite number of speeds. Miko quickly rubbed them with her special salve and pushed one far up into Kathy's vagina and the other she inserted into her sore anus.

"Now, you get what you want."

Miko pulled a chair up beside the bed and sat behind the batteries. She turned the dials of the two dildos. Kathy felt them move inside her openings. They swelled and twisted inside her and then began to vibrate...

...slowly... slowly...

Now Miko touched the dial on the wire leading to Kathy's nipples. Instantly there began a sequence of alternating electric shocks which caused Kathy to jerk against the restraints and try to cry out behind the gag. The shocks came in three second intervals, first the left nipple then the right. With each shock one of Kathy's breasts would jump and the nipple would swell. Her breasts seemed to be jiggling of their own accord. As her nipples swelled, the teeth of the clamps dug into them.

Finally, Miko turned the dial on the control that led to the suction cup. The lubricated bushes flicked over Kathy's clitoris like a thousand miniature tongues. Kathy's first orgasm was immediate. She strained and bucked against the cuffs and straps which held her down. She groaned and made guttural sounds in her throat. Saliva began to trickle from the corners of her mouth. The orgasm had hardly subsided before another one began.

Miko twisted her dials. She fed more current into the clamps. Kathy's body jerked and she twisted her head from side to side with each shock. Miko increased the speed of the vibrations in the dildos while she slowed those in the little suction cup. She made the dildo in Kathy's anus plunge in and out while the one in her vagina swelled and turned. Kathy came again. The sweat poured off her. Saliva streamed from her mouth and down the sides of her neck. Miko changed the sequence of shocks so they both came at the same time. Once more she increased the current. Behind the gag, Kathy began to scream as she came for the third time within ten minutes. After her fourth orgasm, she passed out.

Miko continued to play Kathy's body like an instrument. The brushes in the clitoral cup spun around, then slowly moved from side to side, and then rapidly up and down. The dildos retracted, and lengthened, and swelled, and twisted and turned, and plunged in and out. The current diminished and increased randomly. Sometimes the shocks were delivered together. At other times they alternated. The secretions that flowed from Kathy's cunt puddled under her. She urinated. The bed was soaked.

Miko played with her for more than two hours. During those hours Kathy lost consciousness four times. Miko counted twelve orgasms.

When Kathy passed out for the fifth time, Miko quickly withdrew and disconnected the devices. She removed the restraints, packed everything including cosmetics, ointments, perfumes, shoes, and gowns into her suitcase. Before she and Naka left, they placed a towel under the unconscious girl, took her pulse, and pulled a sheet over her.

CHAPTER TWENTY SIX - FLIGHT

Kathy awoke slowly, drifting in and out of frightening dreams. Gradually, she became aware of the soaked mattress. Then she felt a throbbing pain in her anus and the soreness of her nipples. Her mouth hurt, too, where the ball gag had stretched it. She felt a dull pounding in her head. It took several minutes before her eyes focused.

She struggled to sit up. Except for the ruined mattress, which smelled of urine and was flecked with spots of blood, everything seemed in order. The house was quiet. It surprised her to discover that she was alone. Little by little the events of last night began coming back to her. She remembered Abul - sucking his hideous cock - feeling it tear her ass. She remembered the Japanese woman with her jar of ointment and her silver needles. She remembered the small sound of the whirring camera. She noticed the marks around her waist and thighs left by the velcro restraints. Gingerly, she touched the tiny scratches on her nipples.

Other memories began to come, but she forced them back into her subconscious. She began to convince herself that the most obscene unspeakable events happened in the nightmare dreams from which she had just awakened. Compared to the abuses of last night, Stein's little entertainments were a walk in the park. She should have listened to him. Men like Satomi and Abul were not interested in playing games, they intended to destroy her utterly.

She had to get away. There was no question about that. She wondered why they had not left someone here to watch her. Then she remembered she was broke. They had taken her car, her cash, her credit cards, and closed her bank account. She had signed over the house to them. She had absolutely nothing except some loose change in the bottom of her purse. She thought of calling Ted or Stein or even Brian but after what happened to Richie, she didn't want to get them involved.

Suddenly she recalled the 'Playtime' can. She and Jeff had hidden a coffee can in the back of their closet. They would often put extra cash in it, always bills. From time to time, they would spill the money out on the bed and count it. Depending on how much was there, they would treat themselves to a spontaneous playtime. Most often it would be a big night in the city or a weekend at some bed and breakfast in the country.

She ran to the closet. The can was still there. Quickly she went to the living room and emptied it on the coffee table. She counted eleven hundred and fifty-three dollars. It wasn't as much as she'd hoped, but it would get her across to London. She could stay with her sister-in-law for a few days until she came up with a plan to change her identity and escape to some remote place where Satomi could not find her. She dialled Mary Margaret's London number. She let it ring for five minutes, but there was no answer. Well, it would just have to be a surprise visit. She called the airlines and booked a seat on a U.S. Air flight that was leaving Pittsburgh at four o'clock for J.F.K. in New York. She lucked out and was able to get a seat on Virgin Atlantic that would leave New York at eleven tonight and put her down at London's Heathrow around ten-thirty tomorrow morning. She checked her watch. It was now two-fifteen.

Perfect! She just might manage to escape...

If nothing went wrong! If they were not watching!

She had just stepped out of the shower when the phone rang! If one of Satomi's people were calling and she didn't answer, they would be on their way to her house in minutes. She picked up the phone. It was Miko. "You are accepted," she said. "Limousine be there to get you soon."

She heard the click as Miko hung up. She hastily threw some clothes into a carry-on bag and called a cab. She was still looking behind her as she boarded the jumbo jet for London.

She slept soundly until the flight attendant shook her as they were landing at Heathrow.

Since she didn't have any baggage, she went directly to the terminal exit. There was a long queue for taxis, and she was grateful when a smirking Pakistani took her arm and guided her past it to where a cab was waiting at the curb. "My brother cab," he said. "Very cheap." She worried a little because the driver was another Pakistani, but this was London. She was safe now. She climbed in and gave him Mary Margaret's address. He made no move to start the car. She thought he hadn't heard her so she repeated the address.

Suddenly both back doors opened and two men slid in beside her. As the cab was pulling away from the curb, she wanted to scream but her throat had gone dry and the man on her left was holding up a ball gag and shaking his head. He was a big man with a ruddy face and short cropped hair. The man on her right was the one who had tricked her, younger and thin.

"You can call me Bill," the big man said. "That's Benji." The cab turned into a narrow unpaved road that skirted one of the outer fences surrounding the airport. The driver pulled in next to a small cinder block building and stopped.

"Now we have to have our little talk," Bill said. "Mostly I will talk and you will listen." He made himself comfortable, turning slightly to face her. "You will listen and listen good. Right?"

"Yes," Kathy said.

"Tell me, Kathy," he began, "have you ever ordered a lobster in a restaurant?"

The question surprised her. "Yes, yes I have."

"Do you know what happens in the kitchen when you order a lobster?"

"I think they take it out of a tank and drop it in boiling water."

"Right, Kathy. It's exactly what they do. Have you ever felt guilty about that? I mean you just point to something on a menu and a living thing gets dropped into a pot of boiling water and dies."

Kathy was slow to answer. "No, I guess I never really thought about it."

"Well, let me tell you that Mr. Satomi shares your attitude, not only as it pertains to lobsters, but also in regard to people. To him you and I mean no more than a lobster any one of us might order in a restaurant. He has people killed all the time, everyday in fact, and like you with the lobster, he never really thinks about it."

"You mean that you are here to... to..."

"To kill you?" He smiled at her. "No, no, we're not going to do that, although if Mr. Satomi hadn't been impressed with the video tape, various parts of your lovely body would now be collecting flies in dumpsters scattered around Pittsburgh." He paused, letting this sink in. "Trying to break your contract with one of the world's most powerful men was not a smart move, Kathy. We knew where you were headed almost as soon as you did. We know the details of every phone call you've made in the last couple of months. Mr. Satomi is no fool, believe me. You haven't taken a piss that he doesn't know about."

"Why did you let me get this far?"

"You were to be sent in this direction anyway so we decided to let you come over on your own... First, let me show you a couple of photographs." From his coat pocket he took a packet of snapshots and handed them to Kathy.

She uttered a little cry when she saw that they were of her sister-in-law, Mary Margaret. The beautiful young girl was riding a bike in one. In another she was apparently going out on a date. Another showed her at a beach wearing a string bikini. There were photographs of her studying at a desk in her room, eating in a small cafe, on a bridge looking down at the Thames, on the steps of the library, and one startling picture of her stepping out of her shower. Kathy felt as if she might be sick. Had it not been for Kathy's connection to Satomi, these people would have had no reason to photograph Mary Margaret.

"Please," Kathy said, the tears forming in her eyes, "I'll do anything you say. I'll abide by the terms of the contract. I promise not to try to run away again. Anything, only please, please don't hurt her."

"We know you are going to fulfil your contract, and we know you won't run away again. There's never been any questions about those things. I showed you the photographs just to illustrate a point. I want you to understand that since the day you made the decision to enter the service of Mr. Satomi, any other independent decision you make could affect others. In signing the contract you gave up the right to decide anything. Do you understand that?"

"Yes, now I do."

"There's no need to be concerned. We just wanted you to realize that what you did could have led to an unfortunate result."

He waited for Kathy to calm down before continuing.

"The terms of your contract state that after successfully completing a two months training period, you will enter Mr. Satomi's service as one of his concubines. The training facility is on this side of the Atlantic. That's where we are going to take you now." He picked up the car phone and spoke in a language she couldn't understand. They waited in silence for five minutes. Then, a large private jet appeared slowly moving up to the other side of the fence. "There's our ride," Bill said. The two men and Kathy went through a gate in the fence and boarded the plane.

In the front compartment were several Pakistanis. They turned to look at her. "She's the one," Bill said to them. He reached into the side pocket of his coat and withdrew a video cassette. There was a large TV screen in the front of the compartment. Beside it, was a VCR. Bill slid the cassette into the VCR. "I brought you boys a copy of the tape starring our little runaway," he chuckled.

The young Pakistani took Kathy's arm and led her to the back of the plane as it rolled down the runway and was immediately airborne.

Miko closed the door to the back compartment and locked it. On a stool next to a full sized fibreglass tub sat a young woman every bit as homely as Miko. "This Mi Jong, she Korean," Miko said. "She give you bath. Much to do in short time." The tub had ben filled with scented hot water. Kathy lay back in it and let the soothing hands of the young woman bathe her. "Wash hair, too," Miko said. "Must make beautiful, pleasing to look at."

When she stepped out of the water both Miko and Mi Jong patted her briskly with huge towels. Miko then blew her hair dry and styled it. "Now," Miko said, "make body smooth like silk, make glow like soft lantern."

When they had finished, Kathy turned to Miko.

"Where are we going?"

"We go to training place. In mountains of North Pakistan. Nothing near."

She tensed with dread.

"And who - who is the trainer?"

"Mr Abul."

Kathy jumped up and looked round wildly. She could not stand that, she would run away... but Miko and the Korean woman grabbed her and forced her down on the stool. "They show you pictures, right? Pictures of sister-in-law, right?" Miko glared at her. "If Mr Satomi don't have you, he get pretty sister-in-law. You know it will happen. Now, no more foolishness."

Miko looked across at Mi Jong, who poured a hot liquid into a small cup. "Drink!" Miko ordered. Kathy's hands shook as she accepted the cup and quickly drank the bitter tasting tea. Within three minutes she had stopped trembling. She leaned back, her body relaxed, and Miko picked up her acupuncture needles. The first time, Miko had coated the ends of only four of them with the bright green liquid, now she dipped six in the vial. Soon they let her rest...

"Your promise," Miko said. It was much later. The plane was beginning to descend now. "You remember your promise? The gift?"

Kathy looked puzzled for a moment and then in a dull, flat voice said, "Yes, the gift."

Miko indicated that Kathy was to stand. Mi Jong came to them with a black cotton caftan that covered Kathy's naked body, her hair, and all of her face except her eyes. They slipped her feet into a pair of sandals.

"Abul master here. Now we meet master and go to reception room of training place. Master and friends are there waiting for you."

The plane had landed and rolled to a stop before a small terminal. A few minutes later, three figures dressed in black cotton caftans made their way to a long white limousine which was parked just outside the gate.

WATCH OUT FOR PENITENT II - THE TRIAL

As usual, we start the bonus pages with the first chapter of our next book, to be published in June. It is NAKED TRUTH by Nicole Dere, the author of *Sisters in Servitude, Owning Sarah* and *Virgin for Sale* - need we say more?

1.

Keith had always been fiercely jealous, Vee knew that. Had known it right from the start, when they had first begun going out together, when she was still a fresher at college. She had found it thrilling then, powerfully so. He was quiet, ruthlessly ambitious and determined to succeed. So different from the other loud-mouthed, crude, beer swillers in the set she moved around in. He didn't even seem particularly interested in her, only in his goal of a First Class Honours and a foot on the ladder to high flying success. So he became something of a challenge.

He seemed to stand on the by-lines, as far as the sexual manoeuvres which figured so largely with most of her contemporaries were concerned. He was good looking, in a lean, aesthetic way. His angular face, crowned by a neatly clustered mop of blond curls, had an intensely serious expression most of the time. His smile was guarded, contained, giving little or nothing of himself away. The blue eyes were deep, unknowable, they stared with a cold dispassion that sparked a shivery thrill secretly inside her.

It was her own diffidence that roused his interest. She knew he fancied her, at least physically, in spite of that distant front. He found her gawky schoolgirl charm attractive, he told her later.

After a few close encounters, she had surrendered her virginity a couple of years earlier to a groping friend of her brother's, who had been hasty, messy, and appallingly clumsy. David, her brother, only eighteen months older than she was, had practically played pimp, bringing the 'chum' round when their parents were away for the night, laying on alcohol to oil the wheels of her seduction.

What was really bad, so bad that Vee had almost succeeded in pushing it away from her conscious memory, was that she had secretly wanted her brother to make love to her. She had flung herself against David in torrid open mouthed passion, feigning drunkenness, and he had fled, from his own as well as her incestuous desires, she suspected, and left her to the less than tender mercies of 'chum'.

When it was done, she was glad in a way that she had got it over with, she was like all her school mates now. But it wasn't repeated. In fact, it was what had finally driven her into the arms, and, on one never to be forgotten rainy November afternoon, into the bed of her bosom pal, Ruth, acknowledging at long last the lesbian inclinations she had been fighting against since earliest adolescence.

She was glad the fight was lost. Or won. She and Ruth remained lovers throughout the two years of their sixth form schooling, revelled at how easy it was.

Keith wanted her, she could tell, despite her nervous, schoolgirlish, giggling shyness - maybe because of it. "Vera's a dreadful name, isn't it? Most folks call me Vee." Then they were kissing, seriously clinched against a tree in the breath-steamy dark. His mouth was demanding, hard, his teeth clashed against hers, until the soft inner surface of her lips was cut and tender.

The next time was on her bed. Sunday afternoon was the traditional passion time. She pictured girls groaning, crying, thrummed with buzzing sexuality, abandoning themselves to hot sex. All about sexual odours wafted compellingly on the breeze through the deserted corridors of the building. She was both terrified and damp with weak-kneed excitement at her racing thoughts.

They quickly graduated to the bed, but on top of the coverlet, both minus shoes but minus nothing else. Their mouths clamped together, bodies and limbs heaved and twisted as the bed springs danced to their writhing. She could feel him, he thrust his trapped hardness unmistakably against her, while his sweaty palm inexorably claimed the cold smooth contours of her nylon covered leg, to the swell of her rigid thigh muscle. Eventually the hand extended its claim, under her blouse, to the ticklish bare midriff, and the fragrant sheen of her skin.

His clumsy but determined fingers flipped out her breasts after something of a struggle, and those fingers touched and brushed over the tiny hardness of a nipple, and she flushed.

"You've got an erection too," he teased tightly, and she couldn't force a smile.

Under her skirt, his hand finally slid between her legs, to caress her already wet vulva, tracing the cushiony outline under the protection of her tights and her tiny knickers. Finger pads rubbed up and down the length of her labia, bringing up their grooved outline like a brass etching under the sticky gauziness of her underclothing. She was twisting and shivering, her hips moving in rhythm to his stimulation. The wet patch spread, and she breathed raggedly, moaning through her open mouth. On and on his hand rubbed, until she was sobbing, ready to burst with excitement. He grabbed her wrist with a free hand, pulled her down to the domed bulge of his own excitement still trapped his pants.

"Are you on the pill?" The brutal question smacked her to crimson faced reality, at the same instant as the hand between her thighs ceased its movement. With a wounded howl, she swung her legs away from him, and clutched the creased blouse across her chest, hobbled, doubled over ludicrously, to the tiny basin, hung there, great tears splashing down her shiny cheeks.

"I've got a contraceptive," he said. But it was too late. His own clumsiness made him retreat further. He would not accept blame. He was tight lipped, still cruel in the awful embarrassment. "I'm sorry. I thought it was understood."

Later he returned, courting her with flowers and with a slightly awkward charm. “I had no idea. You’ve never - you’re a virgin, aren’t you?” He mistook her blushing, hangdog silence for consent. And was in turn even more intrigued. Genuinely startled even, filled with the idea that she would be his, belong to him in actuality, him only. No one else before him. He began to love her, in his possessive way.

Ironically, now she wanted to give herself to him. Burned to do so. Wept for it. And now he refused. “We’ll wait. It’ll be good for us. We’ll be really sure. Besides, it’s sort of cute. You know, the way it used to be. The way it should be.”

They did indulge in sex. All the titillating, torturous foreplay, spread out over many hot, sweetly frustrating sessions in each other’s beds, or rather on them. Never under the covers. That helped to fight temptation. But he grew bolder. Bared her breasts, while she tearfully apologised, and pouted at his fond taunts, his mouth suckling as he drove her wild. And, finally, he got round, or through, her knickers, and fingered her, patiently, tormentingly, as she drew nearer to, but not quite over, the crest of her bucking wave. Except that, at last, she did - clenching and unclenching, gasping in the shuddering climax that trapped his aching wrist between her squeezing, convulsive thighs.

She, too, with fearful pleasure, saw and touched his penis, thrusting pole-hard from his fly, learned to stroke and caress, learned the quickening rhythm which brought its culminating, thrilling, scaring reward, of pumping hot, odorous semen scalding her quivering hand and fingers.

“We can’t do this!” she wept one afternoon, when the heavy smell of their sex, and the stains on the cover, lay accusingly about them. Abjectly she begged him to take her ‘properly’, and he was adamant in his refusal. “You don’t really want me,” she cried. “What’s the point of our relationship?” A quarrel grew, got worse. “I think we should stop seeing each other,” she muttered tormentedly. She was desolated by his stiff-necked agreement,

At the end of term party, Keith was there again, coolly observant as usual. She was with a boy called Bill, and she got defiantly drunk. Couples were slinking off, and Bill was almost desperately lecherous. Why the hell not? she thought. Let's get it over with. She had almost come to believe in her virginity herself.

She let Bill take her to a coat-strewn bedroom, and amid the piled up garments she lay, giddy and sick, trying unsuccessfully to feign passion in response to his slobbered kisses. Then, suddenly, he was gone, plucked magically from her. She struggled up in smeary-eyed amazement, to see a possessed Keith delivering a series of sickening kicks to Bill's squealing figure on the floor.

Keith turned, and dealt her a ringing, open handed slap on the side of her bared thigh, and she yelped in agony. The red imprint stood out like a brand for days. He dragged her roughly upright, thrust her balled up pants and tights into her hand and pulled her from the room. Like an irate parent, he led her through the crowd, barging people out of the way. He let her get her coat, but captured her wrist immediately again, and tugged her to the taxi rank.

In the cab, he held her hand in a painful grip, and they exchanged no words. Her tights and knickers, still meshed in a ball, were in her coat pocket now. She was very conscious of her nudity under the silk dress. It had ridden up at the back. She could feel the upholstery of the seat on the backs of her thighs, even on her buttocks. Her vulva was throbbing urgently. She stood, feeling the cold night air on her, while he paid off the taxi, then, grabbing hold of her again, he marched her along the passage of the flat he shared to the austere bathroom.

"Get your clothes off!"

Hypnotically, she obeyed, snivelling softly, like a chastised infant, perversely excited by the knowledge of his unmoving stare. She stripped off, dropping her clothes on the ugly little cream wooden chair, while he ran a steaming bath.

"Get in!"

She winced at the heat, but said nothing. Her skin pinked and glowed. She washed thoroughly under his admonishing gaze, blushing as she did so, but making no attempt to hide even her most intimate ablutions. When she had finished, he held out a large towel to her. It was his, she could tell. It was still damp. He bundled up her clothes under one arm and again drew her after him, naked, to his room.

Inside, he faced her sternly. "Did that bastard do it to you?"

She shook her head, "No one has," she whispered faintly. "I only want you."

He pulled her to him. "OK. You're my girl. I mean permanently. Right? Mine completely, understand?"

His blue eyes held her, blazing at her. She was shivering with fear as he bent her over his knee, spanking her like a naughty child. It excited her almost unbearably at first. She thought she would climax, feeling the rub of his clothing on her fragrant belly, the ferment of her thighs as she squirmed, but then the beating went on, hard resounding slaps, until the pain took over and she was squirming in earnest, her feet sawing the air, burning in real agony, her bottom clenching and unclenching with fire.

She sobbed desperately for him to stop.

When he did, he flung her brutally off him, so that she fell sprawling on the faded rug, weeping blindly, clutching at her stinging bottom. He plucked her up and thrust her on her back, on the bed, parting her legs roughly. She stayed like that, her jutting knees splayed, still sobbing as he tore off his clothing. His prick looked huge, lance like. He entered her at once, thrusting into her, tearing her despite her wet readiness, so that she cried out in pain. He plunged fiercely, and she joined him, flinging up her belly against his, spearing herself sacrificially, overjoyed, embracing the hard, driving burn, lost at the final flooding burst of his manhood inside her.

And now our serial, ERICA (expanded version), by Rex Saviour. This is Episode 8 but that need not stop its enjoyment by new readers. Rex is trying to cure Erica of her fear of being touched, beaten, snakes etc by densensitisation - that is, exposing the patient in gradually increasing doses to what she fears most. So far this is not working out too well!!

2-9

After John had gone, I sat in my armchair waiting for Erica to come down. I finished the wine and still she had not come. I was beginning to get cross.

In the end I had to send the butler for her.

She entered timidly and stood at attention before me, still whimpering a little. It was obvious that she had been crying, but she had dried her eyes. She had put on the short pink smock I allow her to sleep in, it is hip length, and the belt of course. The butler would have brought her through the kitchen, I expect, for the staff usually congregated in the warmth there and would enjoy the chance to touch her up a bit. That was helpful in curing her of her shyness, so I pretended not to know about it.

"Why did you go to bed?"

"Well - I thought - Uncle John went - it's bedtime -"

"But what about your punishment?"

"Oh but I've had my punishment, Uncle Rex!"

"Indeed?" I motioned to her to turn round. The ointment that John had applied before he released her from her bonds had worked its miracle - her bare bottom was round and seductively smooth, maybe just a shade pink but unmarked, unblemished and utterly inviting. I slapped her as a sign to turn to face me again.

"I don't see any signs of punishment."

"I've had it, Uncle Rex, truly I have, from Uncle John, oh truly truly!"

I picked it up the black book. "You had a record number of marks tonight."

"Yes, Uncle Rex, I know. That's why he beat me so hard."

"Did he now? How many do you think he signed for?"

"All of them, it must have been for all of them, it must have been!"

I shook my head.

"Most of them?"

"None of them! He hasn't signed for any of them!"

"Oh God!"

"And that's some more. Did he give you any uppercuts?"

She went white.

"Come now," I said. "I can always telephone him to find out, you know."

Miserably she shook her head. "N-no," she muttered.

"But your bottom is still very sore?"

She nodded.

"We'll spare it then. Uppercuts only. Well, mostly. That means position five. You get ready while I open another bottle."

I find I enjoy punishing Erica better if the wine is flowing freely. Sipping it between strokes while she waits is particularly good, specially if I walk about behind her, which makes her tenser and tenser the nearer I come.

It was half an hour later when I went to the kitchen, where the position five punishment is carried out. I only use it very occasionally, for it is rather erotic and I tend to get carried away. And of course it is an imposition on the staff, who like to watch television there.

Erica was already secured to the stretching frame. The staff must have done that for her. For this punishment she lies face down on the big table and holds onto its far edge. Her bottom is not supported, but goes beyond the table edge, held up by her ankles being strained apart and pulled towards the extensions of the wide table by cords and weights. This presents her bottom with no obstruction above or below, at a convenient height for discipline, and allows for some erotic heaving up and down if she is tickled or struck.

In fact, I noticed that the ankle blocks had been raised maybe twelve inches above normal, to give better access from below. No doubt, then, she had had some tickling already! But I didn't complain - in fact I cranked up the ankles even further, so that the back of the thighs curved down nicely to the twitching bottom. There was a teacup on one cheek, causing some squirming. I went between her legs and removed it - it was its heat that had been causing the squirming.

"Excuse me, Sir," said the Butler. "But are you going to whip Miss Erica tonight?"

"Obviously," I said. "Any objection?"

"Oh no," he said hastily, "no Sir, that is entirely your affair. It is just that her howling late at night has got more frequent lately. It keeps some of us awake, Sir, and we wondered if you could gag her, Sir, if you have to whip her in the evenings?"

"Of course," I said. "How thoughtless of her." I turned in Erica's direction. "You will be more quiet at night in future, my girl," I said. "All this noise is very selfish. Have you no feeling for others? If you start it I shall gag you and then give you double what you have had already."

"Thank you, Sir," said the Butler. "I am sure that will be satisfactory."

"No problem," I said. I glanced at the TV. Some of them were watching a movie. "Let me know when the film is over."

"Very good, Sir. Thank you for your consideration."

It was about three quarters of an hour later that I came back.

Erica was alone now. Her legs were pulled very wide apart indeed, for the frame had been used on a daily basis to stretch them outwards, and the staff had encouraged her in her progress. For stretching, of course, she was laid on her back, not face down as now. An hour or two a day with strong weights on the ropes had worked wonders and she was quite supple already. She could almost have gone in a circus as a contortionist! The frame held her at a convenient height for me, head turned and one blue eye on me in acute apprehension. Her knuckles were white where she gripped her end of the table.

I was busy examining the other end of her, though. The business end, one might say. I turned the smock up further over her waist, then ran my fingers over her sex. It was beautifully smooth, no hair at all, and I noticed that the petals were opened by the stretching apart of her legs, for she was stretched open almost at right angles.

It wouldn't be wise to keep her like that too long, I thought. It looked very uncomfortable. Perhaps she was whimpering because I hadn't started sooner.

I was not quite ready though. This was a situation to be relished to the full. I went back to her head, and stroked that glossy hair. It was a little damp with the perspiration of fear. I used it to lift her head, and put her lips to mine. The tongue was frantic, avid for forgiveness, but she did not dare plead with me, knowing it would be counter-productive.

I was wondering what I could do to prolong my pleasure, when I noticed that she was wearing her snake ear rings. I unclipped one and ran it slowly down along her backbone. It was interesting to see how frantically she heaved and wriggled from it.

What a chance to do a little towards snake desensitisation!

I replaced the earring, and went to fetch the python from its tank.

When I came in with it she went berserk. I have never seen anything like it. I decided to keep that as a threat for another time, and let him crawl around on the floor instead of teasing her with him.

I did not intend to use the belt she was wearing, for I have a thinner one for this position, one that I can crack like a whip, either from above or below her - it is kept in the kitchen, and as I wrapped it round my fist her apprehension grew visibly, and she started to whimper more loudly.

I suppose I should have given her sex some protection against the upwards strokes, as I didn't want her out of action for afterwards, but I am always careful, and so long as I have not had too much wine I usually manage to confine myself to her inner thighs, getting at the sensitive bits nearest her sex quite easily but doing no damage. True, I had erred once or twice in the past. It hadn't mattered then, but it would be pretty frustrating tonight!

I opened the black book and studied it. "Dear me," I said. "This must be quite a record." I caressed her smooth sex, relishing the way it flinched from my intrusive fingers.

"Why flinch?" I asked. "I'm being very gentle, aren't I?"

"I'm frightened you'll pinch."

"Like this?"

"Oh! Oh yes!"

I continued to caress her. "Are you ready?"

No reply, so I started to use the belt, alternating between upper and under cuts - I had to stand back a bit for the under cuts, but they worked well.

It occurred to me that this arrangement about getting double what she had had already if she screamed might interfere with my enjoyment of her in bed, maybe for several nights, so in future - unless of course I was in the mood to get my satisfaction from a buggering or a more prolonged beating - I would bring her as close as possible to screaming point without actually breaking her control. It would be a matter of very nice judgement, because if she did scream I would have actually to double the punishment as promised, or she would never believe me again.

She was soon near to that point. I could tell by close attention to the moans that came from her. At this stage, the best way of prolonging punishment without going over the edge would be a short break.

"You nearly screamed that time, didn't you?"

"Yes, yes, yes -"

"You'd better be very careful."

"I know. Oh God, I know!"

Again I let a blasphemy pass, and released her from her bondage.

"Fetch me another bottle."

She clambered painfully down and dropped to her knees, clutching me round the legs and turning up a tear-stained face, but one eye on the python as he explored a nearby corner.

"Have we finished, then?"

"Oh no, I just need a drink, then I shall continue."

"Oh Uncle -"

"What?"

"Do you think you should?"

"Should what?"

"Start another bottle?"

"Why ever not?"

I knew exactly what she wanted to say. If I started one, I would finish it, and she thought that might affect my aim, I might catch her on the sex. But she didn't dare to say that. She just went and got the wine from the fridge, poured me a glass, and resumed her position, whimpering unrestrainedly as I secured her ankles again.

Soon after I started again I had brought her back to breaking point. Two more of each, upper and under, I thought, then I'd stop. The first had her squirming and choking a scream back.

One last one, then. I would make it the hardest of the lot. She could take one more really good uppercut.

Unfortunately my aim was bad! It produced the loudest scream I had ever had from her. Ordinarily I would have been proud of it, but tonight I was furious with myself as I thrust the gag in.

Damnation! Now the punishment was to do all over again. She would be useless in bed for days, just when she had become available!

I unfastened her and dragged her to the punishment room and secured her to the whipping frame. I tied her wrists to the top corners and ankles to the bottom ones, so that she hung in place facing a mirror.

I fetched one of the whips from above the fire in the den: time to break it in. I made her stop her noise long enough to kiss the whip: her eyes nearly jumped out of their sockets when she saw it.

You can imagine how frustrated I was as I gagged her and then went behind her. She was watching in the mirror, and I saw her body tighten as I raised the whip. After the first few strokes, though, I blindfolded her, thinking anticipation was probably more beneficial, specially if I calmed down enough to space out the strokes a little, and made my timing irregular. I really got to work with that whip, using all my strength and skill. Her body jerked about, covered in beads of sweat, her bottom writhed, and big though the estate is anyone in the grounds would surely have heard her if I had taken the gag out.

I have to admit that I went a bit over the top that night. Too long and too hard. By the time I had finished she was contorting in a way I had never seen before.

When I rubbed the ointment in, she thrashed about like mad...

I left her hanging there and went to bed. But frustration kept me awake until at last I went and fetched her.

She was not, after all, totally useless. In fact I have never known her mouth and tongue so eager to please. But she squirmed away more than I expected when at last I plunged into the cringing softness of her for the first time, and she made those pitiful little mewing sounds all the time I rode her.

I woke next morning to brightness and blue, sunshine through the open window, birds praising a perfect day, a deep feeling of contentment and completion.

I had waited three years to sleep with Erica - she had shared my bed many times, of course, but as a temptation, not as a woman - and now at last my life was fulfilled.

I raised myself on an elbow to look at her, sleeping peacefully at my side. How did she feel? I could have sworn there was the slightest trace of a secret smile on her bruised lips, but that was hardly possible. Or was it?

But to me? To me she was love! Last night had been love!

The realisation hit me like a blow. Vague thoughts from yesterday and before suddenly crystalised, became rock hard and shone with clarity, they had a life of their own.

Rex owns Erica. Rex beats Erica. Now Rex screws Erica.

Rex loves Erica.

There was no escape for me, for either of us. I must expose that perfect body to increasing shame. It was my property, not hers. My property, my problem. The soul within was crying out for help. I was her God, desensitization her future salvation, masochism her kick.

Unless I hardened my aching heart I could never cure her, and to do so was still my sacred mission ...

Next month we begin Part III - Erica: Radio Controlled

A VICTORIAN SCRAPBOOK by Stephen Rawlings
Author of JANE AND HER MASTER

4th Extract - THE DANGERS OF GOTHICK DRAMA

From the Morning Chronicle

(Gentlemen are advised that they should take care to withhold this article from the fair ones who are in their household, since it is not suitable for their eyes. The matter is, however, of such import that we feel obliged to draw it to the attention of the general public)

It has long been known that the female mind can be much injured by the practice of reading novels, either of the Romantic or the Gothick variety. Our attention has been drawn to a new, and even more pressing, danger. There are circulating now, under the guise of Art and Drama, a number of dramatic scripts that are of such a terrifying nature as to turn the female brain completely. Though their content is quite repugnant, we feel justified in offering our male readers a sample, so that they may be aware of what to expect from such pieces of work.

Extracts from RANALDI'S REVENGE or THE DUCHESS DISHONOURED.

ACT 1 Scene i An ante chamber of the Count's castle. Enter Count Ranaldi with his Moorish servant Spika.

Count (to Spika): She inflames my lust, accepts my suit, yet lives herself as bride to that over-bearing Duke. Nay. Whore not bride, for 'tis his estates she craves, not his caresses. I will have her, Spika, despite His Grace. Her golden hair shall be the rope with which I tie her to a prisoning wall; that lush red mouth shall receive my kisses and myself. I will ravish her behind and before and return her to her husband fecund with my seed. Tonight she dines with her cousin, but returns late to her home. See to it that she never reaches her husband's bed. She shall feast on tears, and sleep on stone, before she feels his prick again.

ACT 1 Scene ii The tower room in the Count's castle. Present the Count and a fat cleric. There is a sound of a woman's cries outside, then the door opens and Spika appears dragging Antonia by her hair.

Count: How now Madam. Do you disdain my hospitality?

Antonia: What means this Sir? Your servant has forced me here against my will. You are dishonoured to treat a woman so.

Count: Nay, my lady. It is you shall be dishonoured. Before you leave this place your body shall be forfeit to my lust, to wipe out the slight you did me when you scorned my love, and chose His Grace's gold. I will revenge myself upon the Duke and your falsenesses. When I have had my way between those rosy lips above, I'll take my pleasure between those cheeks below in the secret bud they guard and, when I tire of that, plough your mossy furrow in front. Our bellies shall press and press again, until yours shall swell from our fierce congress. I shall return you to your stiff-necked mate all ripe to burst with alien fruit. *(to the Moor):* Strip her and expose her secrets.

ACT 2 Scene ii A corridor leading from the tower room. Marpley accosts Spika.

Marpley: How does the lady then?

Spika: Hardly I fear. Bent over a rail, her buttocks swelling laciviously, the deep dark cleft inviting invasion, the pulsing probe seeking out her pouting bud. The Count did not spare her, thrusting deep into the steaming depths, leaving behind his spurted seed, useless in the un-fertile ground, leaking stickily from the wounded orifice. She'll feel it keenly there and shrink from sitting for awhile.

ACT 2 Scene iv Within the tower room. Antonia is spread across a bench, her fork held wide by her bonds, bruised teats pointing to the vaulted stone above her. The Count stands with Marpley contemplating the splayed thighs.

Count: See you the tight slit beneath the furry thicket, opening like a flower as warm lubricious flow shows how her lust ignites, shrinking from the brutal ravishment to come, yet yearning to be taken, ravaged, bruised, made to cry out with pain and passion?

Marpley: Indeed, it tugs at my manhood like the lodestone on a needle.

Count: It is a bearing I'll pursue till she is bearing, heavy with a woman's load. I'll plough her long and plant her deep. Her belly will remember me, nine moons from now.

Act 3 scene i The passage outside the turret room. Marpley again encounters Spika.

Marpley: How? Is she ravished then?

Spika: Yes. 'Tis accomplished as he did desire.

Marpley: Went it well with her?

Spika: I fear she feared it, and more than ordinary, for he is determined to have her with child. She begged him to use her any other way, even to take her in her Satan-pit behind, but he declared he'd had his fill of that dark, barren place, and sought the fertile warmth of her moist sheath. She begged and shrieked to be spared. Her delicate feet, like pink mice, curling in terror as the rod approached, spasming with anguish at its cruel bite, but still he sank it in her to the hilt. The long sculpted legs, thighs strained apart, leading to the sacred grove above, but helpless to shield it from the coming storm, which broke, and at its breaking, so did she, shrieking her fear and misery to the cold unfeeling stones above.

Marpley: Then now is her honour truly dishonoured.

Spika: Truly so. Her womb is awash with alien spawn.

<u>Act 3 Scene iii</u> The tower room. Antonia is again crotch wide on the bench. A brazier, stage left, glows around the irons.

The Count: No blood yet?

Spika: No my Lord. I've had her thighs watched these six weeks now, and nothing shown.

The Count: Can we be sure, this soon?

Spika: The maid confessed the Mistress should have bled five weeks since. I think she told truth; she would not wish to face the hot irons and the rack a second time. Her screams gave promise of a truthful tongue.

The Count: Then give me the iron, Moor. No other shall plough this field until my crop is harvested. She shall be sealed until the fruit is ripe for plucking.

(Presses the iron to her nether lips. Antonia screams and faints in her bonds)

The Count: Put a cloak about her and return her to the Duke. Turn her out before his gates. She shall knock and ask for two to be admitted, where only one went out.

(Available from Messrs. Frogg and Duckett. Blackfriars. Price 10s6d Cloth. Library Ed. [illus] 2Gns.)

***

Temporarily out of print

ISBN 1-897809-01-8 Barbary Slavemaster *Allan Aldiss*
ISBN 1-897809-02-6 Erica: Property of Rex *Rex Saviour*
ISBN 1-897809-04-2 Bikers Girl *Lia Anderssen*
ISBN 1-897809-05-1 Bound for Good *Gord, Saviour, Darrener*
ISBN 1-897809-07-7 The Training of Samantha *Lia Anderssen*
ISBN 1-897809-10-7 Circus of Slaves *Janey Jones*

All titles (including above) are available plain text on floppy disc
£5 or $8.50 postage inclusive (PC format unless Mac requested)
or can be downloaded from http://www.thebookshops.com
e-mail james@jamesbrown.com
Credit card Teleorders/Fax orders (UK) 0113 293 0654

All our in-print titles (listed overleaf) can be ordered from any bookshop in the UK and an increasing number in the USA and Australia by quoting the title and ISBN, or directly from us by post. Credit cards show as EBS (Electronic Book Services - £ converted to $ and back!): Price of book (see over) plus postage and packing UK £2 first book then £1.30 each; Europe £3.50 then £2; USA $6 then $4. Please make US cheques payable to Silver Moon Books Inc.

TITLES IN PRINT

+ means Silver Mink

ISBN 1-897809-03-4 Barbary Slavegirl *Allan Aldiss*
ISBN 1-897809-08-5 Barbary Pasha *Allan Aldiss*
ISBN 1-897809-09-3 When the Master Speaks *Josephine Scott* +
ISBN 1-897809-11-5 The Hunted Aristocrat *Lia Anderssen*
ISBN 1-897809-13-1 Amelia *Josephine Oliver* +
ISBN 1-897809-14-X Barbary Enslavement *Allan Aldiss*
ISBN 1-897809-15-8 The Darker Side *Larry Stern* +
ISBN 1-897809-16-6 Rorigs Dawn *Ray Arneson*
ISBN 1-897809-17-4 Bikers Girl on the Run *Lia Anderssen*
ISBN 1-897809-19-0 The Training of Annie Corran *Terry Smith* +
ISBN 1-897809-20-4 Caravan of Slaves *Janey Jones*
ISBN 1-897809-21-2 Sonia *RD Hall* +
ISBN 1-897809-22-0 The Captive *Amber Jameson* +
ISBN 1-897809-23-9 Slave to the System *Rosetta Stone*
ISBN 1-897809-24-7 Dear Master *Terry Smith* +
ISBN 1-897809-25-5 Barbary Revenge *Allan Aldiss*
ISBN 1-897809-26-3 Sisters in Servitude *Nicole Dere* +
ISBN 1-897809-27-1 White Slavers *Jack Norman*
ISBN 1-897809-28-X Cradle of Pain *Krys Antarakis* +
ISBN 1-897809-29-8 The Drivers *Henry Morgan*
ISBN 1-897809-30-1 Owning Sarah *Nicole Dere* +
ISBN 1-897809-31-X Slave to the State *Rosetta Stone*
ISBN 1-897809-32-8 The Contract *Sarah Fisher* +
ISBN 1-897809-33-6 Virgin for Sale *Nicole Dere* +
ISBN 1-897809-34-4 The Story of Caroline *As told to Barbie* +
ISBN 1-897809-35-2 Jane and Her Master *Stephen Rawlings* +
ISBN 1-897809-36-0 Island of Slavegirls *Mark Slade*
ISBN 1-897809-37-9 Bush Slave *Lia Anderssen*
ISBN 1-897809-38-7 Desert Discipline *Mark Stewart*
ISBN 1-897809-39-5 Training Jenny *Rosetta Stone* +
ISBN 1-897809-40-9 Voyage of Shame *Nicole Dere*
ISBN 1-897809-41-7 Plantation Punishment *Rick Adams*
ISBN 1-897809-42-5 Naked Plunder *J.T. Pearce*
ISBN 1-897809-43-3 Selling Stephanie *Rosetta Stone*
ISBN 1-897 809-46-8 Eliska *von Metchingen*
ISBN 1-897809-47-6 Hacienda, *Allan Aldiss*

All the above £4.99 UK $8.95 USA. Postage - see previous page

ISBN 1-897809-44-1 SM Double value (Olivia/Lucy) *Graham/Slade*
ISBN 1-897809-48-4 Angel of Lust, *Lia Anderssen*

£5.99 UK $9.95 USA. Postage - see previous page